The Book
of
Jane

Also by Anne Dayton
and May Vanderbilt

Emily Ever After

Consider Lily

The Book of Jane

Anne Dayton and May Vanderbilt

Broadway Books

New York

PUBLISHED BY BROADWAY BOOKS

Copyright © 2007 by Anne Dayton and May Vanderbilt

Published in the United States by Broadway Books,
an imprint of The Doubleday Broadway Publishing Group,
a division of Random House, Inc., New York.
www.broadwaybooks.com

BROADWAY BOOKS and its logo, a letter B bisected on the
diagonal, are trademarks of Random House, Inc.

This book is a work of fiction. Names, characters, businesses,
organizations, places, events, and incidents either are the
product of the authors' imagination or are used fictitiously.
Any resemblance to actual persons, living or dead, events,
or locales is entirely coincidental.

Book design by Donna Sinisgalli

Illustration by Bonnie Dain for Lilla Rogers Studio

Library of Congress Cataloging-in-Publication Data
Dayton, Anne.
The Book of Jane / Anne Dayton and May Vanderbilt. — 1st ed.
      p. cm.
1. New York (N.Y.)—Fiction. I. Vanderbilt, May. II. Title.

PS3604.A989B66 2007
813'.6—dc22
2006036515

ISBN 978-0-7679-2655-3

PRINTED IN THE UNITED STATES OF AMERICA

1 3 5 7 9 10 8 6 4 2

First Edition

The Lord gave and the Lord has taken away.

Blessed be the name of the Lord.

JOB 1:21

The Book of Jane

Chapter 1

Most people don't know that her real name is Liberty Enlightening the World. It's a mouthful, so people usually just call her Lady Liberty or the Statue of Liberty, but I think you kind of lose something in the translation.

"Are you in charge here today?" I pull my gaze away from my favorite client and turn to see who's talking. I see a young red-haired woman in perfect "political" navy blue. She's the woman behind the mayor.

"Yes," I say, extending my hand. "Jane Williams."

As a senior publicist at Glassman & Co., one of the largest PR firms in New York, I get to work on some great accounts, but none of them give me the same thrill as representing one of the most famous statues in the world. I'm in charge of all of Libby's photo ops. Anytime someone wants to print a photo or do a documentary about her, they have to come through me.

"Sophie Brown," she says, and holds up a finger to me to tell me to wait, then presses her earpiece for a moment. I smile patiently, making a notation in my ever-ready planner. I've gotten very good at dealing with high-powered politicos and their tech toys.

She takes her hand down and gives her head a good shake. "Okay, that wasn't for me. But I have a question for you."

I look around. The red, white, and blue balloon columns look great, even after their boat ride over here. The stage is already set up right at the statue's feet, just like the mayor ordered, and the sound guys are checking the system. It's all going according to schedule. The mayor is championing a controversial minimum wage for New York City. Since many of the hourly workers in the city are recent immigrants, he has initiated a local minimum wage, set much higher than the national one, to protect them. But this change hasn't exactly been popular with big business. And so, to insure that no one misses what's at stake here, the mayor is holding a publicity event on Liberty Island today, in spite of my protests that June afternoons in New York are often plagued with torrential, unexpected rain.

"Sure," I say to Sophie. "Shoot."

Sophie looks around and then drops her voice. "Did someone tell you about the Banks Box?"

I lean in to hear her better. "I'm sorry?"

"The Banks Box," she whispers. She flashes a quick smile to the staffers swarming around us, then drags me away from the thick of things. What on earth is going on?

"No one told you?" she asks. "But I heard *you* had it."

"Had what?"

She holds her head for a moment like she has a splitting headache. "Mayor Banks is only five foot six."

"Really? He looks taller on TV," I say.

"Because of the Banks Box. I mean, he doesn't know we call it that. I need someone to plant it at the podium so that the press can't see it. He always stands on it. And I heard you had it."

I stifle a laugh and shake my head.

"I have to find that box," she says and starts running away. "What a day."

I watch her go, but as she leaves I can't help but notice something on the horizon. Big, dark thunderheads. My heart begins to race. Oh please God. Not this. Not today.

"What's up?" I hear a chipper voice behind me. I turn around and see my assistant, Natalie, her dark-brown hair blowing about her thin face.

I nod at the horizon. "See that?"

"Yeah," she says, brushing a strand of hair out of her face. "That's rotten luck. But you've got the tents ready, I'm sure. You're Jane Williams. You were born prepared."

I frown. "No. The mayor insisted that the event was 'rain or shine' and refused to pay for us to rent them." I shake my head. "He said he didn't want to waste the tax dollars on some silly tents they'd never use, but I think he really just didn't want to block the statue out of the photos."

"Yikes." She looks toward the dock, where the mayor is now stepping off a ferry, wearing a dark suit and a flag-print necktie.

I watch the sun go behind a large, black cloud. A few bright yellow beams burst through holes in the cloud mass here and there, but they mostly just emphasize the size of the ominous cloud.

"Tell me about it. We've got a ninety-five percent chance of rain *and* the Banks Box is missing."

Natalie laughs. "Well then, you'd better start praying to that God of yours. You need a miracle."

"**Where** are you going, love?" Howard asks. Howard works for the National Park Service and is the official keeper of Liberty Island. Liberty Island is technically on the New Jersey side of New York harbor, but New York gets all the credit for her and the Garden State only gets a view of her rear end. Howard is just one of many people who work full time to keep the statue safe and clean. As her publicist, I'm just the proud aunt, which makes Howard her fussy, concerned grandpa. It makes sense that she has a big family. She's a Jersey girl, after all.

"Please, Howard?" I beg, smiling at him. "I won't be long."

He winks at me. "I have to do one last sweep for stragglers on the grounds anyways, and then you and I are both leaving for the night. I've got a wife at home, and she gets jealous of Libby if I stay out all night."

"Thanks, Howard," I say, turning toward the stairs. I grab the handrail and begin to climb. I remember how when I came here as a kid, I counted every stair. There are elevators now, but they haven't been kept in working order since they closed the observation deck in the statue's crown after 9/11. It breaks my heart to know that children can no longer ascend the last flight and see the breathtaking beauty of New York City sprawled out before them. But as a staff member, I can do something that the public hasn't been able to do since 1916. I can keep going up, past the observation deck in her crown, out onto the deck that encircles her torch. The statue was originally designed for people to be able to go out a little door in her right hand and walk around her torch and have a 360-degree view from almost 150 feet in the air.

As I climb, I begin to pray. To me the staircase is like a labyrinth in an old cathedral in Europe. The dark, quiet corridors and the creaky metal stairs are a chance for me to move my body in a repetitive, circular motion and focus my mind on higher things. I begin to climb. With each rotation up the circular staircase, I list one thing I'm thankful for.

One, thank you for not letting it rain today so that I didn't look like a laughingstock. Whew. Natalie was probably kidding when she suggested that I pray for a miracle, but I gave it a shot anyway, and the thunderheads rolled past us without ever breaking open. She got a real kick out of it, saying that the universe favored me. *Two, thank you for helping us find the Banks Box.* Who knew the mayor was so short? But when I found the little wooden box underneath the stage where someone had forgotten about it, I thought Sophie was going to cry with relief. *Three, thank you for a mayor who cares about the poor and the meek. Four, thanks for Tyson, the best boyfriend in the world. Five, for Lee. Six, my family. Seven, my health. Eight, Raquel. Nine, Charlie. Ten, New York.*

When I finally reach the top, I am panting and lightheaded,

but overwhelmed by how blessed I am. I lean over my knees for a moment to catch my breath and steady myself. Soon my breathing slows, and I stand up. I put my hand on the door that leads out to the statue's torch, and a chill runs through my body. This statue stands for truth and for freedom. She stands for liberty. And it is impossible not to feel her power and the importance of her message at this threshold. Finally, swallowing back a lump in my throat, I push the door open and walk out, a little unsteady.

Manhattan is a shimmering sea of lights, delicate and peaceful. It's better than the best Christmas tree you've ever seen. It's better than New Year's Eve fireworks or the candles on your birthday cake. It's better than anything you can imagine. I grip the railing of the veranda in the torch and stare at the city, sparkling and buzzing with life below me, the city of freedom and refuge. I take a deep breath of night air and smile, thanking God for allowing me to live in such a magical place.

This is what it's like to be alive. This is what it's like to be happy. And I'm the happiest girl in the best city in the world. *Thank you, God.*

I stand on the subway platform, tired from the day, but very fulfilled. I actually feel like my job mattered today, that the bakers, the waitresses, the cashiers, the hotel maids, and the janitors are finally being given a helping hand.

I look down the long, crowded platform and smile as

the illumination from the coming train lights up the dark tunnel. These are not the modern monorail-looking machines that you see in Paris or Washington, D.C. They are real live locomotives that screech and scratch their way through one-hundred-year-old tunnels, sending sparks flying and rats running for cover. In some ways, the subway is a symbol for New York itself: it's dirty, it's a loud talker, but it's also a minor miracle of engineering. I step on and ride a few stops, holding on to the handrail lightly, then exit and begin the long trek up the stairs. No matter how much respect I have for the subway, it's still always a pleasure to ascend the worn, grubby steps and leave it behind, stepping back into the magical world of Manhattan.

Above ground, I stroll down Bleecker Street past the cheesemonger and the Italian grocer and begin to weave my way home. I inhale a deep breath of moist summer air. I love my neighborhood. The West Village is a tiny corner of heaven tucked into one of the biggest cities in the world. The West Village refused "the grid system" when it was introduced in the mid-1800s, so my neighborhood's streets run at crazy angles and stop and start without warning, an unknowable maze. This means that we get the occasional tourist wandering around nearly in tears mumbling, "How can West Fourth street intersect West Eleventh Street?!" and cabs avoid our neighborhood if at all possible, not wanting to deal with our ancient cobblestones and narrow driving paths. The relative quiet, combined with the charming, crumbly brick and brownstone

homes and old, swaying trees reaching up for stories and stories, makes it feel like my own secret garden.

I live on Bedford Street, just a block down from Chum-
ley's, an authentic speakeasy that even today has no sign. You
just have to push on the unmarked door at 86 Bedford, and
you'll find it. I put my key in the front door and begin to climb
to the top floor. My building is a three-story brownstone that
once housed a wealthy family but, in these expensive times, it
has been turned into condos. I could only afford the top floor,
a smallish one-bedroom apartment, but I do have a skylight and
a rooftop deck.

I put the key into my apartment door and let myself in.
Home at last. Charlie is there wagging his little tail at me as I
come in, and I scoop him up and give him a kiss. Charlie is a
milk-chocolate-colored Chihuahua, and like a lot of dogs in
New York, he uses a litter box. My parents think it's insane, but
I argue that what is more insane is coming home by five-thirty
to walk your dog. Who gets off before seven? Besides, Charlie
was Best in Class at Puppy Kindergarten, so he can handle the
challenge of the litter box.

My apartment is dark but it smells good, like detergent,
since I've recently washed my sheets and towels. I throw my
purse and keys on the couch and scuff my way to the bedroom,
worn out. Charlie trails behind me. I check my watch. Hmm . . .
ten-thirty. I decide to throw on my pajamas and go outside on the
roof for a bit. I need to unwind. I walk to my kitchen with Charlie on my heels.

The rooftop deck is really what sold me on this apartment. Just a handful of people in New York can climb a flight of stairs and walk right out onto a fenced-in little paradise. Mine has a view of downtown Manhattan that could break your heart.

Charlie rings the bell I hung by the door with his front paws. I taught him to do that when he wants to go out.

"Ha ha, okay, boy. We're going on the deck," I say. We climb the worn stairs and push open the door to the roof. I see a man sitting on my furniture in the dark. I sigh instead of scream, although the first time it happened I definitely screamed.

"Hey, Lee," I say, rolling my eyes. Lee turns around and looks at me. He is stretched out across one of my loungers in bright red Capri pants and a tight white tank top. "Oh, hey. Just counting the stars," he says and turns back around, talking to Charlie, who has jumped up next to him and is licking his face. The ambient light of New York blocks out most of the stars in the night sky, but Lee likes to look for the few twinklers still mustering through. I can't blame him. Who doesn't love to see the underdog win?

Lee is an interior designer who lives on the second floor. The couple that lives on the bottom floor gets the backyard. Since I live on the top floor, I get the rooftop deck, but Lee, the pickle in the middle, gets nothing but a lower mortgage payment. When he first moved in, I invited him up for a glass of wine on the roof deck. We really hit it off, and before long, we decided to exchange keys for safety reasons. That way, if we ever got locked out, we could call each other to come to the rescue. Now Lee is like a brother to me, a part of my found family.

I plop down next to Lee on a teak chaise-longue. "I'm sorry, but do you live here?" I ask, laughing.

"Apartment Two, Lee Colbert. Nice to meet you." He extends his hand.

I wave it away and see that he is sipping something frozen. He's on a big smoothie kick at the moment and doesn't have a blender, so he finds it perfectly logical to come up to my apartment at all hours and make himself smoothies and sit on my deck. I would complain, but if it weren't for his smoothie making, I'd never eat. "Did you at least make me one?" I ask.

"It's in the fridge. We're doing Banana Wheat Grass Wonder tonight."

I frown.

"You'll like it. Would I fail you, Miss Jane?"

Lee's from Charleston, South Carolina, which he describes as "the Southernest place in America" and also "the only civilized place to live," and so he has a lovely drawl and insists on calling me Miss Jane, no matter how many times I've explained that "my people" come from "Yankee territory." I get my smoothie and plop down next to him. It is cold and sweet.

"What's Ty up to?" he asks, sucking on a straw.

"Writing," I sigh. My boyfriend, Ty, is better known as Tyson R. Williams and is an up-and-coming writer. A young editor at Anchor signed up his first novel a year ago on the strength of some short stories he'd had published in *Tin House,*

Boulevard, and *The Virginia Quarterly*. It wasn't a major book deal, but we thought it was exciting all the same.

"Hey, what's that?" I ask, squinting at a large piece of metal on the other side of the deck.

"Elvis," Lee says and continues to coo at my dog.

I squint harder. It is Elvis. A giant, four-foot-tall metal statue of Elvis. "So he's not dead after all."

"No, it seems he was living at the Flea Market in Queens. I rescued him. Two Hercules types delivered him from the back of a van. I thought he needed some air."

I stand up to inspect the statue. It's not young, sexy Elvis, which I could probably deal with. It's Vegas Elvis, complete with a paunchy body and realistic-looking suede pants. There's even a "hound dog" at his feet. "Lee, he can't stay."

Lee looks at me, horrified. "Jane, have you no roots? This is Elvis."

"I can see that," I say and rub Elvis's tummy for good luck. "And he's ugly. He can't live up here."

Lee's shoulders sag. "Please? Just for a little while? He's a huge mistake and, well, you've seen my place. I can't fit another thing in there."

Lee works out of his apartment, and it looks like a flea market itself. It's crammed from wall to wall with his "finds." Sure, sometimes he palms them off on his clients, but mostly he just grows attached to them and refuses to ever part with them. "What happened?"

"Look, she said she was into kitsch. What's more kitschy than Elvis? How was I supposed to know that she's a Manilow fan and that she positively hates Elvis?" He holds his head in his hands.

"You bought the Pelvis for a client, and she refused it?"

" 'Refused it' makes it sound so rational. I think people in New Jersey heard her screaming at me. And I scoured this state for days just to find that for her. I can't even look at him."

I stare at Elvis, his face twisted into his patented snarl. "Well, okay," I say, sighing. "Just for a little while."

"Really?"

I shrug and sit down on the edge of his chair. "Sure," I say. "You'd do the same for me."

"I would," he says and sighs. "Of course, this kind of thing would never happen to you, Jane."

I squint at him. "True. I tend to avoid buying statues of dead pop icons."

"Oh, come on." Lee laughs and throws his hands up in the air. "Hello? Jane, you're perfect. I can't believe I can even stand to be your friend. It's not easy, you know."

"I'll remember your generosity at Christmas."

"With your stupid blond hair."

I roll my eyes. "It's just hair. It grows out of my head this way. Nothing I can do about that."

"And your perfect boyfriend who is perfect for you. You even have the same last name!"

"Williams is a really common last name. Look in the phone book. It can happen."

"And your perfectly organized cabinets and your neat little day planner." I have the world's cutest Kate Spade day planner that I could not live even one day without. Sure, some people like those little organizer gadgets, but I'm old-fashioned. There's just something about being able to write out events and cross them out when you're done.

"And your adorable family and your great job. Aaah!" he screams and throws his hands up in the air. "Even your dog rings a bell on command. I mean, that's insane, Janie."

"Look, Lee. My life is good. I know that. And I'm very grateful for it. God has really blessed me, and I'm—"

"Oh please. You're always talking about God," he says, shaking his head. "What if you didn't have it so easy, Miss Religious? Would you still be so 'God is my best friend' all the time? I don't think so. You'd be down here in the trenches with the rest of us."

I take a deep breath. "I suppose the less you have, the more you have to trust God," I say, but it sounds a little hollow, even to my ears. I walk over to Elvis to inspect him again. He's really not so bad. "I have been very fortunate," I say and nod, thinking. "But you know, even if tomorrow it were all gone, I'd still be thankful for all that God has done."

"Would you?" Lee asks, narrowing his eyes.

"I would," I say, sitting back down on the lounger. "Absolutely."

"I hope you never get the opportunity to test that statement," he says.

"I hope I do," I say, locking eyes with him. "Then you'd see."

Lee shakes his head and takes a sip of his smoothie. "Whatever," he mumbles, and we both fall silent, looking up at the stars.

"What are you thinking, Lee?" I finally ask.

He looks at me, his face composed and serious. "You should really consider getting a mini fridge out here for us."

Chapter 2

Okay, it's pin candy time!" Raquel says. I'm sitting in a circle with twelve eight-year-olds decked out in "Brownie" brown and orange and covered with patches and pins. Raquel and I sit next to each other in the circle so that we seem to be in charge, although I'm never sure. They're eight-year-old girls. They could make a Navy SEAL cry.

Raquel is my best friend from my church back home. Even though she's a few years older than me, we were always close and reconnected when we both ended up in Manhattan. She's an Upper East Side supermom with two darling children, and I'm a working girl with, well, a very smart dog and a boyfriend who sometimes bathes. Raquel married Jack Hardaway, her college sweetheart, at twenty-one and moved with him to the city, where he had landed a great job at Brown & Walton after passing the New York bar. I think she had intentions of getting a job since she was a computer science major, but, whoops, wouldn't you know it? She got pregnant two months after the wedding, so she just stayed home instead. Nine years later, she's the leader of Troop 192 of Manhattan, a ragtag bunch of little girls that includes her own precocious daughter, Haven Hardaway. The troop meets in our church's basement, and Raquel talked me into being her second in command. I must admit when I signed up I was hoping it was temporary, but I've gotten very attached to the girls now and could never leave. If I did, how would I ever find out who ended up getting picked by Tommy Drake at kickball? Tommy is apparently the only boy at their entire school who is cute. How can a whole Girl Scout troop have a crush on just one boy? I don't know. But I pity poor Tommy. I know these girls.

"I can see your bra, Jane of the Jungle," Bella says and rolls over in raucous laughter into the arms of Kaitlin. Bella, Kaitlin, and Haven are the popular girls in our troop. I look down and discover that my conservative collared shirt has become unbuttoned at the top so that the girls can see a tiny inch of my black bra. Bras are the kind of thing the troop lives for. I button it up and shrug. Rule number one of Scouts: never show you care when they tease you. They can smell weakness.

"Bella, excuse me! It's pin candy time. Let's all zip our mouths shut and open our ears," says Raquel. The girls all make a zipping motion across their mouths and toss an imaginary key over their shoulders, then put their hands over their ears and slowly lift them to reveal their "listening ears." Raquel has somehow made being quiet a game. In the beautiful, peaceful silence that follows I worry about the day when they'll outgrow this game. May the good Lord help us.

Raquel turns to the girl on her left. It is Abby, as always. Abby is pudgy and clings to Raquel as if she were her mother. Meanwhile Haven, Raquel's real daughter, wouldn't be caught dead sitting next to her mom. "I see that Abby has remembered to wear all of her pins, her sash, and even has on her sock tassels. Good job, Abby!" Raquel hands her four pieces of candy, and Abby's eyes light up. I thought up the "pin candy." The girls are supposed to wear their uniforms to Brownies, but ever since they turned eight, half of them have decided the outfits are uncool and started showing up in T-shirts with Shakira on the front instead. So now we reward wearing your pins with pin candy. The most you can get in any given week is four pieces, and Abby always makes sure to get all four. She lives for candy. We go around the circle, and everyone gets a few pieces of candy, but no one else gets four pieces because only Abby would wear her sock tassels. I definitely understand. I mean, sock tassels?

"This week, we're going to learn how to pitch a tent. . . ."

Eight hands shoot up, and Raquel looks around.

"Yes," Raquel says to Haven. I smile. Raquel is way more patient than I am.

"Mrs. Hardaway?" Haven refuses to call her "Mom" in Brownies. "Can I pitch the tent with Kaitlin and Bella?" The three girls lock arms together, and I groan inwardly.

"*I'll* put you into groups in a moment." Raquel motions to Abby for her question.

"How are we going to pitch a tent inside?" asks Abby.

Raquel smiles, and Abby begins to pick at the scabs on her legs. "Right on the floor. You can pitch a tent anywhere, and we need to learn how before our big campout next month."

A lot of the troops in Manhattan take wilderness walks in Central Park and "field trips" to the Toys "R" Us in Times

Square, but Raquel and I had agreed that our girls were actually going to learn useful skills. We would hike, camp, tie knots, sail.

"I don't want to pitch a tent," says Haven, crossing her arms over her chest.

"My mom said that sleeping in a tent is ree, ree, ree-diculous."

"Do you think we're going to get our brains sucked out by ghosts if we sleep in the woods?"

"Can I be in your group?"

"Tommy talked to me in Social Studies, I swear."

"Twee-r-wheet!" I whistle shrilly through my teeth. The girls all stop chattering and put their hands over their ears. There will be no anarchy on my watch.

"Listen up!" Raquel says. "I'll take questions at the end. We're going to divide into two groups, one with me and one with Jane, and we're going to learn to pitch a tent." Raquel eyes the girls warily. No one dares raise a hand, so she continues. "Sleeping in a tent is fun. Pitching a tent is fun. When we go on our big fun campout, no one will have her brain sucked out by a ghost. We will instead have a lot of fun building campfires and singing songs, which are fun."

I stifle a laugh. Boy, I'm convinced, Raquel. Sounds like fun.

My group is doing just fine pitching our tent. I've been assigned Abby and Haven, but Raquel wisely took Kaitlin and Bella, and we have all been working together as harmoniously as can be expected. We have just correctly assembled the little flexy-poles when I steal a glance at Raquel's group, which is nearly done with their task.

"Okay, girls," I say and they turn to look at me. I'm holding the instructions in my hand and reading them out loud, thinking that somehow, between all of us, we'll figure this out. Six little pairs of eyes stare back at me, confused. I try to pretend that I'm in a board meeting for an important client. "Great. Well, this should be a snap, right?"

"Do you know what you're doing?" Abby asks.

I look at her, feigning shock. "Of course I do."

"Duh, Abby. She's the grown-up," Haven says, as if any grown-up is trained in all manners of knowledge, not excluding tent pitching.

"Okay, what I want you all to do is get one of those poles over there and begin to thread it through the fabric loops. Start at the bottom."

A few of the girls get the first pole and Haven holds the tent material so that they can put it through. "Great work, guys. See. It's a little bit like that sewing badge we earned." They guide the first pole through a series of loops and down to the other side. It's really starting to look like a tent now. My phone rings, and I can see that it's Tyson. "Great. Now do the other one on the opposite side. I'll be right back," I say, walking away to the corner to talk.

"Hey, you," I say into the phone.

"Hey yourself," he says. "What's the plan for tonight?"

"Well . . ." I say, stalling. My eyes sting from three late nights in a row, my body aches, and all I want to do is go home to my dog Charlie, eat a pint of ice cream, and go to bed early.

"Oh no you don't," he says. "You're not canceling on me again. All work and no play makes Jane a dull girl."

I melt. "Okay," I say.

"How about Alice's at nine? That will give you some time after Brownies to relax. We'll just get some dessert."

"Deal," I say. Alice's is a little café around the corner from my apartment. We go there weekly. Since Tyson's a full-time writer, he's been really nice to accommodate my schedule, which is a lot more hectic. "See you there."

I hang up and turn back to my group, gasping. Somehow all the tent poles are now out of the shell and Abby has wrapped the material around her body and is pretending to be the Statue of Liberty. Two of the other girls are sword fighting with the Flexomatic poles, and Haven is singing "Greatest Love of All."

"Girls!" I say, loudly. "What on earth is going on?"

They all freeze. Raquel looks over to our half of the church basement and frowns. I give her a confident smile to reassure her I have it under control and then plant my hands on my hips.

"Haven said this was stupid," Abby says in front of the other girls, pointing at Haven. Haven pinches Abby on the back of her arm. I sigh for Abby and regret I even asked. This is the sort of behavior that makes the other girls resent her.

"It doesn't matter what happened. Let's just build the tent now. We're way behind the other group," I say. I give each girl a specific task, and slowly but surely we assemble our tent. At the end we all clap and then rejoin Raquel's group, which has been playing "Duck, Duck, Goose," waiting on us to finish up.

"Everything okay over there?" Raquel asks under her breath when we rejoin the Brownie circle for closing songs.

"I broke the second rule of scouting," I sigh.

"Never turn your back on them?"

"Exactly."

"Right on time," I say, brightening as Ty walks up to the table at Alice's. We always sit at the same small round marble table in the corner. We even have a favorite waitress, Simone. Ty leans over and kisses my nose. I smile and sigh. "I've really missed you."

"You too," he says, sitting down beside me. At six foot one, he is lean and muscular and has sparkling blue eyes and light blond hair. After dating probably every available guy at my church and then dating every available guy that Raquel knew who wasn't married yet, I'd given up hope. And then, poof! I met Ty on a stalled A train, going downtown. He'd just moved here and hadn't found a church yet, so I considered it my Christian duty to get him installed at mine immediately. On our first date we went to Coney Island, where we rode the Cyclone and ate cotton candy, and he pitched softballs at milk cans to win me a stuffed animal, a giant pink elephant, which I pretended to really want. I still remember how it felt, standing there on the boardwalk in front of a pretzel stand, kissing him for the first time. I had never felt anything so perfect. And before I knew it, we had become Ty and Jane.

Simone comes over, and I order a shot of espresso, immune to caffeine after all these years, and a slice of apple tart, and Ty gets a ginseng tea and crème brûlée.

"I have big news," I say, sitting up straight in my chair and clapping my hands as Simone places our orders in front of us. I have been waiting all day to tell him this. He's going to flip.

He cocks his head to the side. "Well, spill it."

"Hamilton's going to let me do it," I say and knock twice on the table for good luck, then realize it's made of marble and shrug. Hamilton is the CEO of Glassman & Co. and has been my boss for the last five years. The company was started by Hamilton's father, the notorious Herb Glassman, who retired a few years back and now spends most of his time in the Hamptons. I've been stalking Hamilton around the office, trying to make him give me fifteen minutes of his time to tell him my new idea. And today, he finally listened.

"What?! How on earth did you pull that off? Wow, Jane. You could convince anybody of anything. That man has a heart of coal," he says and shakes his head.

"I've been praying about how to tell him that I want to pursue charities and nonprofits for accounts, and then last night the perfect idea came to me." I take a sip of espresso. I'm so happy I can barely sit still. "The solution is Matt Sherwin."

Tyson looks at me like I've lost my mind. "The actor? Married to Chloe Martin?" I smile at Ty. It's been a lot of work, but he is finally starting to learn the difference between Lindsay Lohan and Ashlee Simpson and last week he correctly listed the names of Angelina Jolie's children.

"They're only engaged," I say. Okay, so celebrity gossip is a minor habit of mine. I get all the magazines. Don't judge. At least I don't chew my nails. "He's going to solve all of my problems."

"I don't know how," he laughs, "but I'm happy for you."

Ty knows me better than anyone, so he knows how much this means to me. I love my job, but . . . well, I just always thought that I'd end up helping people. In college, I knew that someday I'd be out there in the streets passing out bowls of soup and bread or working long hours organizing campaigns against pollution. Seven years later, the Brownies are the only semblance of the life I wanted. But about a month ago, I saw a solution. I needed to convince Hamilton to let me do pro bono PR for charities.

"Matt Sherwin was just signed up to be the spokesperson for the charity World Aid," I say, taking a sip of my espresso. "They are helping feed the poor, *and* he's a celebrity. He's the perfect middle ground that will make Hamilton happy and allow me to do something to effect change."

"And Hamilton took the bait?"

"He was skeptical at first, but he likes the idea of Glassman & Co. working with A-listers, so I have the go-ahead to pursue them. I just hope they bite," I say.

Tyson takes a long sip of tea. "You really are incredible."

"So are you," I sigh.

"And I have good news too." He takes a bite of crème brûlée. "I'm over the writer's block."

"Hooray," I say, and toast him with my espresso. His book comes out just before Christmas, and he's currently putting the final touches on a critical scene, but Ty has been stumped about what to do. His character is literally standing on the edge of a building, thinking of jumping, and he hasn't been able to figure out how to get him down again.

"I'm so relieved. For a while there, I thought I'd blow my deadline."

"That's so wonderful," I say. "Wow, soon you're going to be a real, published writer. I'm going to say I knew you when."

He smiles and blushes a little. "I'm sure it will only sell two copies."

"Are you kidding me? I'm going to buy a hundred of them myself so you'll at least sell one hundred and two copies."

He laughs for a moment, but then he looks down at the table and picks at a hangnail. "Jane, do you ever wonder what would happen if my book were to . . ." His voice fails and he blushes again.

"What?" I ask, studying his face.

"Take off," he mumbles.

Tyson is so gifted and smart. Sometimes our relationship feels like a downhill, out-of-control slide, but Raquel says that's what love is. All I know is that I can never see him enough. I can never kiss him enough. There isn't enough of him in the world. I'll always be on a quest for one more look from him, one more laugh.

"Of course I've thought about it. It's going to be a best-seller."

He shrugs and smiles. "Well, no matter what happens I'll be getting my final payment for the book in a few months," he says.

"Wow," I say. "That's so wonderful. We'll have to do something fun."

He smiles, a little lopsidedly, and takes a long drink of water. "Maybe. I might save it instead . . . for a big purchase."

My heart swells. A ring! A ring! He's saving for the ring. "That's a great idea," I say. I burst into a big, wide smile.

"Like an apartment or something. I've been thinking of buying a little place to call my own."

Even better. Our place. I don't want to burst his bubble by reminding him that even four of his books won't be enough for a one-bedroom apartment here in Manhattan. "That's right. You just keep saving, and one day you'll have enough for a down payment," I say, and then add in my head, Especially when we sell my place and pool our money. How responsible of him.

He looks down at his tea for a minute. I wonder if we should have a fall or a spring wedding.

"Jane," he says suddenly. "What do you think about New York?" He looks intently into my eyes.

"What do you mean?"

"I know you're from around here, but could you see yourself settling down here?"

He's definitely going to ask me soon. Why isn't he using

his money for a ring? Did he already buy it? No. I'll bet it's a family ring. That would be very special.

"Oh yeah. I'd love to settle in New York. In fact, I always imagined myself bringing up my family here." He looks at me and plays with his fork. He's nervous that I'll want him to move to the suburbs once we're married. He's a writer. He needs to be right here in the heart of the city. I get that. "I'd never want to be one of those moms out in the 'burbs. I mean, all the best schools are here in the city, right?" He shrugs and coughs. "Exactly. And my family's right up in Westchester so if I had kids"— I change that to "if we had kids" in my head—"then I could just leave them with Grandpa and Grandma when I go away on vacation. It would be perfect to never leave here. Just like I always dreamed."

He nods and smiles. "Right. That's how I thought you felt. Just wanted to make sure." He smiles back at me his patented crooked grin, and we just sit and stare at each other a moment. I'm so excited at the way our lives are finally coming together.

Chapter 3

Jane, can you hand me that olive oil?" Raquel says just as the timer on the oven starts to buzz. She whips around, opens the oven door, peers in, and takes the chicken out.

"Mom?" Haven yells from the living room. "Where did you put my sunglasses?"

"Why do you need your sunglasses now, Haven?" Raquel yells. Without missing a beat, she grabs the olive oil from me and sprinkles some over the spinach leaves she has poured into a bowl, then tops it all with goat cheese and apples. I stand by, trying to stay out of the way. Raquel looks at the back of the house again and belts out, "It's almost dinner time. Can you go grab your sister?"

"But I need them," Haven yells. We hear the thud of toys being thrown on the floor of her bedroom, and Haven singing "This Kiss."

"Would you mind bringing this to the table?" Raquel asks me as she shoves the salad into my hands. I shake my head and walk to the dining room. I see Haven has set it tonight. The forks and spoons are reversed, and she has given her father a giant serving fork instead of a regular fork.

"Jack, where's Olivia?" Raquel yells to her husband,

who is on the computer in the living room. Olivia is their younger daughter and a real live miracle. When she was born, she was completely deaf. Raquel and Jack were devastated when they found out, and their doctor was not optimistic that Olivia's hearing could ever be improved. After visits to several specialists and a lot of prayers, they heard about a new and somewhat experimental surgery that might be able to help. Their insurance didn't cover it, and though it cost them their savings, Raquel and Jack never thought twice about getting Olivia's cochlear implants put in. Now except for a small square pack she has to wear in her pocket every day, you'd never be able to tell she is deaf. Olivia is as talkative and outgoing as any two-year-old.

"She's probably with Haven, honey," Jack calls. It will never cease to amaze me how hard it is to keep track of a two-year-old in a two-bedroom apartment. There just aren't that many places she could go.

"Haven, bring your sister to the table," Raquel yells, placing the grilled asparagus on the table. "I'm so sorry about all this," she says to me, shaking her head.

"I'm almost ready," Haven calls from the room the girls share. "Olivia, stop touching my things," she shrieks, and we hear a crash, followed by the high-pitched crying of a toddler.

"Don't ever have kids," Raquel says under her breath before rushing out of the room.

I look around at the photographs on the wall, framed Christmas portraits of the family. Jack and Raquel have to be the hottest couple outside of Hollywood. With his blond hair, huge build, and blue eyes, he looks like an old-fashioned superhero. She is a taller Salma Hayek, and was elected homecoming queen her senior year in an unprecedented landslide. I always wanted to be her, but eventually I realized I was never going to have a mother who danced to salsa music or a cousin who starred in a telenovela. I am just Jane. Plain Jane. I look at the picture a little closer. Their daughters should really model, though I know Jack would never go for that. They practically radiate wholesomeness, their light-brown curls springy above their lacy dresses. Olivia even got Jack's blue eyes, which are just stunning on her. They're all so perfect. It's hard not to envy Raquel.

"You are not wearing that at the dinner table!" Raquel yells over her shoulder as she comes into the room.

"I just want to show Jane," Haven whines, coming into the room, followed closely by little Olivia. And God forgive me, but I can't help it. I burst out laughing. Haven is dressed in a rolled-up denim skirt, a tight pink shirt, and patent leather Mary Janes. She has pulled her hair into a high ponytail and is wearing giant dark sunglasses. She is also wearing bright red lipstick and has blue eye shadow above her eyes, around her eyes, and, inexplicably, on her left cheek. She has dressed Olivia in pink leggings and a pair of her mother's heels and has painted her face in a similarly clownlike fashion. "Do we look cool, Jane?" Haven asks, putting her hand behind her head and sticking out her left hip.

"Very cool," I say, trying to stifle a laugh. Raquel glares

at me. "I mean, not too cool." Haven's face falls. "I mean, um . . ." I look at Raquel.

"Are we ready to eat?" Jack asks, coming into the room, and Raquel just shakes her head and collapses into her chair.

"**Are** you okay?" I ask. Raquel is loading the last of the dishes into her dishwasher while Jack gets the girls ready for bed. "You look very pale all of a sudden."

"I'm fine," she says, smiling weakly as she straightens up. "I'm just tired."

"I know what will help," I say, pulling down the box of cannoli I picked up at Veniero's from on top of the refrigerator. "You want some coffee to go along with these?"

"No coffee for me," she says. "I think I'll just sit down for a bit." She walks to a chair by the table.

"Raquel, I've known you since we both ate boogers. Tell me what's going on," I say, pulling out a chair next to her.

"This can't be happening," she moans.

"You're freaking me out, Raquel," I say, leaning in to her. "What's up?"

"I'm pregnant." She looks at me blankly.

"You're what!? That's so great," I say, clapping.

"Shhh . . ." She hushes me. "I haven't told Jack yet."

I cock my head at her. "Why?"

"You couldn't tell?" she asks, turning to show me her profile. I had noticed that she'd put on some weight lately, but I had attributed it to her passionate embrace of snack cakes. Having young kids around the house isn't easy.

"No way," I say. The truth is not what a pregnant woman wants to hear. "Why haven't you told Jack?"

"I'm in a little denial, I think." She rubs her stomach, which is definitely a bit domed. "My cycle has been somewhat irregular for years, so it took me a while to realize it. I'm three months already, and I just got up the courage to tell you."

"But this is great news." I lean in to give her a hug. "You should tell him."

She purses her lips and slowly exhales. "It's not the best timing," she says, shaking her head. "Things are really hard for Jack at work right now, and there have been rumors of downsizing, and with Olivia's medical bills, he's just worried sick about it. And look at this place," she says, gesturing around at the laundry pile on a chair in the corner and the toys scattered across the floor. "Do I look like I can handle another child right now?" A tear leaks out of her eye, and she wipes it away.

"Oh Raquel," I say, leaning in to give her another hug. "I'm sorry." And then, because I can't think of what else to say, I add, "God will take care of this too."

"**Honey**, do you want some more lemonade?" Mom asks as she walks by.

"No thanks, Mom," I say, looking down at my glass, still

half full. I stretch my legs out on the patio, enjoying the sunshine. I love Saturdays in Westchester. All my friends are back in the city dodging cabs and pooling sweat on the grimy streets, and I'm lazing on a lounge chair under towering sycamores about to enjoy my dad's famous burgers.

"Ty?" she smiles at him, lifting her chin and winking. "One for you?"

"No thanks, Mrs. Williams," he says, flashing her a sweet smile.

"Tyson? What have I told you about that?" She turns to him and puts her hand on her hip.

"Oh, sorry. No thanks, *Elizabeth*." He grins at her again.

"That's better." My mom blushes. I make puking noises in my head. She's so funny. She has a complete crush on Tyson. In fact both my parents do, but I guess I'm thankful. After all those years of bringing home boyfriends that they hated, it's something of a relief.

"I want one," Jim yells from a raft in the middle of the pool. Jim is technically my older brother, but he acts like he's five. He's currently applying to an alternative medical program where he'll learn ancient Chinese medicine, but this summer he's living in his childhood bedroom again and playing World of Warcraft. He says he doesn't want to be "on the great hamster wheel of life" like me. He has already tired of being a volunteer firefighter, a real estate man, a tennis pro at the club, and a food co-op produce manager, but not one of them made him "want to get up in the morning."

"Are your legs broken?" Mom says to Jim over her shoulder as she laughs and strides away. Mom's happy to have Jim home, but she's also hilariously sharp-tongued.

"Jane, get me one," he says from the center of the pool. "Please?"

"What, am I your slave?" I laugh. "I'm nobody's slave. Except maybe Zac Posen." I take a sip. "But you're no Zac Posen. Zac Posen has a job."

"Aw, come on," he whines, paddling his raft slowly to the edge of the pool. "She comes home for one day and suddenly she's royalty?" he yells, grabbing the pool wall.

"We've got a crown we're presenting her with later," Dad says from behind the grill. He's wearing a very tall, white chef's hat and an apron. He's grilling today with a new birthday present—an electric meat thermometer.

"Why is she so special?" Jim huffs as he gets out of the pool.

"Because I'm employed," I say, as he passes by me, dripping wet.

"You've really lost that old humor I used to love in you," Mom says to Jim, who is wrapping a towel around himself and pouting.

"That's why I'm home," he says. "To get it back."

"Really? And here I thought it had something to do with Patrice Lovell next door," I laugh. Patrice, our next-door neighbor, was Jim's first girlfriend.

He rolls his eyes and walks inside. I look at Ty, who is

turning a gorgeous bronze in the sun. "Aren't you glad my family just lets it all hang out when you're around? I mean, some families might actually try to be normal around guests."

I look back at Mom and Dad. They still make a handsome couple, after all these years. My dad has the über-blond hair my brother and I inherited, although his has turned a respectable snowy white. My mother keeps her chestnut hair in a fashionable low ponytail. Mom always stayed home with us when we were kids and took us to church every Sunday, but since we moved out (in Jim's case, for the first time), they've reinvented themselves. Mom now works part time at the church, and Dad retired last year. They're happier than they ever have been, and they're more in love. But they're still completely dorky.

Tyson gets up and walks over to my father and the two men begin chatting about sports, and Mom comes over to take his chair for a moment.

"I'm so excited about your World Aid thing," Mom says.

"Thanks," I say. "I still can't believe they agreed to my proposal. It's going to be such a big account for me."

"I can believe it," Mom says and nudges me. "You're the best publicist in all of New York. They're lucky to have you. And you'll be working with that Matt Sherwin, right? I can't wait to tell everyone I know about that little tidbit."

"Yeah," I say and blush a little. It's still sinking in that I am now the official publicist for World Aid and will be spending a lot of time with an A-list celebrity. Matt Sherwin is as Hollywood as it comes. And World Aid is doing so much to feed the developing world. It's the opportunity of a lifetime.

Squinting into the sun, I look at Dad and Tyson. They seem to be in a serious discussion and their voices are low.

"What's that all about?" I point at them.

Mom looks at them and then shrugs. "Beats me." We both watch as Dad offers his hand and Tyson shakes it. Tyson looks back at the two of us over his shoulder. I could be crazy, but I think . . . did he just ask for my hand in marriage?

Dad turns around with the biggest grin on his face. "I propose a toast," he says. He waits as we all raise our glasses. "To the Williamses."

"To the Williamses," we echo. Except I'm pretty sure I hear Jim say, "To Captain Morgan." But as I say the words, a chill runs down my spine.

"Come on, Charlie. Let's go. Ring the bell." Charlie looks at me holding his leash and then rings the bell by the door. We're off on our scheduled evening stroll. I have Charlie penciled into my calendar for a walk every evening for the rest of his life. As I descend the stairs I hear a loud commotion below. It sounds like Lee is moving his furniture around inside. I knock on his door.

"Who is it?" an older lady's voice calls, and then I can hear Lee's muffled voice, tight and strained.

"It's Jane," I say. I wait a moment longer and then the door swings open. "Hi," I say to Lee, who does not look like himself. His eyes are puffy, he has a bandana tied on his head, and he's wearing cutoff denim shorts and a sleeveless Bon Jovi shirt. "What in the world?"

But before Lee can answer, a slim woman comes from behind him, pushing him out of the way, startling Charlie, who starts to bark.

"Shhh. Shhh . . . Charlie. This is a nice lady. She's our friend." I pick him up, and he calms down but continues to eye the woman.

"I'm Mary Sue Colbert, Lee's mother. Just call me Mary Sue, shug," she says and presses my hand in some kind of old-fashioned, dainty handshake.

I snap out of my shock. "Oh. Hi. Nice to meet you. I live upstairs. I'm Jane Williams, and this is Charlie."

"Oh. We're going to be neighbors then," she says. She reaches out, lets Charlie sniff her fingers, and begins to scratch behind his ears. He starts wagging his tail and squirming to get down, so I let him down, and he practically leaps into the arms of Mary Sue. "Aren't the little 'uns the best?" she says and scoops up a very happy Charlie. "Come on in, Miss Jane," she says and opens the door to Lee's living room. Lee's apartment is even more cluttered than normal, but this time every available surface is covered with boxes.

"Can I get you a glass of water?" she asks.

"Sure," I say. Mary Sue goes into the kitchen with Charlie on her heels and leaves me alone with Lee. I sit down next to him on the couch.

"What have I done?" he whispers.

I keep my voice low. "Please tell me what you've done. I'm at a loss. Your apartment has doubled its furnishings somehow, your mother answers the door, and you look like you're from Queens all of a sudden. What's up?"

He puts his head on the coffee table and mumbles, "I told my mother to come and see me. She took the next plane up here. That was Saturday. Her 'personal effects' arrived today."

I start to chuckle at his dramatic despair when Mary Sue comes back in with a glass of water for me. She pinches Lee on the cheek. "So you're the Jane that Lee is always talking about. I tell you what, shug, when Lee first mentioned you, I thought to myself, Now Mary Sue, I think your son has finally found himself a bride, but he says you're just friends and you have another beau."

I smile. Mary Sue is sweet, if a bit meddling. "Yes. I have a boyfriend named Tyson. I . . . don't think I'm really Lee's type. But Lee and I are good friends."

"That's nice," she says, taking a sip of water herself. "He's such a good boy, Lee." I look at him, a bit uncomfortable that we're talking about him as if he weren't in the room. "I'm afraid I just wore him plumb out with the big move. But isn't he a dear? Why, you know, he positively insisted I come up here and live with him."

"That's nice, Mom, but I'm sure Miss Jane needs to take Charlie on his walk now. I'll come up and see you later, Janie."

"Oh hush," she says to him. "He just gets so embarrassed, you know. But when I told him I had the cancer—shug, I got cancer of the bosoms—then he said, No mama of mine is going to get treatment at some second-rate hospital and be surrounded by perfect strangers during her time of need, so I just obeyed him and came right on up here, though, you know, leaving Charleston is never ideal."

I look at Lee and can see this is true. I stare at my glass of water not sure of what to say. Poor Lee. Why didn't he tell me? Did he just find out? I search for something to say and come up with nothing that doesn't sound trite.

Mary Sue sees my shock and pats my hand. "Don't you worry now for one moment. I'm gonna lick this silly thing, and we'll all have a big ol' time here in New York in the meanwhile."

I try to smile at her, and Charlie jumps up to her lap and kisses her on the face. She laughs and pets him. "Buck up, Miss Jane. I'm serious. It's gonna be just fine."

When we walk through the door in the ballroom I feel light as air, with Tyson's hand on the small of my back. I'm wearing the long black gown that I always wear to formal events. Thank God for Valentino. Tonight is Hamilton Glassman's fortieth wedding anniversary, and he decided to surprise his wife Genevieve with a party at the Four Seasons. He keeps saying that only a few personal friends have been invited, but since I ended up having to do most of the planning for the event, I happen to know that for him "a few personal friends" translates to the mayor, several senators, and about four hundred other beloved guests, including the entire company. Must be nice to be a Glassman. But the good news is that I'm not working tonight and aside from a few unavoidable meet-and-greet moments, Ty and I will get to dance to a real big-band orchestra and drink the finest of champagnes all night, which is something his writing does not normally afford us. All around us couples are dressed to kill and swirl and sway to the music.

"Ooh la la," I say and wriggle my nose at my handsome date.

He shrugs. "Pretty fancy in here."

We walk over to an empty table covered in a crisp, blindingly white tablecloth with a tasteful centerpiece of calla lilies. I look around and see Hamilton and his father, Herb, talking to a group of sycophantic men in tuxes. Tyson and I have a seat at the table and chat and nuzzle each other for a few minutes, when a slick businessman plops down next to us. Before I know it, he has Ty trapped in a discussion about "the real estate game." I hate party bores and decide the best thing I can do to make it up to Tyson is to fetch a plate of hors d'oeuvres and a glass of champagne for us to share.

I make my way over to the food area first and queue up behind a tall man, but just as I'm coming up, someone comes over to him and they begin to chat. I wait politely for a moment, then I discreetly slip around them and then hit the rest of the spread. I pick up a knife and spread a bit of pâté on my plate and take a piece of baguette.

"I saw you cut in line," a voice from behind me says.

I turn around and look up at a tall, dark-haired man. "I'm sorry," I say, looking around to see if anyone notices this strange person accosting me. "You seemed to be occupied. Please, go ahead, then."

No guy in his right mind would actually cut you back, but sure enough the man gets a very pleased look on his face and cuts in front of me. I sigh. Chivalry is truly dead. I comfort my-self with an interesting-looking canapé.

The man turns back to me again. "Was that you who took the last of the duck pâté?"

I look at him, confused. "What? Oh, no. I have this other kind," I say, pointing at my plate. He studies my plate with in-terest and then looks at my face, as if trying to discern if I'm telling the truth.

I snatch my plate away and say, "If you'll excuse me, I'm not feeling hungry anymore," and stomp away. The nerve of some people. These rich, important types are always the same. They think that everyone will bow down to them and kiss their feet. I glance over to my table and see that the real estate agent has not even come up for a breath, and Ty, bless his heart, is still listening intently, so I decide to go and get a glass of champagne and cool down for a moment.

Armed with a glass of champagne, I turn back toward the party and watch people dancing to a George Gershwin song. It is beautiful. I love watching the guests, swaying perfectly to the music, dripping with diamonds and sequins. People just don't know how to dance anymore. It's only the older generation that has charm and class. And then I think about Lee's mother, Mary Sue, with her lovely, thick drawl and can-do spirit. The week has been so busy, I haven't had even a moment to stop and process what she told me the other day. Poor Lee. I need to have coffee with him soon. Maybe there is something I can do for the two of them.

"You sure seem to be enjoying that champagne."

I look up and see the rude man again. What kind of night is this? I'm a publicist. I can handle this. I will not be intimidated. I will not yell. I will be in control.

"Jane Williams, nice to meet you." I thrust my hand forward.

"Coates Glassman," he says, clipping off each vowel. He shakes my hand roughly. "Charmed, I'm sure." He takes a sip from his glass and smirks at me. "If you don't mind my saying it, you are sucking down that champagne as if it were a Malibu Sunrise and you an eighteen-year-old coed."

I look at my glass, and it is indeed nearly empty. I look into Coates's eyes to show him I'm not afraid, even if he is related to my boss. "I beg your pardon?"

"Oh come on, it's natural," he says, looking around the party. "Something as romantic as this is sure to get you worked up about how you still don't have a boyfriend and you're, what, thirty-f—"

"Look, nice guess, Coates, if I may call you that, but I *do* have a boyfriend, and I *am* in love so such a romantic affair as this is just, well, that. Romantic."

Coates raises his eyebrow at me.

"And I'm only twenty-eight."

Coates laughs as though he's just been told a very good joke, and I blush. I really am twenty-eight. What is he implying?

I decide to just walk away and not let him spoil my evening any further, but just as I am turning to go, Coates says, "May I ask you five questions?"

I turn back to him and cock one eyebrow. "I thought it was usually twenty questions for parlor games."

"I'll only be needing five."

"I get one first."

"Sure. If it will make you feel better, then ask away."

"Why?" I ask him.

"I'm an actuary. Do you know what that is?"

I shake my head no.

"It's my business to ask the questions no one wants to ask themselves. I have to know things about people that they don't want to admit they know."

"What?"

"Sorry. You had your one question. Now I get my five." I shrug. "Good then, we'll begin. Where is your day planner right now?"

I look down at my feet. "I don't have one."

Coates frowns at me playfully. "Now, Jane, this will never work if you lie to me."

"How do you know I'm lying? I'm not lying," I say, lying through my teeth.

"I would say it is uncharacteristic of you to lie, if I had to guess, but I assume you are right now. You're a young, driven businesswoman whose entire appearance screams, 'I keep my life just so.' Ergo, you must have a planner or a calendar of some sort."

I look at my feet again. This guy is pretty good. I look up at him and say finally, "It's in my bedside table. Left-hand drawer."

He smiles arrogantly. "Good. Next one. Did you grow up in Westchester or Connecticut?"

I narrow my eyes at him. "How is this fun for you if you already pumped someone I know for the right answers? Who was it?"

"On the contrary," he says, his eyes crinkling in delight. "I just happen to be good at what I do. So is that Westchester? I'm leaning toward Westchester, and I'm rarely wrong."

I roll my eyes at him. "Yes. Westchester. But how did you—"

"I've known other women who grew up there."

Great, so I'm a Westchester type now. I look down at my manicure and wonder if that's what gave me away. Or was it the shoes?

"Three. Did you cry when Ross and Rachel got back together?"

"Yeah, but who didn't? That's hardly revealing. What are you trying to figure out, anyway?"

"Four. Which one is your boyfriend?"

I smile and turn and point at Tyson, who is looking adorable with his floppy hair.

"Really?" Coates says, as if surprised.

"What? *Now* you're surprised? Not when you correctly guess where I came from?" Tyson and I are such a good couple we practically match. Once someone stopped us on the street and said we looked good together. This Coates guy must not be that much of an actuary, whatever that is.

"I'm just surprised, is all. I'm surprised that *that's* your boyfriend."

"It's not like you're Miss Cleo."

"*That's* never going to last." He raises his eyebrows.

"Do you have another question for me? I should really be getting back."

Coates looks over at Tyson and shakes his head again. "Yes. One more. What is it that you really want to do with your life?"

I rear my head back. "Saving the biggest one for last, I see."

"Is that how you see it? It could be the easiest one, really. Depends on your perspective."

I look at him sideways. It is the hardest question, right? I mean, how does anyone really know what she wants to do with her life? Or what God wants her to do with her life? I might already be doing it. I'm not sure. Marry Tyson? Start a family? Climb through the ranks at Glassman & Co.? That's what I have planned. So that's the answer, right? I open my mouth to tell him, with confidence, what I really want when Hamilton walks over to us and claps Coates on the back.

"Coates. Good man. Nice to see you." Hamilton turns to me, surprised to see us standing together. "And Jane. I see you've made the acquaintance of my roguish nephew. Got all the looks in the family, this one." He winks at Coates. I look at Hamilton to see if he's serious, and he most definitely is, and then I look at Coates. Huh. He is kind of good-looking. I hadn't noticed. Nothing like Tyson, who has women gaping at him on the street, but rather cookie-cutter handsome. Dark, straight shiny hair, conservative cut, blue eyes that are rather cold, square-boxy face, no facial hair. He's a tie-advertisement kind of guy. And Hamilton is implying that we are flirting with each other.

"We've met," I say, trying to think of an exit strategy.

"Well, now. Don't lose your heart to this one. He's got quite a path of broken dreams strewn out behind him."

I look at Coates. Any decent man would deny this or blush at such a ridiculous statement, but instead Coates is simply standing there with his arms crossed across his chest, beaming with joy.

"He's the family black sheep, you know," Hamilton says, laughing.

"I'm not particularly surprised," I say.

"Pardon me, will you?" Hamilton asks and then slips away at his wife's beckoning from across the room.

"It was nice meeting you," I say to Coates and turn to go. But at the last moment, he catches my wrist.

I turn around and look at him. "What now?" I ask.

"Don't you want my assessment, Jane? Here I've been working so hard on it for you."

"Not really."

Coates laughs as though I've said something hilarious. "Exactly!"

"I'm sorry?" I say. I know I shouldn't let him goad me on, but I can't resist.

"That's exactly my assessment."

"What is?"

"Jane, you're a very smart woman. You're ambitious, organized, well liked, successful, but you don't ask yourself questions if you don't like their answers."

"What?"

"You lie to yourself."

Chapter 4

Lee is standing in my doorway holding two pints of Ben and Jerry's and smiling guiltily.

"I know I was supposed to bring sandwiches," he says, cringing. "But I just couldn't face it. Mom's got me on an egg-salad sandwich regimen I can't even discuss." He brushes past me and flops down on my couch, putting his feet up on my coffee table. "I'm going to have to spend hours on the elliptical machine to make up for this, but I need some Chunky Monkey right now."

I grab the other pint out of his hand and sneer. "You get Chunky Monkey, and I get reduced-fat vanilla yogurt?"

"It's better for your figure," he says, sinking down into the cushions.

"Hey!"

"Now, Jane. You know if you got off your routine you'd be unhappy. I'm just watching out for you." Charlie comes running out of my bedroom and jumps into Lee's lap. Lee pats his head absently and then puts him back on the floor.

I walk to the kitchen to get spoons. "Rough week?"

"The worst," he says dramatically, burying his face in a throw pillow. "I just need some time to unwind." I toss a spoon at him, and he lets it land on the couch next to him. He picks it up, then turns to me very seriously. "My mother is driving me crazy."

"Mary Sue?" I sit down next to him and dig into my tub of frozen yogurt. "But she's so sweet," I say through a mouthful of vanilla.

"She is sweet. But she is driving me crazy. She has completely taken over my life. It's like high school all over again, except this time she can't make me take Tina Elliot to the prom."

"Huh?"

"She was the daughter of my mom's friend. She didn't have a date, so I had to take her or pay for my own car insurance for the entire summer," he says, digging out a chunk of banana. "And I was saving up to buy a bread machine, so I didn't really have money to spare, you see."

"A bread machine?"

"They were just out. Everyone who cared about fine food was getting one." I nod. "She wore headgear." He shudders.

I cringe. "What does this have to do with now?"

"My mother is trying to take over again. She has to be in control of everything. She wants to know where I am at all times. She spends all day cooking and gets mad when I don't eat an entire ham every night. She is redecorating," he says, examining a bit of chocolate on his spoon. "She says my apartment is too eclectic." He takes a deep, dramatic breath. "Jane, she hung flowered wallpaper in my bedroom."

I nearly choke on my frozen yogurt, envisioning Lee Colbert in his new floral paradise. "Floral wallpaper?" I laugh. "Does it make you dream of English rose gardens?"

"I wouldn't know," Lee says, rolling his eyes. "I'm sleeping on the couch." My eyes widen in surprise. "Oh, come on, Jane. Have a little more faith in me. Even if it is my apartment, which she invaded uninvited, I'm not going to make my own mother sleep on the couch."

"Uninvited? I thought you said——"

"*She* said. She said I forced her to come up here, Jane. What actually happened is I said that it was a shame she was so far away and would she like to come up and visit? She showed up with all of her stuff and doesn't seem to have any intention of leaving."

"Oh, Lee, I'm sorry. Is there anywhere else she could go sometimes so you could get a break?"

"My aunt lives in New Jersey, so she'll go out there some, I guess," he says, digging his spoon down into his pint. "But it looks like she's here for the long haul. And she's acting crazy, Jane," he says, turning to me. "She's never been so clingy before. When I was growing up, she was always out at society functions and volunteering at the Historical Society. She let me do my own thing. But now it's like she's possessed. She wants to know where I'm going, what I'm doing, who I'm going with, and whether she can come."

"She's going through a lot right now." I look at him. He's biting his lip. I have no idea what to say. Why am I so bad at this?

"And with moving up here, she's probably just having a hard time adjusting." I take a deep breath. "Maybe she just needs some time, Lee."

Lee stares straight ahead. "When she called and said she had cancer, it was like my heart stopped," he says, looking down. "I couldn't breathe. I couldn't think. I felt numb."

I look at him and squeeze his shoulder. I'm so glad he's talking about her cancer. I had begun to worry he was in denial.

"Jane, when my dad died, I thought I would never be happy again. I can't lose her too. This is just too soon, too sudden, and it scares me half to death."

"Didn't she say that she has really good odds?" I say. I'm racking my brain. No one in my family has ever died early, and unfortunately, my words sound hollow and stupid. I keep searching.

He sighs and pinches his lips together. For a moment, I think he'll cry. He shakes himself, takes a deep breath, and continues. "She says they caught it in time. But I haven't been able to go to the doctor with her yet, so I'm not sure. She's awfully private, old-fashioned, you know, and keeps insisting I not come."

I slide over and give him a side hug. He puts his head on my shoulder and quietly sniffles.

"It's going to be okay," I say again and again in the quiet of my apartment.

After a while, he pulls back and wipes his face with his hands. "Sorry I'm such a mess."

"Nonsense. You're not a mess."

"It's just that she's so brave. Do you know how much her

'bosoms' mean to her? She always says, 'Dolly Parton ain't got nuthin' on me.' "

I burst out laughing, and so does he.

"And all I can do is complain about her. I'm a monster."

"No, you're not. Tell you what. When anyone else asks you about how it's going, you be the hero. But with me, you tell the truth. You're not going to get through this all alone. And I won't judge you for hating floral wallpaper or for wondering why there's a crocheted doll on your toilet paper. I know you love her. I'll just listen and laugh with you."

"Thanks, Jane," he says.

I smile, thankful to have thought of some way to help my friend. Charlie whimpers at our feet and then jumps up and begins to kiss Lee's face again and again while Lee laughs.

"And I can rent this mutt out for a small monthly fee too if you need him."

I like to get into the office at least an hour early. It's my time to read the paper online, consult my day planner to see what the day has in store, and get some coffee into my veins. It's a great way to start the day and I look forward to the serenity of the quiet office. My assistant, Natalie, will be in about a half hour from now, and I want to get my tasks organized.

I take a sip of my coffee and begin to scan the *Times* online. I gasp, sputter, and spit out the coffee onto my desk. It's not that it's piping hot. It's the headline I just read: BAD BOY PHILANTHROPIST? The picture underneath it is of a handsome man smirking arrogantly—it's that guy I met the other night, Hamilton's nephew, Coates. I wipe up the coffee with a napkin from my desk, then read the article.

It reports that Coates Glassman is making waves in the New York socialite scene, but not just because he's handsome or a do-gooder. Sure, he gives away untold millions of the Glassman Foundation's money, but he also can't keep a personal assistant, and now two of his former assistants have banded together in a lawsuit against him, stating that he dismissed them unfairly without pay and asked them to work seventy-hour weeks with no overtime. The article also notes that Coates has angered many of his family members by converting to Christianity but that his behavior seems no better since this development. It seems the *Times* had no trouble finding people to give anonymous quotes about this self-absorbed behavior.

I roll my eyes. This is the problem with being a Christian. For every ten good deeds done in silence by humble, devoted followers, there is one yahoo who is publicly acting like an idiot and giving a bad name to all of us. I click on an article about time management strategies, hoping to calm down for a few moments before I begin work for the day, when my personal cell phone rings.

The screen flashes "Unknown" and I hesitate. I decide to answer. It's probably just a wrong number.

"Hello?"

"Hello. Jane Williams?"

"Yes?" I say.

"Jane, this is Matt Sherwin. . . ."

A pause hangs in the air. I process what these two words mean. Matt. Sherwin. Okay, Jane. Don't panic.

"I'm from, uh, the charity?"

I recover. "Hello, Mr. Sherwin. Good to hear from you. Sorry about that." Why is he calling me on this phone?

"Please call me Matt."

We are both silent for a moment. What should I say?

"I'm so glad you called. Is there something I can help you with?" We publicists have to be good on our feet. That's why they pay us.

"Huh? Oh yeah. I just wanted to say, like, how important Aid World is to me, and I hoped that we could schedule a time to meet together."

Aid World? The charity he represents is called World Aid. We'll have to work on that. "Sure. When's good for you? I'd love to meet to discuss *World Aid*."

"I'm only just now back from Bali, so, like, maybe sometime this weekend?"

Meet during the weekend? A tad inconvenient, but oh well. "Sure. Love to. Bali? What were you doing there?" This is a classic trick. Make some chitchat with the client so that he feels important to and loved by your company.

"Bali? Oh right, Bali. There was this convention of actors who are concerned about, um, some animal there. What's it called? Do you know? It's the endangered one?"

"I'm sorry?"

"Oh, the animal I was trying to protect? In Bali? You know it?"

"No," I answer slowly. "But isn't that great of you? You really have a heart for—"

"The giant sea turtle . . . or was it a yak? I think the yaks were in Tibet though."

"Hmm," I say, trying to sound interested.

"Can't be sure. Anyway, let's meet this weekend at the pool at the Hotel Gansevoort."

My eyes get wide. The rooftop pool at the Hotel Gansevoort is the celebrity hangout of the moment, replete with bone-thin women and ultra-tan men. "Su-sure. What time?"

"Let's say Saturday at three, but I'll have Nina call you to confirm."

I jot down, Nina to confirm. Three at Gansevoort. Who is Nina? "Splendid. It will be great to meet you and pick your brain about what you want to do to help with the Strike Hunger Campaign."

"Yep. Um, bye."

I hear a dial tone. "Bye-bye," I say to no one. I've talked to the occasional celebrity now and then, but never anyone on his level and never on my personal cell phone. How did he get the number? What have I gotten myself into?

Chapter 5

I look around uncertainly. The sleek glass fence of the rooftop pool deck reflects the bright sunlight. Thin, tan bodies lounge on the stylish deck chairs, and small groups of perfectly toned socialites gather under the umbrellas. Beyond the glass, the Hudson River glistens, and the deep turquoise pool glows softly in the sun.

The Hotel Gansevoort is a boutique hotel in the gritty-chic Meatpacking District. Celebrities love to come to New York, and specifically the Meatpacking District, to get away from the paparazzi in Los Angeles that surround even tiny cafés, waiting for just a glimpse of someone famous. And the Hotel Gansevoort is this year's beehive for the moneyed and famous. Upon seeing the forty-five-foot rooftop pool, I realize that the entire hotel is rather beside the point. The hotel exists to hold this pool high above the hoi polloi. The pool is the scene. This season, anyway.

I scan the area again. I don't see him. Surely I would recognize Matt Sherwin, right? Every woman in America knows what he looks like. He must not be here yet. I walk slowly to an available lounger on the far side of the deck. I feel out of place in my dark jeans and heels. A few people look up at me as

I walk by but, quickly recognizing that I am not famous, look away. I sit down on the edge of my chair and take it all in.

It's one of those stiflingly hot days when summer feels like punishment, but despite the heat, the pool is almost entirely empty. Just one couple sits on the low steps, chatting quietly. Everybody else is just here to see and be seen. A skeletal blond girl sips something cool and clear through a straw under an umbrella, looking around vacantly. Next to her is a pretty auburn-haired friend. They look kind of familiar, especially the redhead. I rack my brain for a name. The redhead glances up and sees me staring at her, and I quickly look away.

Where is Matt? I should have known better than to show up on time for a celebrity. Maybe I should roll up my jeans and dip my feet in the pool. I lean forward in my chair and begin to roll up my pants, looking up every few seconds to make sure he hasn't arrived. No luck. I start on my other pants leg, looking around.

I stand up and walk toward the edge of the pool. I stick my toes in, then crouch down to sit on the edge. I swirl my feet around in the water. The sound of swishing water is soothing in the moist, silent air.

I don't hear the door open, but I notice every head swivels when a large, perfectly muscled man walks out holding a glass. I look quickly. Oh my gosh. It's him. Two girls to my right lean toward each other and whisper. I take a deep breath. Be cool, Jane.

Matt strides confidently to an open lounge chair, gives a quick wave to the two twittering girls, and sits down. His broad tan shoulders contrast with the white towel on his chair, and his gray swim trunks hug his lean hips. He looks just as good in person as he does onscreen. No, better. I watch as he leans back in his chair, slides his sunglasses down over his eyes, and puts his arms behind his head.

I stand up and pull my pants legs down, slide my shoes back on, remind myself to act confident, and walk toward him. Out of the corner of my eye I catch a woman snapping a photo on her digital camera, trying to be discreet, and I realize that everyone on the roof deck is watching me right now. Matt doesn't seem to notice me coming toward him, and when I get closer, I notice his eyes are closed.

He wasn't even looking for me?

"Excuse me?"

"Uh?" Matt mutters, opening his eyes lazily.

"Hi, I'm Jane Williams," I say, thrusting my hand out. "I'm the publicist for World Aid."

He stares at me confused. "World Aid?"

"Yes, World Aid. For the Strike Hunger Campaign? Your personal assistant, Nina, confirmed that we were to meet here." He looks at me, then looks up at the sky. He looks back at me and starts to smile. I can actually see the recognition dawning.

"Oh right, World Aid," he says, smiling good-naturedly. "That's right." He takes my hand and shakes it. "Jen, you said?" He raises his sunglasses and looks me in the eye.

"Jane."

He nods, taking a long sip of his drink. "Have a seat," he says, gesturing to the empty chair beside him.

"I brought the press kit Glassman and Company is putting together for the Strike Hunger Campaign, and I thought we could go over it and discuss what you're going to be doing," I say, pulling a folder out of my bag. "The first major event we're going to be doing is a benefit party at the Pierre to help relief efforts in Guatemala, and——" I look up to notice Matt has closed his eyes and is making punching motions with his fist. "Are you okay?"

"Wha?" he says, opening his eyes in surprise. "Oh, I was striking hunger," he laughs. "Maybe I'll make that my campaign catchphrase."

" 'Catchphrase?' " I repeat blankly.

"Yeah. My catchphrase." He takes another gulp of his drink, finishing it. He shakes the glass, then looks in it, apparently hoping to find more liquid inside. He looks up at me and smiles from ear to ear. My stomach drops for a moment. Looking at his dimples and white boxy teeth, I understand what makes some people stars. He has *it*. That star quality.

His phone rings, and even though we're working, he answers it. After listening a while he says, "Yeah, dude. Cool. Okay, so St. Tropez. I'll get Nina to set it up. Okay, bye." He snaps his phone shut and smiles a big glitzy grin at me. "Sorry about that. I'm going to St. Tropez with some friends of mine. We're coordinating. Well, I'm not really coordinating, Nina is, but you know."

I nod. "Right. Your personal assistant. We spoke on the phone."

"Yup. My right-hand lady. She handles the finer details of

my life. She can find anything out. She's the one who got me your phone number."

I nod. She's the puppet master. I see. "She sounds great."

"She really is. She's, like, the best . . . Do you want a drink, Jen?" he asks, placing his glass down on the ground. "We could go inside to the hotel bar and grab something cool."

"Su—Sure," I say. "A drink would be good. It's hot out here."

"All right," he says, standing up slowly and stretching. He picks up the towel from his chair and turns toward the glass doors. Matt punches the air several times and says, "Strike hunger!" as we walk. I follow him across the pool deck, acutely aware that every eye is on us as we walk inside the hotel.

As we begin our hike to the pond, the girls whistle the work-camp theme song from *The Bridge on the River Kwai,* also known as "the cool whistle song from the 'old' *Parent Trap*." We had them watch a couple of camping-themed movies before we left, as many of the Brownies have never been camping. In fact, some of their parents have never been camping before. These are Manhattan tykes born into typical New York families. Good people, but not exactly the rough-and-ready type. Luckily, both Raquel and I went with our families growing up, so we feel fairly confident we can build a fire at the very least.

The car ride up here was pretty stressful, with Raquel and me both driving SUVs borrowed from the girls' families. Like most displays of wealth, buying a giant car in Manhattan makes

little sense and is insanely popular, so we had no problem securing transportation, but we had some trouble getting all the
girls and their luggage into the cars. Some of these kids could
have been going on a three-week vacation to Paris for the
amount of stuff they brought. Most of them showed up in what
their parents thought might make good camping outfits. Kaitlin
had on a pink Juicy Couture terry sweat suit with her name
embroidered on the butt. Bella had on stylish camo capri pants,
a matching camo head scarf, and a little white tank top with
rhinestones. Haven had, of course, done her own makeup and
was wearing dark shades, although Raquel had apparently
forced her to wear a sensible outfit from Old Navy. Once we
got everyone into the cars, though, and on the road, we had rel-
atively little trouble getting to the campsite, despite several
potty breaks and an endless game of MASH in the backseat that
almost made me want to drive off the road. After we arrived
we pitched tents, just as we had practiced, and loaded up the
girls for the brief hike to Lount Pond to rent canoes and swim.
They even seemed to be enjoying themselves on the way, which
was as shocking to us as it was to them.

Now we're at the pond, Raquel and I have just made
arrangements for six two-seater canoes and a single canoe for
me. I start passing out the life vests to the girls.

"I don't know how to canoe," Bella says and hands me back
the life vest. "I'm just going to tan on the shore instead." Bella
is the heir to a considerable fortune from a high-end jewelry
store in Manhattan. I'm sure she talks to her nanny this way all
the time and gets away with it.

I bend over so that I'm eye level with her. "We're a troop. We're earning our Water Everywhere badge, and we're doing it together." I hand the vest back to Bella. "So suit up."

Bella makes a snotty face but takes the life vest as if it's crawling with maggots. I move on. I figure she'll give in and actually put it on in a moment.

We all sit onshore while I demonstrate how to paddle a canoe and the girls and Raquel watch. Raquel has finally told Jack she is pregnant, and he is ecstatic. So ecstatic he has become a bit protective, so she promised Jack she'd be really careful this weekend. I break them into pairs, splitting up Haven and Kaitlin and Bella. I hold each canoe, put two girls in it, and send it off. One by one, as the girls get the hang of paddling, the canoes begin to make slow progress across the lake. I hop into my own canoe and paddle out to keep an eye on all my little ducklings. As I approach one of the canoes, I hear trouble brewing.

"Stop it, Abby! Stop it! You're ruining everything!" Bella screams. Haven and Kaitlin seemed to be doing just fine across the lake with their respective partners. But perhaps pairing Bella with Abby wasn't the best idea, even though I did it with the best of intentions. I always think that if the girls would just spend more time with Abby, they'd see how fun she is.

I paddle up to the troubled little canoe. "How is it going, guys?"

"I want a new partner," Bella says, standing up in the canoe. "She doesn't know how to paddle. She's ruining it for me," she says, pointing a finger at Abby. Bella looks a little bit like a modern-day Shirley Temple, with a headful of luxurious brown curls.

"Bella, you don't speak to adults that way."

Bella puts her hand on her hip. "I'm not kidding, Jane. I hate Abby."

I look at poor Abby and see her wilt.

"Bella, we don't 'hate' people in the Girl Scouts. Hate is a very ugly word. What if you heard someone else say they hated you? How would you feel?"

Bella doesn't sit down, but studies my face. "Fine. I don't *hate* her. May I have a new partner?"

I smile. "Absolutely not. There will be no changing of partners. And Bella, if you don't straighten up and fly right, Miss Raquel and I are going to have to talk to your parents about your behavior." Bella juts out her lower lip. "Being in Scouts is a privilege. If you don't behave, you don't get to be a part of our troop." Bella looks at the other canoes, which are a good distance from them now. I pray it doesn't occur to her that her mom is on the local council, which would technically make it a bit tricky to kick her out.

"And I really hope you choose to stay in the Scouts, Bella. We love having you," I say, nodding confidently.

"Fine," Bella finally says and plops back down, the canoe rocking wildly. She crosses her arms across her chest, and Abby begins to row them toward the other canoes. "Great work, Abby," I say. "You have a perfect canoe stroke."

Two hours later, we are all worn out. And even though two canoes have completely capsized and every single girl ended up jumping into the pond, they are having the time of their lives.

By nightfall, the girls are exhausted. We spend our time around the fire recounting the canoeing adventure. Finally, as many of their eyes are drooping, Haven gets everyone to sing "Unchained Melody," which Raquel and I decide is close enough to a campfire song. When they're done, we tell them all to go to bed, and they don't fight us on it.

Raquel and I stay up a little later, make another s'more, and chat and laugh quietly, thankful to have a little time away from the girls. She's sitting across from me on the picnic table, and I'm telling her how Haven screamed in the pond when a fish swam past her, and we're both dying laughing.

"Jane," she says, recovering, "I have to tell you something. I was going to wait until we got back but . . ." She shrugs.

"It's okay. Tell me now. I'm sure it's fine, no matter what."

"I've already informed the Girl Scout Council. I'm retiring."

"What?!" I screech, forgetting the sleeping girls. I lower my voice to a whisper. "You're quitting?"

She looks at the table and picks at a splintered piece of wood. "Jane, I know I dragged you into this, and I want to come back to the troop someday, but I just can't do this anymore. I'm so tired. I'm going to pieces. Jack and I agreed that I need to cut back, or I'll go crazy."

I let this wash over me. She's right. I know she is. Lately, she's been looking stressed and worn out and she's already got Haven and Olivia to deal with at home.

"Okay," I say slowly. "I understand." Okay, maybe that's a stretch, but I am trying to understand. "We'll figure out something."

She looks up at me and smiles. "Thanks, Jane." She rubs my shoulder a little. "I guess I'd feel better if I knew that you were going to take over the troop. I know that's a lot to ask of a single girl, but they love you so much, and I don't know what some of them would do without Scouts."

I am shown to a table in the back at Spice Market, which looks like a fancy market in Marrakech or Bombay. Matt Sherwin is actually waiting for me, which is good, since he just told me an hour ago that he made dinner reservations so we could discuss the Strike Hunger kickoff party. I had to drop everything, including my date with Ty, to rush over here, since I wasn't about to let this campaign slip through my fingers. All eyes turn and watch me as I approach the table, and out of the corner of my eye I see a flash go off as he stands up and gives me a kiss on the cheek. I blush. Just great. Today I discovered a weird spot on my face and didn't have time to do much in the way of covering it before I came.

"Jane," he says, pulling back and holding me by the shoulders. "It's so good to see you."

I want to be mad at him, but I simply can't. It was rude of him to book a last-minute dinner, but as he comes around and pulls out my chair for me and is so polite, I hate myself for it, but I melt a little. He's very, very good, this guy. Oh, star quality.

"So," I start once we're seated, "how's Chloe doing?"

He smiles. "Chloe's so great, you know? She's like this amazing person."

"That's great. You guys seem really good for each other. And she's filming something? Or she's here in New York too?"

"She just wrapped a new Penny Marshall film and now she's at home in Maryland at her mom's." I smile. It's so cool when stars make family time a priority.

The waitress comes and takes our drink orders, and Matt begins to tell me about his new idea for a Greek gods theme for the Strike Hunger kickoff event. Across from us, I notice two girls watching us intently. One of the women has lovely auburn hair and the other is a brunette. Hmmm, red hair must be coming back in. Then I study her closer. Have I seen her before? Maybe she's a New York party girl? She turns and catches me staring. I look away, but not before I see her smirk.

Chapter 6

Tyson stumbled over his words when he suggested we meet in Union Square Park tonight, and he seemed really out of it when I called him to say goodnight before I went to bed last night. Of course, this means that I have to leave work early to get ready for the big night. I have to make sure I look good. This night has to be perfect.

I sneak out around four—I get in early enough that I don't feel too bad—rush home on the subway, and run up the stairs to my door. Tyson and I are meeting at six-thirty. I give Charlie a quick hug for luck. He licks my face in return.

I go into the bathroom and check out my skin. Ugh. Why is that spot still there? I can't believe this is happening tonight of all nights. I dig in my makeup bag for the pressed powder and dab it over a red patch. I could swear it's gotten bigger. Okay. There. That looks better. Then I slick on some sheer lip gloss. Ty always says he likes it when I wear the lip gloss. I check my fresh manicure. It's unchipped. I grab my digital camera from the living room, flooded with light from the skylight above. I smile as I picture my mother opening the e-mail with a photo of my bejeweled hand attached.

I open the fridge, pull out the cooling bottle of champagne, and put it in my bag. Tyson will laugh when he sees how prepared I am for the big "surprise." But what does he expect? We talked, long ago, about getting married after a couple years, and I really like to keep things on schedule. I unlatch the lock and take one last look around my "single gal" apartment, my heart dancing. I take a deep breath, smile, and walk out the door to meet Ty.

"There's something I've been meaning to talk to you about," Tyson says, pulling his hand away from mine and turning to face me. I take a deep breath. This is it! I look around slowly, drinking it all in. The trees arch above us, creating a deep green canopy of sweet-smelling blossoms. All around us lovers laze on the neatly manicured lawn, and the dog run across the park fills the evening air with sounds of joy and life. Broadway curves behind us, and cabs whiz down the backbone of the greatest city in the world, providing the perfect urban backdrop for this fantasy moment. The skyscrapers downtown twinkle, and the night is warm, thick, and heavy, full of promise. We lie on the warm grass, nibbling the cheese I bought from the farmer's market at the north end of the park. Union Square has never been more beautiful than tonight.

Ty pushes his white-blond hair back behind his ear. He has been fidgety and nervous all evening. I smile at him, encouraging him. This is the moment I've been waiting my whole life for. A little behind schedule, but I'll take it. We're meant to be. Tyson and Jane Williams. We're so adorable it makes you want to puke.

"Jane, you're an amazing person," he says, looking into my eyes.

I am? I smile and give myself a little pat on the back. I guess I kind of am. "Thanks," I say and take his hands in mine.

"And we've been together for a while," he says, taking a deep breath.

"Two years, six months, thirteen days," I say, smiling. He looks at me, confused, then looks away.

"And in that time we've gotten to know each other very well." He watches the skateboarders practicing their tricks on the steps at the bottom of the park.

So he's really going to do it. I guess I pictured it differently all along. He's not on one knee, he doesn't seem to have a ring . . . but then, it's Ty. What did I expect? This is exactly the way he'd do it. Forget all that embarrassing fuss, right?

"I agree," I say. "I know you better than my own feet."

He looks back to me and half-grins. I beam back at him. Jane and Ty are getting hitched, ladies and gentleman. In sickness and in health, here we come.

"Probably better than we know anybody else. And I really care about you," he says.

"I really care about you too."

He waits, looking away, absently putting his hands in his pockets. Go on. I hold my breath. "I've been thinking a lot recently about the kind of person I want to spend the rest of my life with." I smile, nodding and pursing my lips. Just spit it out.

"And, well . . ." He looks at me, then looks away. I touch

his arm softly. "Jane, I think you're going to make a great wife. . . ." I can't contain myself anymore.

"YES!" I yell.

He stares at me, wide-eyed.

"Yes, I'll marry you!" I repeat.

"What?" he mouths weakly.

"Ty, you're perfect. It wasn't an accident that God brought you into my life. You're who I've been waiting for my entire life. I love you so much." I reach over and pull his face toward mine, forcing him to look at me. It's so like him to be nervous. "Of course I'll marry you," I say, leaning in to him and closing my eyes. I've known he's the one since the day we met, and I've been praying about this ever since.

"Jane, I . . ."

My eyes fly open.

Uh-oh.

Why is he looking at me like that?

He pulls his hands out of his pockets and places them on mine.

Oh no. Why isn't there a ring in one of them? "Ty?" I look at him. He doesn't meet my eye.

He places his hands on mine. "I was trying—I wanted to say that, well, I think you're going to make a great wife some-day. . . ." He takes a deep breath.

I look at him. He looks like he's about to pass out.

". . . for somebody else."

The words echo in my head. Despite the warm night air, a chill runs down my spine.

"What are you saying?" I ask, mouth gaping in shock.

"You're great. But I just don't think it's going to work out for us," he says, looking down.

"What?!" I nearly yell, stunned. "You don't want to marry me?" This has to be some kind of cruel joke.

"I wish I could," he says, pushing the stubborn lock of hair back behind his ear again. It is time for him to get it cut. I make a mental note to mention that later on. How would he ever remember things like that without me? He's always so wrapped up in his writing he forgets about practical things. "But I just don't think we're right for each other."

"Why not?" I ask. "We're perfect for each other. Everybody says so."

"No, we're not," he says. "Jane, you're beautiful, and talented, and successful, and funny. But——" He breaks off. "We just don't stand a chance for long-term happiness."

I can't even bring myself to say anything. I wait, openmouthed, for him to go on.

"You're so wrapped up in your career, and——"

"This is about my job?" I swallow hard. I will not cry.

"No, it's not just about your job," he says slowly. "It's about your way of life. It's about——"

"I can quit," I say. "Who cares about stupid old Matt Sherwin anyway? Someone else can deal with him, and——"

"Jane, you're not listening. It's this whole life," he says, gesturing around. A bus honks, and I turn around to see a man peeing on a tree behind us. The deep rumble of the subway below us sounds like the earth is grumbling. The thick hot evening air, which only moments before felt full of promise, now just feels oppressive. "I can write anywhere, and now that the book is going so well, I am seriously thinking about settling down, and—"

"With me," I say, gasping for air. "You're supposed to settle down with me." This can't be happening. "I can work fewer hours. I'll cut back."

"It's not just hours, Jane. It's—I want something else entirely. I want a nice quiet life somewhere where I can just write all day, and where it doesn't cost a fortune to rent a tiny apartment just to live in squalor, and where life moves slower, and . . . Jane, I want a family. I want kids, lots of them, and a wife who wants to take care of them—"

"I'd take care of our children!" I say, enraged. I bite my lip. I will not cry. I will not cry, but my nose begins to sting as I try to fight the tears back. This can't be happening.

"Jane." He looks into my eyes. "Would you really give this all up?" he asks.

I look around slowly. The soft music from a radio fills the park with a low mellifluous sound. I look down Broadway. I can just barely see the sign for the Strand, my favorite bookstore in the world. And a few blocks below it is my church. Our church. I think about all that it has meant to me, keeping me grounded in the big city. I look uptown. The soft glow of the lights of the skyscrapers fills the streets with a cheerful radiance.

I worked so hard to get to where I am. And the campaign with World Aid is going so well, and I am really starting to feel like I'm doing something that matters. Could I really just quit?

I look up at Ty. He's looking straight ahead, staring at nothing, his deliciously handsome profile still. He's everything I've always wanted. The subway rumbles beneath us again, and this time I smile.

I love this city. New York is my home. I'm living the life I've always wanted, that I worked so hard for. The city is a hard place to live, but we're called to be in the world. I have always felt like this was where God wanted me to be, working and living with people who don't know him. Would I really give this all up?

I look around again just as the first raindrop hits the ground next to us. Slowly, a tear works its way out of my eye.

"No," I say quietly.

"I know." A raindrop hits his cheek, and I nod. I stare at him, unable to move. I don't know what to say.

"You'll make some lucky man very happy someday," he says, squeezing my hand.

I look at him. I know he means it, but what a terrible thing to say at a time like this. I want to sock him in the stomach.

"But wait," I say, trying to take this in. "What were you talking about with my father the other day?"

Ty looks at me sideways. "When?"

"At my parents' place," I shake my head back and forth, realizing that I had wanted this so badly that I had imagined it was finally happening, "I saw you and my father talking at my house."

"Oh," Tyson says. "The Yankees. I bet him they'd lose to the Sox this year." Their handshake flashes before my eyes. "Oh Jane. You must have thought . . ."

I nod a few quick, angry nods.

Tyson puts his face in his hands. "I'm so sorry." We sit in silence for a moment while I think about all the miscues I've had. He shakes his head.

"Jane, I'm a fool."

I nod in agreement.

"But hopefully I can make this easier on you. I'm moving to Denver at the end of the month," he says as he stands up.

Denver?

"The pace is slower there, and I can get a lot more for my money, and I will be close to the mountains for snowboarding in the winter, and I can settle down and write. . . ." He trails off.

I just nod, not bothering to wipe away the tears that are now streaming down my face.

"You'll be fine," he says, nodding. "You'll always be fine. You're strong and smart. You're the kind of girl who always lands on her feet." I look away. "In a few weeks you won't even remember my name," he says, smiling weakly.

"Please leave," I whimper, looking down at the pattern the raindrops are making on the ground.

"I love you," he says, turning slowly.

He has never said that before.

I watch him as he walks to the subway entrance, then stare after him when he disappears down the steps.

I pull my purse into my lap to have something to clutch to my shivering body and the cold, hard bottle of champagne feels like a concealed weapon. I don't move, even when the rain begins to beat down on me, even when the air darkens into night.

Chapter 7

You look like you've seen better days," a deep voice says from across the elevator. I have been trying to keep my head down so no one could see my face, which is puffy and red from crying, not to mention covered in a hideous rash that is definitely growing. I figured if I could make it to my office without being recognized, I could close my door and hide out until the hemorrhoid cream does its magic. It sounds kind of gross, but I have to admit it really does get rid of eye puffiness. It takes a little while to work, though, so I have kept my eyes focused on the ground all morning. What kind of boor is this who can't recognize that I don't want to chat? I look up to see Coates Glassman smirking at me. And here I had thought my morning couldn't get any worse.

"I don't know what you're talking about," I say curtly, looking down at the floor again. This must be the slowest elevator in the world. Of all the mornings for his little visit to Glassman & Co.

The elevator dings, and the doors open. I quickly walk out into the lobby. Coates follows me out and opens the glass doors leading to the row of offices. I mumble a polite thank you and scurry to my office, waving at Natalie.

I fall down into my chair and turn my computer on. Work will take my mind off all this. I have a campaign for Astor National I'm working on, and I have to review some permission requests for photos from the Statue of Liberty archives. I type in my password and hit Enter. Weird. I try it again. My computer isn't letting me log on. What a morning. As I'm picking up the phone to call the computer help desk, I hear a knock at my door.

Natalie opens it and pokes her head in. "Hamilton would like to see you in his office."

"Right now?" I ask, horrified by the image of my puffy, tear-streaked face confronting my boss.

She nods and turns away. I stand up, take a deep breath, lift my chin up, and walk toward Hamilton's office. I stop in my tracks when I see Coates inside. Hamilton sees me, nods, says a quick good-bye to Coates, and motions at the chair for me. Coates passes me on his way out, looking at the floor, and walks away. I take a seat and stare at my hands.

"Jane, your personal life is just that, of course," Hamilton says, ruffling a stack of papers on his desk. Oh no. How does he know? I haven't told anyone about Ty. "But when it becomes public, it is no longer none of my business. Especially when it involves one of our clients." He coughs. "One of our most visible clients."

I look up at him. What? "I'm not sure I understand what you mean," I stammer.

"I am referring to this," he says, pushing a glossy magazine toward me. I recognize it immediately as *Star Power*, the weekly gossip rag that fills newsstands and mailboxes across America, including mine. Its circulation is almost as high as *People*'s, mostly because they have dispensed with those pesky words almost entirely in favor of photos of celebrities. I lean in to look and gasp. There is a picture of me! From the pool deck at the Hotel Gansevoort with Matt! But why would they print a bad picture of me in *Star Power*? I look up at Hamilton uncertainly. "You've seen this, Jane?"

"No," I say, looking back down at the page. There's another one. I look closely. It's Matt Sherwin kissing me on the cheek, though from the angle at which the picture was taken it almost looks as if we're lip-locked. It's from that night at Spice Market. And then I see the worst part. The title. PLAIN JANE STEALS MATT FROM PREGNANT CHLOE? And next to it is a picture of me squinting at the sun at the pool, making me look very devious and conniving. I look at Hamilton, then back down at the page. The "article" underneath the photos proclaims that Matt seems to have forgotten about Chloe in light of his new love, an ordinary working girl named Jane Williams who is in fact his publicist at Glassman & Co. for the World Aid campaign. It insinuates that we have been seen gallivanting all around town, while his pregnant girlfriend waits for their child. It even suggests that Matt and I stayed in the hotel together. I look up at Hamilton, wide-eyed.

"But it's not true," I stammer, trying to think. Why would someone do this?

"Whether or not it's true, it's in newsstands everywhere. As you can imagine, this sort of thing looks very bad for us," he says, taking a sip of coffee from the ceramic mug on his desk. "The World Aid people are livid. Instead of helping them promote their cause, you have gotten your name and image into the public eye." He picks up a pen and rolls it around in his hand. "Honestly, I don't think you did this on purpose, Jane, especially because of your . . . church thing." He blushes, but I am too shocked to say anything. "But unfortunately, this is out of my hands. The reputation of Glassman and Company has been impacted, and someone has to take the fall." I look down at his hands. "The board has asked that you be let go."

My mind, in its slow state, takes a few minutes to grasp what he's saying. "What?" I finally manage. "You're firing me? But it's not true!"

"I'm afraid so," he says simply, closing the magazine and putting it on top of a pile of papers on his desk. "I don't have much choice."

"But sir, I—"

"Go ahead and pack up your things. Your password has already been changed, and your company cell phone has been shut off. We'll need to have you out by noon."

"By noon?"

"Yes, Jane," he says, nodding. "Go now and pack."

I am dumbfounded. Speechless. I try to make myself move. Hamilton watches me as I stand up and walk toward the door. Shell-shocked, I walk toward my soon-to-be-ex-office. Fired. For dating Matt Sherwin. What is going on?

I sit down at my desk to think. What just happened? I try to motivate myself to get up and start moving, but I can't. I stare blankly at the wall. This job means everything to me. God? Are you still up there? I was just starting to do something that would make a difference. What possible good could come from this? What will happen to World Aid?

People walk up and down the hall, going on with their jobs, but no one looks in. I take a deep breath and sit up. I look out at the hallway and see that empty boxes have been placed outside my office door. I guess I really do have to move my stuff out. The sooner I get this over with, the better off I'll be. I force myself to rise and walk to the doorway. I reach for a box and am startled to see Coates standing in the doorway. I brace myself. Whatever he's come to say, it can't be good. It's a little too convenient that he made his little visit just before I got the ax to believe he's not involved in this somehow. The board, indeed. I take a deep breath as he opens his mouth.

"I told you it wouldn't last," he says, smiling.

I wait a moment and give him my most piercing glare. His face lights up like a lantern, and he breaks into a huge grin that only eggs me on. A thousand insults flash through my brain.

But I can't get them out. I just run around and begin packing up my things. I can feel Coates standing behind me, awkwardly. He waits for a moment and then walks away. As I hear him leave, I sigh with relief, knowing I'll never have to see him again.

Out on the street, I walk to the subway station, not knowing what else to do. Maybe I'll go get some coffee. I look around to see if there's a Starbucks around, knowing full well the closest one is never more than a block away when you're in Manhattan.

"It's you!" yells the man behind the counter at a newsstand I pass, shoving a copy of *Star Power* in my face. "You're the girl in the magazine." I grab it from him angrily and put my head down and walk away.

"Hey!" he yells. "You have to pay for that!"

I turn around, put a few dollars into his hand wordlessly, and head for home.

When I walk through the door, I am so stunned I just retreat to my bedroom, pull down the shades, and cry in complete silence. The love of my life and my job, all gone in a few short hours. I ask God just what exactly his plan is in all of this, but hear nothing back, only the sound of my tears splatting on my pillow.

Hours later, my tears have run dry, and I am not any closer to comprehending how it all happened or what I am supposed to learn. I decide I need to talk to somebody. My first, involuntary thought is to call Ty—how could he leave me at a time like this? Surely he still cares; surely he will be willing to talk to me right now. But even as I dial his number, I know I shouldn't. I'm not surprised when he doesn't pick up. Even if he misses me like I miss him, he is the kind of person to sever all ties and move on without looking back. I think about calling Raquel, but the image of perfect domesticity she represents is too much for me to handle right now.

I scoop up Charlie to snuggle with him for a while, but he just lies there listlessly. He is cocking up one of his eyebrows lazily. No tail wagging. I guess it's true that a dog always knows when his owner is feeling blue.

I have to go somewhere, I decide, and I have to talk to someone. I have to get out of this stifling room. I pull myself up, say a quick prayer for strength, and slip my flip-flops on. I stumble down the stairs to Lee's apartment and knock timidly on the door. Lee isn't home, but his mother takes one look at me, pulls me into her arms, and hugs me. For the first time today, I feel loved.

Chapter 8

Now don't you worry, shug," Mary Sue says as she pats my back. "It's going to be all right." She squeezes me tightly, then pulls back and motions to the couch. "You sit there, and I'll go get us some sweet tea, and you can tell me all about it." I nod wordlessly, not knowing what else to do.

From the kitchen I can hear her saying, "You know in Charleston we just call it tea. If a person says, Why I do want some tea, they mean sweet tea of course, but Lee told me up here I had to get more specific-like and call it sweet tea. But I said to him, now why don't . . ." I stop listening, drowning in a dark tidal pool of my own thoughts. How have I lost my boyfriend, my job, and my reputation? I am worse than a country music song.

"Do you want some lemon bars?" she calls from the kitchen, poking her head around the corner. Not sure what to say, I nod. A few seconds later, she appears with a flowered enamel tray filled with lemon bars and two glasses of cold, dark tea. She sets the tray down on the table and hands me a glass. I take a long sip of the cool, sweet tea and smile.

"Now," she says, settling into the couch and looking concerned, "Do you want to tell me what's wrong?" I take a deep breath and nod, but as soon as I open my mouth to tell her, I start bawling. Mary Sue doesn't say a word but puts her glass down softly and leans in to give me another hug. She lets me cry on her shoulder for what seems like hours, holding me while my body is racked with sobbing. She pulls tissues out of her pockets to wipe away my tears, and she rocks me gently. The evening light in Lee's living room softens into twilight, and the room slowly darkens. When I can't cry anymore, she smiles at me, switches on the lamp, refills my glass, and starts to talk. Her smooth, buttery voice and soothing accent lull me into relaxation as she tells me about her childhood, growing up among the sweeping verandahs, cobbled streets, and lush trees of Charleston, about the lavish parties her parents threw and the friends she had, the world of trouble she got into when she put a bug in her sister's knickers. I know she's trying to distract me, but it works, and I am transported far away from my own sad world to another time and place.

It's ten-thirty when she finishes telling me about her debutante ball, and slowly, she helps me to my feet. At the door Mary Sue gives me a final hug, and I squeeze her back. "Thank you," I whisper.

"Hush now," she says, shaking her head. "We'll talk more tomorrow." I tread the stairs to my empty apartment, and it isn't until I'm inside that it occurs to me that I should have asked how she's doing.

"**Is** he going to be okay?" I ask, nervously holding Charlie on the icy-cold steel examining table. He looks so pitiful and small in this large, stark room. I can feel him shivering. My eyes ache because it's midnight, and I've been crying all day. This is the worst possible end to the worst possible day in my life.

"I'm not sure," the veterinarian says, making a notation in Charlie's file. Her stern face and graying hair are not comforting, but this pet hospital is supposed to be the best in the city. "Pancreatitis is a serious infection, but it's treatable. I want to keep him here tonight and get an IV into him to get him hydrated again. He's dangerously dehydrated. I also want to run some blood work on him and take some X rays to confirm that he hasn't eaten anything toxic and that there's not something lodged in his intestinal tract," she says. I bite my lip. Oh Charlie. A night in the hospital? Poor thing. I fight back the tears as his little face wanly peers at mine. I need to be strong right now. He'll sense it if I'm nervous.

"You'll take good care of him?" I ask. She smiles at me like I'm an annoying child, while she caps her pen and places it in the pocket of her crisp white lab coat.

"That's what we do," she says, reaching across the table for him. Normally, he'd back away, but he's so weak he allows her to scoop him up into her arms.

"Be good, Chuck," I say. I walk around and kiss him on the head. He looks at me listlessly.

"He'll be fine," she nods. "We'll call you tomorrow with an update."

I nod, pick up my purse, and walk back to the reception area. On the way, I stop and steal one last glance at him as the vet takes him deeper into the hospital. With red eyes, I approach the front desk to make sure they don't need anything more from me.

"Um, hi. My Charlie is going to stay here tonight," I say to the elderly lady behind the big desk.

From behind a nurse hands her a file, and the receptionist peers into it. "Here's his file. You're Jane Williams?" I nod. "Okay, Charlie Williams is admitted at this time. I just need a deposit from you for the visit. I'll print out your estimated costs, and tonight you just pay half of them." I nod again.

While the woman turns around to the printer, I read the sign that says, "All payment is due at the time of treatment. There is no payment plan." I gulp. Charlie has never had to go to the twenty-four-hour emergency pet hospital before, so I hope it won't be too much. At least I've got about two thousand saved up for emergencies just like this. Nothing is too much to make him feel better.

The woman grabs the three-page printout and brings it back to her desk. She slides it over to me. I take it and instinctively flip to the back page while she discusses everything on the itemized invoice. I nearly pass out when I see the estimated total is $643.57.

I am awakened by a loud beeping. I reach out and smack my alarm clock, but the noise continues. I sit up, disoriented. Sun is streaming in through my windows. What time is it? I look at my clock and gasp. It's almost eleven! I overslept, and I am going to be late for work, and—slowly, it dawns on me. I am not

late for work. I don't have anywhere I need to be. And that in-
cessant beeping is my phone. I grab it and flip it open to stop
the noise. "Hello?" I mumble without looking at the caller ID.

"Jane?" a deep voice says.

"Yep," I say, falling back into my pillows. It's all coming
back to me now.

"It's Matt Sherwin." I stifle a groan. Matt "career death"
Sherwin. Why is he calling me? "Did you see the article in *Star
Power?*" he asks and laughs.

"Yeah," I say. How can he think this is funny? "I don't know
where they came up with that stuff." I take a deep breath. "How
did Chloe react to it?"

"Who?" Matt asks. "Can I have some cream for this coffee?" he asks, away from the phone, then turns back to me. "I'm
sorry, what did you say?"

"Chloe? How did she react to the article?" I say. No sense
in being fakey-professional anymore.

"Oh, she thought it was hysterical," he says. "We had a
good laugh over it." He is silent for a moment. "Chloe's so
great, you know? She's like this amazing person."

"Is there something I can help you with?" I say, sitting up.

"Huh? *Can I get another spoon?*" he says, away from the
mouthpiece. "Oh yeah," he says. "I tried calling your work
phone, and it was like shut off. What's up with that? Nina had
to track down your personal cell number again. I had this great
idea for the big party. I was thinking we could have these big
columns, you know? And what if I dressed up like Zeus for the
big speech? And we could have someone dressed like Hera run

around terrorizing people all night, you know, with like, water guns or something."

"Matt, I'm afraid I'm not working on the Strike Hunger Campaign anymore," I sigh.

"But you were, like, so good at it, and we had so many ideas," he says.

"I was fired because of that article."

"Whoa, bummer," he says. "Over some stupid little pictures in a magazine?"

"I'm afraid so," I say.

"Can I have the check please?"

"What?"

"Sorry. Man, Jane. That's a real downer. Oh, I'm getting another call. I'll talk to you later?" He hangs up before I can get a word in, and I fall back on my pillows, cursing him.

After the call the room is silent. What am I going to do with my day? After fifteen minutes of daydreaming, I force myself to get out of bed and stumble into the living room. I can tell that my eyes are puffier than Angelina Jolie's lips, but I realize I left my hemorrhoid cream in my office yesterday. That will be a nice treat for whoever gets to move in next. I almost smile at the thought but can't quite do it.

Not knowing what else to do with myself, I go and open my day planner. I had a whole week's worth of meetings, but now I'm not going to be attending any of them. I look for something else I have scheduled, anything to look forward to. I see "Date with Ty"? scribbled in for next Friday and then throw the planner across the floor. For a moment, I'm appalled at myself, but then I leave it there and switch on my computer. I quickly check my e-mail and scan the headlines at cnn.com. I click around for a bit and then run out of websites that I like to check in on. I've never been much of a Web surfer. Let's see, I can check the weather. So there's a storm coming. Interesting. But there must be something else—oh, good idea. I sigh in relief. I should research pancreatitis. Poor Charlie. I Google it and find a few articles about the symptoms and how to treat it. After an hour, I'm nearly an expert on the disease and force myself to stop. I check my e-mail again. No new messages. I stand up and get a glass of water. I lean against the counter. Should I paint in here? A nice sunny yellow? I think back over yesterday and wonder if I should start looking for a new job, but I can't bring myself to face that yet. I go back to my desk and sit down in front of my computer. I tap my fingers and look out my window. I pull up Google again. What is it that he does? I type in "actuary" and hit Enter.

Chapter 9

This was a good idea, I think, as I ride in a cab through the familiar streets of my hometown, comforting even in the rain. Maybe especially because of the rain. This is where I belong. After moping around my apartment, noticing that the rash on my face was getting larger, and watching bad daytime TV for several hours, I decided I needed to get out. And what would be better than to go home and surprise my parents? They will be happy to see me, and being in familiar surroundings will be soothing. I packed a few things to take with me, and I rushed to Grand Central to catch the 5:17 train.

On the train, Charlie is all I can think about. I called the pet hospital today, and they said he was doing much better, but they recommended he stay another night. I wanted to visit, but they said he was sleeping and suggested it might be harder for him to see me and not get to come home. I sigh aloud, thinking of him in that cold, scary place for another night. He must think I've forgotten about him.

I look out the window at the trees whizzing by. I should probably also think about getting a new job. But my lack of a job only reminds me that there is something worse. Tyson is gone. For good. And that place is still too dark for me to visit, so I push it aside.

As the cab from the train station pulls up in front of my house, I smile, thankful I have such a support group nearby. The lights are on in the living room, and my parents' cars are both in the driveway. I throw some bills at the taxi driver, walk around to the trunk to get my bag, and stride quickly up the flagstone path to my front door. I push open the door and step inside the cool house. "Mom?" I call. I place my bag down in the entryway. "Dad?"

I hear voices in the kitchen and walk in to see that my parents, brother, and a very pretty brunette are sitting at the table playing cards. "Hi guys," I say. They all turn and look at me.

"Jane!" my mom exclaims, jumping up to give me a hug.

"Honey," Dad says, laughing. "When did you get here?"

"What are you doing here?" Jim asks.

"I just thought I'd come home for a quick visit," I say. They all stare at me, confused. "So here I am," I say and laugh.

"Well . . . welcome," my mom says. "We're just playing a little game of hearts. Why don't you pull up a chair until we finish this round? Oh, you remember Patrice?" she asks, gesturing to the woman.

I glance at the beautiful brunette with the deep blue eyes and the perfect heart-shaped face. *This* is our next-door neighbor Patrice Lovell? We used to make mudpies together and launch them at innocent passersby. She was pudgy and had a boy's haircut last time I saw her, and though she and Jim dated in junior high and have always been friendly, she never used to just come over and hang out.

"Hi," I say, and she smiles back. I pull out a chair and sit down.

"Do you want some wine?" Dad asks, gesturing to the glasses at everyone's place.

"Sure," I say and bite my lip. Why is everyone looking at me like that?

"Honey, are you okay?" Mom asks, looking concerned. I realize my eyes are probably still puffy and red. Plus moms can always tell when something is wrong.

"Of course I am," I say, smiling cheerfully. "I just wanted to see you guys. Is that okay?"

"Of course," Mom says. "It's just . . . we've been getting a lot of phone calls. So many we had to take the phone off the hook. And they're from magazines." She looks at me questioningly. "Something about Matt Sherwin?"

I sink my head into my hands.

"And I couldn't reach you at work or on your cell phone so I was getting worried."

Oh. Mom always used my work cell phone number. I was kind of hoping to avoid getting into this right away, and with Patrice here, I really don't want to talk about it.

"Dad, do you need some help with the wine?"

"I've got it, honey," he says. He sets a glass down on the table in front of me. "Are you in trouble?"

"Can we talk about this later?" I ask, reaching for the deck of cards. "How are you, Patrice?"

"Great." She smiles at me shyly. "We're celebrating Jim's acceptance to Montauk School of Alternative Medicine tonight."

"You got in," I say to Jim, trying to smile. "That's great." He smiles proudly, then sticks his tongue out at me. "When do you start?"

"September." He takes the cards from me and starts to deal another hand of hearts. "What's wrong with your face?"

"Jim!" Mom says. I put my hand up quickly to cover my rash. "I've almost won this round, Jane," she says. "We'll deal you in next game."

I nod and take a sip. The wine is light and refreshing.

Mom puts a smile on her face, trying to help me out. "So how's Ty?" she asks and beams at me. I freeze. I had also hoped to avoid talking about this. I take another sip. Mom looks at me.

"Mom, Ty and I broke up," I whisper. I feel so small.

"*What!?*" Dad yells.

"No!" Mom says. "When? Why?"

And now they're shocked. Great. I wait for a snarky comment from Jim, but he just looks at me sadly, which actually hurts more. I *am* pathetic.

"It just wasn't going to work out," I say, biting my lip.

"Of course it was," Mom says. "You guys were perfect for each other."

I take a deep breath. "I thought so too," I say, taking a long drink. "But apparently he had other ideas. He's moving to Denver."

"Denver?" Dad asks, flabbergasted. "Why would he want to live there?"

"Honey," Mom says, patting my hand.

"Mom, I—"

"Maybe you could give it another shot?" She smiles at me hopefully and pats my hand.

I look around at them. "I wish we could, more than anything. But I think it's a more permanent break." Before they can say anything, I stand up and walk to the door. "I'm going to go to bed now," I say. Dad nods, stunned. Mom looks like she's going to cry, as if Ty broke up with her.

"Honey, check my vanity. I've got a great Dr. Hauschka product that will help your face."

I ignore her, trudge to my childhood room, and collapse on the bed.

The next morning, I stay in bed for as long as I can, listening to the rain drum against the roof, praying for wisdom, but the smell of bacon fights against my desire to remain cocooned in my own world. Finally, hunger wins. I have to go face my family.

Dad is cooking while Mom reads the paper and drinks coffee at the table. I can hear vague computer-generated explosions coming from Jim's room.

"There you are, honey," Mom says, smiling sweetly as I trudge down the stairs in my pajamas. "Did you sleep okay?"

I nod as I walk toward the pot of freshly brewed coffee.

"Do you want some orange juice?" Dad asks, flipping the bacon in the pan.

"No thanks," I mumble, then take a seat at the table.

"How are you feeling today?" Mom asks.

"I'm okay."

"I didn't sleep very well myself," she volunteers. I nod. "I was up all night, thinking." I don't say anything, so she continues. "I realized what the problem is. I think you just don't understand what a man really wants."

I look up at her, eyes narrowed. "What's that?"

"They want to feel needed, honey. They need to feel like the provider. It's an ingrained thing from way back in the caveman days. He went out hunting, she stayed in and took care of the children. He brought home food at night, and they were all happy. Men are still the same today." She smiles and hands me a napkin.

"You think I should hang out in a cave and Tyson will come back?" I ask in disbelief.

She laughs. "No, honey. What I mean is, Ty is probably uncomfortable with the fact that you make more than he does and that you place so much value on your career. You just need to be more supportive of his career."

"You mean I should quit my job."

"Not yet. But you do need to let him know that when you get married you will." She smiles.

"But I won't."

"That's what I'm saying," she says, as if I'm a petulant five-year-old. "Maybe you should."

I take a deep breath. Please, God, don't let me punch my mother.

"I lost my job, Mom. So waiting until I get married to quit it seems a little ridiculous now."

I watch as her face registers shock, surprise, and, finally, delight.

"But that's perfect! Does Ty know?"

I close my eyes and place my fingers on my temples. I can't even begin to deal with the fact that my own mother is delighted that I just lost my dream job.

"No, Mom. I—" I take a deep breath. "I love Ty. I miss him more than you could ever know. But it's just not going to work. He dumped me, and he's moving on, and there's nothing I can do about it." I start to cry. "I lost my job, but I'm going to get another. I love working; I love doing something to make a difference in the world."

"But honey, your job wasn't really about making—"

"I am proud of my work," I cut her off. "And I was just starting to be able to do what I really wanted with the charity work. And a magazine printed a lie about me and Matt Sherwin, and I had to take the blame." She nods, taking it all in.

"So that's what it was," she says, looking at me. "I wondered."

"Are you okay?" Dad asks, sitting down at the table.

"I'm fine. I just . . . need some time to think."

"Honey," Mom says, taking a sip of coffee. "Take some time. You deserve it. But why don't you give Ty a call?" She looks at me sweetly.

"Mom, I can't," I sigh. They don't get it. I know she's trying to help, but I didn't come here for advice; I came because I needed someone to take my side. I came here because moms are supposed to protect you and defend you against the world.

"Of course you can. Ty loves you," she says, placing her cup down precisely.

"You're acting like this is all my fault," I say, sitting up straight. I look at one, then the other, and they're both shaking their heads.

"Sweetheart, that's not what we're saying," Dad says and then glares at my mom. She ignores him and looks at me, pursing her lips. I wait, but she doesn't say anything.

I nod, then stand up and walk to the stairs to gather my things. I don't need this. I'll take the first train out of here.

I trudge up the stairs to my apartment building slowly, closing my umbrella and shaking off the water. I'm so glad it's pouring. I couldn't deal with the world being sunny and beautiful while I am so miserable. I spent the whole train ride thinking about what they said. Is it all my fault? Is this whole thing one big mistake? What is God trying to teach me in all this? All I know is that I couldn't stay there any longer. I know they loved Ty, and they were disappointed, and they'll come around, but I can't stand to sit and be judged until then.

After I drop off my bag, I'll head to the animal hospital to pick up Charlie. It's just a short walk from here, and maybe on the way I can even find him a Welcome Home from the Hospital toy. I think about how good it will be to see him. At least he still loves me.

But at the top of the stairs I stop and sniff the air. It smells weird up here. Damp. Like mildew. I'll have to contact the building manager about that. It feels damp too.

I put my key in my lock and push the door open. Why . . . what? Why is there water all over the floor? Is that some kind of trash? My couch? My couch is all wet. What happened? I look down. I'm standing in an inch of water. The entire floor is covered with debris. And there, in the middle, is Elvis. The giant statue is lying on its side on my living room floor, his stupid mouth still open in a ridiculous grin. But how did Elvis get— oh no. I look up slowly.

The skylight is gone, the broken pieces of glass littering my floor. The wind from the storm must have knocked the King over onto the skylight. He crashed through. And judging by the amount of water in my living room, it happened quite a while ago. I can't move. I'm frozen in shock in the doorway as it begins to register that Elvis has crashed through my roof and destroyed my living room.

Chapter 10

I knock on Lee's door and prepare to meet Mary Sue. She's a mom. She'll know what to do about my roof. But when the door opens, I see Lee smiling at me.

"Look what the Chihuahua dragged in," he says and crosses his arms over his chest. "How is Mrs. Matt Sherwin doing today?"

"Can it," I say and push past him. I do a quick sweep of his apartment looking for Mary Sue. "Where's your mom?"

Lee strolls over to his sleek designer couch, now strung with a giant lace doily, and plops down. He's smirking. "She's not here, and you're avoiding my question." He pats the seat next to him. "Why don't you come sit over here and tell me all about it. Is it true he had his teeth capped?"

I walk over and collapse for a moment, my head spinning.

"Well?" he says.

"What?" I wish he'd stop teasing me. I'm overloaded. I need to think.

"Jane, you're going to have to tell me eventually. You should just be glad I'm not mad that I had to find out from the tabloids."

"Lee?" He keeps mumbling about loyalty and friends and telling each other all of our secrets. "Lee!" He looks up at me. "I am not with Matt Sherwin." I take a deep breath. "My roof caved in. Tyson dumped me. I lost my job. Charlie is sick. My parents think I'm a failure. And I don't know what to do."

He stares at me in shock.

"Your mom didn't tell you any of this?" I ask. "I saw her the other night, and she was a big help."

"She mentioned you'd had a bad day and that I should call you immediately, but something was wrong with your cell phone, and I couldn't get through. I guess she thought you'd want to tell me yourself."

"That must have been my work cell phone. They confiscated it. Along with my Blackberry and my dignity. The way those people were looking at me that day . . ." I lose myself for a moment thinking about it, but then I remember why I came down here. "Lee, I need you. Come upstairs. Now."

As we open the door to my apartment, he gasps. "Well, I'll be," he says quietly. I flip on the light to better assess the damage. The plaster around the skylight is soaked and has started to crumble onto my wooden floors. The rain has soaked my couch, and from what I can tell, the books on my shelves. I can see a good inch of water on my bedroom floor. I walk over to the desk and pick up my laptop. Water comes pouring out and splashes onto my shoes. Lee takes a deep breath and finally speaks. "I'm so sorry, Jane. This is really bad. Historically bad. It's almost like, like, you're cursed. And that statue—I'm so sorry."

He's so dramatic. "Lee, I'm not cursed."

"I don't know, Jane. Are you sure you haven't angered that God of yours that you're always going on about?"

"This from the guy who won't go outside if his horoscope is bad? Look, forget it." I should have never come to him for help. I wish Mary Sue had been home. "Lee, I just need help right now. What should I do?"

"Let's go back down to my place and call the building manager. We'll figure something out."

Lee and I call the animal hospital and arrange for Lee to pick Charlie up in an hour. The nurse reassures me three times that he is 100 percent better and out of danger. Then we locate Robert, the building manager, on his cell phone, and he gives me a contractor's number to call first thing in the morning. But he also warns me that I will have to cover the cost of the repair because it happened due to my own negligence in not securing the statue. I gulp, but I can't think about that now.

I go back upstairs and pack everything I can think of into a big rolling suitcase. Lee graciously offers to let me stay with him, but warns I'll have to fight with Auntie Di, who is coming over from Jersey tonight to stay, for a space on the living room floor. I can't do that to him. I'll figure something out.

As I start to trudge down the stairs, he calls after me. "So you really didn't kiss him?"

I shake my head.

"Well, good," he says. "Because I really think he got his teeth capped and you can tell that when you kiss someone."

I am standing outside my building, about to dial Raquel's number, when my phone rings. "Hello?" I say quickly, putting it to my ear.

"Is this Jane Williams?" an unfamiliar voice intones. Whoever she is, she is all business.

"Yes," I answer, my heart falling. She doesn't sound happy.

"This is Margaret Ann Markelson, for the Girl Scouts of Greater New York," she says. "Bella's mom?"

"Oh, um, yes. Hi, Mrs. Markelson." Why is Bella's mom calling me?

"I am afraid I have to inform you that we have found it necessary, in light of your recent . . . indiscretions . . . to ask you to relinquish all ties to Troop One Ninety-two. We the parents felt it is in the best interest of our children. Effective immediately."

"What?" I screech, but inwardly, I'm not even surprised anymore. Of course the girls' parents don't want a harlot like me teaching their children values. "But that story about me in *Star Power* isn't true," I say. "You can't fire me for something I didn't do." I know I hadn't decided whether or not I would take over the troop, but now that I don't have any choice, I know I want them. They can be frustrating at times, but the look on their faces when they have just mastered a new skill or learned a new song . . . It breaks my heart to think I'll never get to help them again.

"I'm afraid I have no choice," Mrs. Markelson says. "I am very sorry."

"But I showed them how to roast marshmallows," I say. "And canoe."

"Well, isn't that nice?" she says. "Perhaps you should have thought about how much those little girls looked up to you when you were cavorting all over town with that actor."

"But what I'm trying to tell you is—"

"Please, don't explain. I know everything already. The problem is you young, unmarried troop leaders never seem to realize that you're always a Brownie. You're not just a Brownie on the clock, during troop meetings or on campouts. You're a Brownie every day, and you should act like one, no matter who is watching."

"I know that. I did. You've got to believe me."

"I don't *have* to do anything."

I shrug in helpless anger. What can you say to a livid Brownie mom?

"Look, the troop is now in the hands of a mother. I will take over for now. A mother will better understand the full responsibilities it entails."

"Fine," I spit. "But I gave my everything for those girls. And I, for one, think we did all right."

Mrs. Markelson laughs. "All right isn't good enough for the Brownies, dear. Good night."

I stare at my phone in disgust. Raquel warned me that some people in the local Brownie council were a little crazy, but that call was worse than the Inquisition. I sit thinking about our first campout. I love those little girls. I can't believe they're taking them from me. My head spins at all the rumors that are inevitably being spread about me by the Upper East Side moms. I shake my head in disbelief.

I can't worry about this now. I think about the puddle on the apartment floor. I need to call Raquel about staying over. Maybe we can talk about the Brownies tonight, and she can fix it. I dial her number, and the phone rings for a while before Raquel breathlessly picks it up. "Hello?" she asks wearily.

"Raquel, it's Jane," I say, cringing. She sounds really tired. Wait? Has she seen the article? Does she know about the Brownie thing? "Look, I'm sorry to do this to you, but I was wondering if I could come crash at your place for a few days. My roof caved in, and I—"

"Your what?" she asks distractedly. I hear a shrill yell in the background.

"My roof caved in, Raquel. And I need a place to stay while I figure out what to do, and I was hoping—"

"Haven, put that down!" Raquel shrieks just before a large crash erupts in the background. Raquel sighs. "You're welcome to come over, Jane," she finally says. "You're always welcome. But, as you can probably tell, it's not the best time for us."

"Raquel," I say, unsure how to react, "I really appreciate that. You know I wouldn't ask if it weren't an emergency." I realize she doesn't know a thing about the *Star Power* nonsense or the Brownies. I've never heard her sound so frantic.

"Jane, if it's an emergency, why don't you go home to your parents?" she asks. "They're right there, and they have the resources to give you anything you need." I have to admit that from her perspective it probably seems like the obvious solution, but I can't go back there. Not after the way I left things today. I need space and time before I can face them again.

"I would," I say, "but I went there last night, and they—they don't really understand my current situation, and—"

She sighs. "You're being silly, Jane. Swallow your pride and go back to them. Remember the prodigal son? Parents are always willing to take their children back and give them another shot, trust me," she says, and I wince as I hear Olivia yelling for her father.

"Raquel, you just don't understand," I begin, but she interrupts me.

"I understand that your parents are there for you if you'll just use them. That's the practical thing to do. You're single and mobile and should take advantage of it. Someday when you have a family, you'll understand," she says.

My plan to crash at the Hardaway Hotel crumbles with her words. I know she's stressed out, and maybe logically what she's saying makes sense, but it's certainly not what I need to hear right now. "Um, I guess you're right. Okay, I'll do that," I say, lying to get her off the phone.

"Listen, I remember when I was single," she says, her voice softening a little. "You have these little problems, and you think they're the end of the world, but I can assure you, they're not," she says. I feel myself getting angry. Thanks for the condescension, Married Lady. "Someday, you'll be a mom and you'll see what I mean."

"Whatever," I say, amazed at my own composure. Some friend. "I have to go." And while my voice is clearly saying to her, You'd better not let me hang up like this, I'm so angry at you, I could scream, she says a quick "buh-bye" and is gone.

I sigh. I take a moment to calm down and think of who to call next. I scroll through my phone, but no one I call picks up. It's like the whole world has conspired against me. I keep scrolling and realize I only really have one option.

As I begin to walk resolutely to the subway in the darkening evening light, I remember in a panic that I've left my day planner behind, and I run back for it. At least that hasn't been ruined in the unexpected flood.

Within a half hour I am at Tyson's apartment in Brooklyn with a lump in my throat. Thank goodness he hasn't moved to Denver yet, because I need him. He'll understand. I know I can depend on him. I thought of calling first, but remembered that he was screening my calls, so I decided I might as well just show up on his doorstep. He can't turn me away once I'm already here.

I knock on the door. "Who is it?" he asks through the door.

"It's me," I say, and then swallow. "It's Jane."

A long moment passes, and I get the feeling that he's looking out the peephole at me. I smile to appear happy. I don't want him to think I've been crying over him all night and have come over in some misguided attempt to get back together.

He opens the door. He is wearing the reindeer pajama

bottoms that my mom gave him last Christmas and a white T-shirt. He stares at me but doesn't say anything.

"Um, hi," I say, my voice wavering. "Sorry to come over in the middle of the night, but the thing is—"

"Jane?"

I stare at him and take a tiny step back. A vein in his neck is throbbing, and his Adam's apple is moving slowly up and down. "Huh?" I muster.

"It's not true, is it?" He looks mad, and a little sad too. I sigh, knowing immediately what he's talking about. I can't believe Tyson, of all people, would even question me. Doesn't he know me better than that?

"Of course not." He nods, and I take a step toward the door.

"I didn't think so, but . . ."

"Ty, I need a place to stay tonight," I say quickly. "Can I crash on your couch? Just for one night?"

"I don't think that's a good idea." He steps back so the door is in front of his body.

"My roof caved in. I have nowhere to go. Please, just let me—"

"I'm sorry, Jane, but I have to do this, or it will only be harder tomorrow." He steps back, and closes the door calmly. I listen as he turns the lock.

I stand there for a moment in the silence, looking around, his words echoing in my head. The world has gone mad. I just try to take a moment to breathe. Eventually he turns off the stoop's lights, and I'm standing in darkness. I almost knock again, but I know it's useless. I look at my watch. It's already ten o'clock. Even if I wanted to go home to my parents now, I'd miss the last train out of Grand Central. My lip quivers for a moment, but then I tell myself that I'm not going to cry any more. Instead, I pray as I walk to the subway. Where has God gone?

Back in Manhattan, I walk until I find a Starbucks, roll in with my big suitcase, and get a cup of coffee and a stale scone. As the dry pastry crumbles in my mouth, I realize that I haven't eaten since the ill-fated breakfast this morning with my parents. I take a sip of coffee, and it warms me. My phone rings, and I grab it. See, I tell myself, a little prayer was all it took. God knows what I need. I flip the phone open, expecting it to be Raquel, or possibly Ty, calling to apologize for what he said.

"Hello?" I say.

An automated recording begins. It tells me about all the new text-messaging benefits they've added to my cell phone plan. I hang up and begin to bang my head on the table until I realize I might be causing a scene. I look around to see if anyone is laughing at me, but no one has even noticed me, which is even worse somehow. Okay, back to the task at hand. Enough with the self-pity. I just need to think of a place to sleep tonight, and I'll worry about the rest tomorrow. Suddenly, an idea pops into my head. I'm in Manhattan, for crying out loud.

There are hotels on every street corner. I'll just go check in and get a good night's rest. I finish my coffee off and wheel my way out. I should have done this hours ago.

I start out at the Marriott. We always stayed at Marriotts on family vacations and while they certainly aren't a Westin or the Plaza, a Marriott is pleasant and safe. But a Marriott in Manhattan is two hundred and fifty bucks a night, I am told by the night clerk. I am aghast. I only have a little in my savings and soon an expensive contractor is coming to fix my apartment and, what's worse, my mortgage is due. Oh, and I am now unemployed, so no money will be coming in for a while. I have to find somewhere cheaper. I turn around and wheel my suitcase out the door. Holiday Inn, here I come. I wheel myself in there, all set to go, only to find out that it is hardly any better. One hundred and eighty bucks. I steel myself to keep from crying. I know I could get a cheaper price on the Internet, but it is eleven, and I just need this day to be over. I go back outside and crane my neck to see if I can find a cheaper chain hotel. At the end of the block, looking a bit down at the heels, is the Big Apple Inn. I trudge toward the flickering neon sign and look through the windows uncertainly. It looks pretty dingy. Is it worth it? I take a deep breath and walk inside. If it's around a hundred bucks, then I will just have to take it. I need to get off the streets, literally. I ask at the desk, and it is a very reasonable $89.99 a night. I sigh with relief.

I wheel my suitcase up to Room 182, my eyes burning

from exhaustion. I can't wait to get inside, take a shower, and go to bed. I play with the tricky door lock for a moment and finally get inside. I turn on the light and sweep my eyes over the room. I am horrified. There is a burn mark in the bedspread and two small, suspiciously shaped holes in the wall. This can't be happening. I run to the bathroom and discover the ceiling is sagging and brown, and I have exactly three squares of toilet paper and two tissues in the tissue box. The grout in the shower is brown, and there is a thick film on the surface of the tub. I shudder. I walk back into the living room and take a deep breath. It's okay, I tell myself. I can stay here one night. I resolve not to take off anything but my shoes, otherwise I might contract some weird disease from this place. I just need to wash my face and brush my teeth and go to bed. Morning will come soon enough, and everything will look different. I open my suitcase only to realize I've forgotten my toothpaste and toothbrush, so I dial the front desk.

"Front desk," a bored voice says.

"Um, hi. I seem to have forgotten my toothpaste and toothbrush. Can you send some up?"

"Hey, Vinnie!" the voice shouts into the background. "Do we have toothpaste? Oh. Okay." After a shuffle the voice speaks into the phone again. "The toothpaste is on order."

"So you only have toothbrushes?" I ask.

"Yup."

I pause, unsure of what to say. "Okay. Well, guess I don't need one without the other."

The man on the other end slams the phone down. I put

the phone down too, find my purse, and dig out my cell phone. I'll call Lee for an update about Charlie. I dial his number, but realize that I don't get any cell phone service in this hotel room. I look at the landline and see that all local calls cost money. I sigh and grab my purse. I'll try again outside the building.

As I walk down the hall to get back to the lobby, I hear a couple screaming at each other inside a room. A creepy man wearing nothing but boxers smiles at me from his open room door as I pass by. I try to ignore him and run quickly outside. Once on the sidewalk in front of the hotel, I look down at my phone. Good. I seem to get reception out here. I walk away from the door a little way and dial.

I am leaving a message for Lee when I feel somebody grab my arm. I try to scream, but suddenly a hand covers my mouth and another arm grabs me, pinning my arms at my side. I try to fight, but I am literally frozen in fear.

"Give me your purse," a husky voice says in my ear. "If you try anything funny, I'll shoot." I hear the click of a gun being cocked and realize he means business. Please God, I pray, please help me. My arms are trapped, but I open my hand to let the purse drop on the ground. I hear it hit the pavement, and I feel something small and hard and cold press into my back.

"Do not turn around," he says, emphasizing each word in a threatening whisper, "or I will shoot." I nod, as tears stream down my face. "I want you to close your eyes and count to ten." He presses me up against the cold stone of the building and smashes my face against the wall.

Quickly, before I even know what's going on, I'm free, and he's gone, the sound of his running footsteps disappearing in the distance. I don't know where he is or if he is still watching me, so I dutifully count to ten, praying for strength and protection. I wait quite a while before I turn around. No one is there. My purse is gone. I walk quickly back inside the hotel, still clutching my phone, and between sobs ask the desk clerk to call the police. He looks bored as I tell him what happened and suggests I go back to my room and wait, promising to make the call for me. I nod and trudge back to my room.

Locking the door behind me, I look at the bed and cringe. Slowly, I sink down to the floor and cry. Thank you, God, I repeat again and again. Thank you for sparing me. A few minutes later, I hear a knock at my door, and I pull myself up. Through the peephole, I see a badge. I pull the door open, and two cops enter my room. It takes a full hour to fill out a report and explain what happened, and they promise to try to find the assailant but warn me how slim the chance is that they will actually find the man. I nod, feeling no comfort in their words, then show them out the door. I lock it carefully behind me.

Not knowing what else to do, I lie down on the bed. Out of the corner of my eye, I see something moving. I sit up and watch in horror as a rat scurries across the floor of my hotel room. A day ago I would have screamed, but now after everything I've been through, a rat is only a mild annoyance. I lie back down and stare at the stained, sparkling ceiling plaster.

How on earth did I get here, God? What is going on? What

are you trying to teach me? I think about my perfect life, crumbling under me. It's easy to be a Christian when life is good. But what happens when life doesn't turn out the way we plan? My mind whirs, thinking back to Lee's suggestion that I'm cursed. Has God abandoned me? Was he ever really there to begin with?

Chapter 11

I am awakened by a knock at the door of my hotel room, but when I look out the peephole, no one is there. Despite the heavy curtains, the room is flooded with light, and I deduce it must be morning. I quickly toss my belongings back into the suitcase and walk to the front desk. The clerk took my credit card information when I checked in, so I sign the forms quickly and burst out the front door. I don't know where I am going, but I have to get out of here.

Outside, it is a beautiful, warm sunny day. All around, New Yorkers are going on with their lives as if the world hasn't gone mad. I shake my head and wander west, dragging my suitcase behind me. I stroll aimlessly amidst the rush hour chaos, wishing I had fifty cents to buy coffee from a little stand. For lack of a better plan, I decide to just keep on walking until I hit the river. I'll rest on the little stretch of green that runs up and down the west side of Manhattan along the Hudson. When I finally get there, weaving my suitcase in and out of traffic and elderly people out for an early morning stroll, I find an oasis of peace in this crazy city. The only people here are joggers running along the path, and I have the small green lawn all to myself. I sit down on a patch of grass and take a deep breath.

This is exactly what I need, I decide. The sun is shining, the park is peaceful, and I can think. I will sit here and close my eyes and relax and figure out what I'm going to—

"You look terrible."

My eyes fly open, and I gasp. Just what I need. Coates Glassman. Of all people. Coates Glassman, wearing running shorts and covered in sweat. Shirtless. What a way to start the day. You are a cruel God.

"You look like you need a shower," I counter before I can stop myself.

"I could say the same about you," he smirks, wiping beads of sweat off his brow. He surveys my tangled greasy hair, my rumpled clothes, and my giant suitcase. "I just ran six miles. What happened to you?"

"Oh, just thought I'd get some fresh air," I say, trying to sound carefree. "You know, it's such a beautiful day I thought I'd just make sure to take advantage of it." I force my face into a smile, even though all I feel like doing is crying.

"Really?" he asks, smiling skeptically. I notice the thin layer of sweat covering his body creates a sheen that sets off his taut muscles. I look away. It shouldn't really be surprising he is built, right? He probably tramples puppies every morning for exercise. It's funny, because no matter how much Tyson worked out, he was always so thin and lanky.

"Are you okay, Jane?"

I look up to see what, if I didn't know better, might actually pass for real concern on Coates's face. I cringe.

"Of course I'm okay," I say, and I think I even manage to

sound convincing. "Why wouldn't I be?" I look at him, then look away.

"For one thing," he says, plopping himself down on the grass next to me, "you have a rash that needs to be looked at." I try to hide my face, reddening. "And I'd guess there has to be something drastic going on to keep you from taking care of it." I refuse to look at him. "And you have big bags under your eyes, you look like you slept in your clothes, and you're wheeling around a suitcase large enough to fit a small child in. I'm just guessing that things may not be going well for you at the moment," he says. I keep my eyes on the ground as a tear leaks out. I will not give him the benefit of looking at him. I will not give him the satisfaction of knowing he is right. He sits beside me, silently, waiting.

I look out at the river. New Jersey looks so peaceful from here. Small pleasure boats out to enjoy the beautiful summer day and large oceangoing vessels move slowly up and down the river. Down there, at the mouth of the river, stands the Statue of Liberty. I take a deep breath, remembering how everything I was unwilling to give up for Ty a few days ago has been taken from me anyway. And I lose it. Tears come quickly, and I can't hide them. My shoulders shake, and I bury my head in my hands. This can't be happening. Coates slips his hand onto my back and begins to rub. While Coates is sweaty, and smelly, and despicable, it is somehow comforting.

"My parents hate me," I finally stammer. "Because Ty broke up with me." He nods. I cringe, remembering how he was shocked that Ty was even my boyfriend. I shouldn't have told him that. But I can't stop my mouth from continuing. "And we were supposed to get married. My Girl Scouts were taken away from me. And my roof caved in, so now I'm homeless," I say wiping my eyes with my hand. "My best friend's mom is dying, and my other best friend doesn't have time for me. I got mugged last night. I thought I was going to die. I spent the night in a dirty hotel where I was afraid for my life, and none of my friends seem to believe that I am not the most selfish person on the planet with silly little problems."

So this is what it's come to, then. Spilling my guts to my ex-boss's nefarious nephew. I really have never been lower. Slowly, I turn my head to see how he is reacting to this news. He is looking across the river, stone-faced.

"And what do you plan to do about it?" he asks, turning back to me, squinting at the sun in his face.

"I'm still trying to figure that out," I laugh, looking around. "I'm sure if I sit here long enough inspiration will come to me."

"Perhaps," he says, nodding. "Or maybe," he says, brushing his damp hair back, "this isn't yours to figure out."

I look at him, lifting my eyebrows. "What do you mean?"

"I just mean, maybe this is bigger than you are, Jane. And maybe you are just supposed to trust."

His turns his face away from me, looking at the river. His profile is clean, even a little handsome. I have no idea how to respond, so I just nod.

"I'm sure it'll all work out," Coates says abruptly, then begins to stand up.

"Yeah, maybe," I mutter.

"You'll be fine," he says, then turns and begins to jog away. I watch him go, openmouthed.

I tell him everything, and he begins to act like a human being, then he just jogs off? Unbelievable. I watch his tan shoulders as he runs uptown. He really is despicable. I should have known better than to trust him, I think, kicking myself as I watch his inky black hair vanish into the distance. The nerve. What was I thinking, talking to him? I don't need his sympathy—or his derision.

And then and there I make a decision. If I'm stooping low enough to talk to Coates, I know it's time to stop feeling sorry for myself. I take a deep breath. I am still here. And though I don't know why this all happened, maybe it doesn't matter. Maybe I'm just supposed to trust. The sun is still shining, and though he hides it well, God must still be in charge. He always is, right? I sigh. How did I let the things I did and the things I owned become who I was?

Looking out at the river, glistening in the sun, I feel better already. Why, this isn't the end of everything. This is the beginning. Maybe it is tough to tell the end from the beginning, but the more I look at this situation, I know that this too is God's plan. A whole new Jane. I'll start over from scratch. After all, this is New York. People do it every day here. I lie back in the grass and let the sun warm my face, at last at peace. Thank you, I pray. Thank you.

I wander through the streets, watching New Yorkers go about their day. I walk past Union Square but can't bring myself to stop there. I wander into a Starbucks and wash my face, and I try to brush my greasy hair out as best I can. I manage to get in touch with the contractor, who says he can't begin work on my apartment until Monday. I call the bank and cancel all my credit cards. They promise to send replacement cards immediately. I try calling Raquel, but she doesn't pick up. I think about my parents. Maybe Raquel is right. Maybe I should just call them. They would bail me out. But when I think of their disdain, I can't bring myself to dial the number. Maybe in a little while. I wander through Times Square, looking at the bright lights, trying to enjoy them, but mostly I find myself annoyed by the throngs of people staring up at the giant billboards. Where can I go? I feel awful, and all I want is a hot shower, a bed with clean sheets, and a roof over my head without a hole in it. I stumble across Seventh Avenue.

My phone rings, and I stop and pull it out of my pocket. Maybe it's Lucifer calling to say there's more in store for me. Perhaps I'll suddenly go blind? When I see it's a Manhattan area code, I decide to risk it and answer the phone anyway. Satan doesn't use Verizon, right?

"This is Janice from the Four Seasons Manhattan. I'm looking for a Ms. Jane Williams. Is she available?" the woman asks.

"This is Jane," I say, waiting for the other shoe to drop.

"Ms. Williams, I am calling to let you know a room has been booked in your name at our hotel. I have been asked to let you know you are free to stay for as long as you need to, and you can check in immediately," she says, as if this were an ordinary task for her. "Do you need directions to the hotel? Or should we send a car?"

"What? A room?" I ask, trying to figure out what is going on. "Is this a joke?" I am going to kill my brother. This is not funny.

"No, ma'am," she says. "I am one hundred percent serious."

"But, how?" I stammer. "How did you get this number?"

"I am afraid I am not in a position to tell you that," she says. "The room was booked under the agreement that it would be absolutely confidential. My job is to call and offer it to you. I can't make you accept it, but as the first night has already been paid for, it seems to me that you— I'm sorry, did you need directions to our hotel?"

"No, thanks," I say. "I, um, I know where it is." We used to send our most important clients there when they came into town. Who on earth would do such a thing?

"Then we look forward to seeing you," Janice says and hangs up the phone. I look around, waiting for the hidden cameras and Ashton Kutcher to pop out of the bushes. Surely I'm being punk'd. But I don't see anything. What do I have to lose? I shake my head. Even if they laugh at me as I walk though the door, I won't be any worse off than I am now. I turn and begin to walk uptown.

Chapter 12

The doorman eyes me warily as I wheel myself into the lobby of the Four Seasons. I feel like I have a sign taped to my back that says, "Satan's Plaything" or even just "Kick Me," but I try to hold my head up and at least pretend I belong here. And just a few days ago this wouldn't have been a stretch for me. But I'm painfully aware of my disheveled state now. No matter. The Four Seasons called *me*. *They* invited *me*, not the other way around. I'll just check in and go and repair myself upstairs.

I stop dead still after my first few steps into the lobby, fully appreciating how gauche my blue Saucony sneakers look here. They seemed so retro cool when I bought them. But this place is breathtaking. I feel as though I have stumbled into a modern Egyptian mausoleum. It is dim and cool inside, but lit so magically from within that everyone looks beautiful in such friendly lighting. The marble floors are covered by huge rugs, and on the desk stands a large bouquet of fragrant, exotic flowers. I don't think I ever appreciated how beautiful it was all of those years that I worked at Glassman & Co. I don't think I even wanted to. Why fall in love with something that is not, nor will it ever be, intended for you? But now that I have a ticket to all of this beauty, I feel like Cinderella.

"Ahem." I look up and see a huge man stuffed in a blue blazer with a Four Seasons patch on his pocket. I smile at him. "May I help you? The hotel lobby is only for our guests. Their privacy is important to us," he says.

I laugh and walk over to the security guard to introduce myself and explain the situation. That is, I try to walk over to him. Instead, my sneaker tread catches on the edge of the carpet, and I trip and fall. It all happens so fast that I don't process it. I suddenly realize that I'm staring at what must be the cleanest hotel carpet in the world. It's really very impressive at this proximity. Next, I feel the security guard gruffly pick me up, and I swear he's trying to smell me. I don't smell that bad, do I?

"Please, ma'am. Let's just collect your, um, things, and I'll escort you out quietly."

I know I should be concerned, but in light of everything that's happened to me, it's really very funny for some reason. I laugh and say, "Okay, I'll go 'quietly.' " I even make the little quote marks with my fingers.

He walks over to my sad, worn-out suitcase—I can never find even a moment to shop for a new one—and begins to walk back to the door. I stay where I am, doubled over in laughter. This is too much.

The goon soon realizes I'm not following him so he abandons my suitcase just inside the main door and goes off. While he's gone, I decide to have a seat for a moment. I can't believe how cool and quiet this lobby is. You can't appreciate this sort of magnificence without at least one night at the Big Apple Inn.

The hotel guests move around the lobby, oblivious to how good they have it.

Soon the goon reappears. On his heels is a stern-looking woman in a power suit, her dark-brown hair in a tight bun. I study them as they whisper and point at me. This is just getting silly. I take a deep breath, pull myself together, and walk over to them, but as I approach I make out the word "homeless." I stop. They think I'm homeless? And then, I realize something. I feel small inside. My cheeks flush with shame. While I'm not truly homeless, in these past few days I've gotten a brief taste of just how easy it would be to become so and how you're treated if you are.

I storm over to them to take control of the situation. I stop just short of their conference, put my hands on my hips, and cock my head to the side. "Um, hi," I say to both of them.

The goon and the woman exchange a worried glance. The woman begins to speak, "Look here, I'm afraid that—"

I extend my hand to them. "Jane Williams. You called me about my reservation? I have a room reserved in my name?"

Instantly, recognition washes over the woman's face. "Oh. Ms. Williams. Terribly sorry. There was a misunderstanding, I'm afraid." She shoots the security guard a look of death.

I'm jumping up and down on the bed in my pajamas when I hear a knock on the door. I run across my giant suite, grab my big, fluffy terry-cloth robe, throw it on, and answer the door. A sheepish young man stands there with a silver cart covered with a white linen cloth. On the cart I spy a giant basket wrapped in cellophane. I stifle a small squeaking noise welling up within me. I will not be a teenaged girl, squealing with glee.

"This was ordered for you, Miss Williams. May I bring it in?"

I open the door slowly and stare at him, dumbfounded, as he places the huge basket on the coffee table and then produces a tray of chocolate-covered strawberries. He bows at me (bows!) and turns to leave.

I have no money for a tip but resolve to bring him a large one as soon as my new debit card arrives. After he leaves, I press my back to the door and just look around at my suite, the view, the basket, the strawberries. How am I ever going to thank whoever did this?

I dig into the basket, tearing off the cellophane to find the card. Strange. I don't see one. And the basket is crammed with girl stuff. I shake my head in disbelief and then begin to examine the ten shades of nail polish, the emery board, the mud mask, the aromatherapy lavender bath oil, the skin-firming cream, and best of all, the foot sloughing scrub. I wonder who . . . ? Aha. Buried down at the bottom is a bar of Ghirardelli chocolate, a package of cookie dough, and a pack of Hubba Bubba bubble gum. Raquel. We used to save up our allowances and walk to the 7-Eleven downtown to buy the precious fruity gum when we were kids. The fact that the flavor never lasted more than about thirty seconds never mattered to us, and we spent entire summers scheming about how to make money to buy more gum. And she knows I love cookie dough. It must be an apology from Raquel for being so awful to me last night. She probably woke up, realized what she'd done, and made the arrangements. I can contain myself no longer and squeal loudly, just like I did when I had braces. But as I pick up my phone to call her, I remember that she was worried about their finances. Now that I think about it, it's not at all like Raquel to spend money so frivolously. But, if not her, then who? A flash of dark hair races through my mind, but I dismiss the thought. That's just silly.

I walk to the bathroom, which is larger than my bedroom at home, and turn on the water in the Jacuzzi tub. While it's filling, I walk to the curtains and throw them open to discover I have a terrace. I unlatch the sliding glass door and walk outside to behold Manhattan in all her shimmering beauty.

How could anyone ever leave her? I know, in my darker moments, that I had considered it, but looking around, I realize now how right Tyson was. This city is my home. I couldn't leave it. It's in my blood. I was meant to live here.

I walk back inside the quiet suite and check on the tub. It's only a quarter full. It could easily fit four people. I wander back out to the bedroom and feel the sheets, smooth as silk.

Matt! It must be Matt Sherwin. That makes perfect sense. Who else would have money to throw around like this? And since it was his fault I got fired, this must be his way of apologizing. I grab the tray of chocolate-covered strawberries and thank God for Matt Sherwin.

After four chocolate-covered strawberries and a bottle of San Pellegrino, I slide off my clothes, slip into the robe and fuzzy slippers, and make my way to a giant Jacuzzi that now looks like a frantically whipped cappuccino. I pour in the aromatherapy bath oil and the scent of lavender fills the room. I turn down the lights, light the candles around the tub, sprinkle the water with rose petals thoughtfully placed in a bowl on the counter, and open the window that overlooks Manhattan. I drop into the bath, and the world melts away.

Fifteen minutes later, my cell phone bleats out in the darkness, and I give it a pleading look. "I'm sorry, but you usually bring me harm," I say to it. It continues to ring, and I finally cave in and slide over to answer it. I see from the screen that it's Raquel. She must be calling to apologize.

"Hi Raquel," I say and sit back to enjoy my bath.

"Jane, look—" she says quickly. "I need your help." I scowl. So she's not sorry. "I need you to come and get Haven." Oh, so she calls me when she needs help? Where was she when I needed a place to stay? I'm just about to open my mouth to really let her have it when she continues. "It's Olivia. She's having some kind of complication with her ear implants. We need to go to the hospital right now."

I swallow hard and look around me. I take a deep breath. Yes, I'm tempted to just tell her I can't come. I can't leave all this. It's paid for and I have no way to get to her apartment. She'll have to find some married person who can understand her problems to help her. But when I open my mouth to tell her I'm not coming, what comes out is "Okay. I'll be there soon." I can walk to her place and borrow a few dollars to get back here.

"Oh thank God, Jane. You're a lifesaver."

I screw up my face, not sure how to feel. "Um, no problem. I'll pray for Olivia tonight."

Raquel sighs. "Thanks, Jane. So fifteen minutes?"

"Sure. And tell Haven to pack a swimsuit. I've got a big surprise for her."

Chapter 13

Onyourmarkgetsetgo!" Haven squeals as she takes off. I follow behind her, running down the dark hallway. She turns around to see if I'm following and smiles when she sees me close behind her. We round a corner and sprint to the end of the corridor, her little legs pumping as fast as they can go. It's impossible not to laugh as her terry-cloth robe, a miniature version of mine, sails out behind her and her feet in little white terry slippers slap against the plush carpet. She is having the time of her life.

"I beat you, Jane!" she yells proudly as she touches the ornately carved mahogany table at the end of the hallway.

"But that wasn't fair," I whine as I straggle in behind her. "You totally cheated. You didn't even wait until you finished saying go before you took off. I demand a rematch," I say, feigning indignation and leaning dramatically on the table. Her smile only grows wider.

"Onyourmarkgetsetgo!" she yells, and takes off again back down the hall toward our suite. She slaps the door just before I do, and we both giggle as we stumble inside to rest. I fall down on the leather couch, pretending to be exhausted, while Haven sits on the edge of the bed and bounces up and down. "You want to ride up and down in the elevators again?" she asks, her eyes lighting up.

"I think we got a pretty thorough tour last time," I say and laugh. "We did see every floor. And that man who was stuck in the elevator with us didn't seem to enjoy it nearly as much as we did."

"We can race in separate elevators and see who gets to the top floor first," she suggests, undaunted. "Or crank-call the front desk again," she says. "We could call them and make fart-ing noises with our mouths!" The very idea causes her to dis-solve into giggles.

"Nah, that was only fun until I realized they knew exactly who was calling." Who knew they had caller ID for every room? "Plus, it's getting late, Haven," I say. "It's about time to let the other guests rest. Why don't we stick around here for a while? You can go in the Jacuzzi again. Or we can eat some cookie dough and watch trashy television," I say, throwing her the remote control.

"Ooh," she says, her eyes lighting up. She turns the set on and flips quickly to Nickelodeon. They're showing a *SpongeBob SquarePants* marathon. Her eyes become glassy as they fixate on the television.

"This is trashy TV? *SpongeBob*? Isn't *The Bachelor* on or something?" I say. She shushes me without turning her eyes away from the screen for a second. She may try to act grown-up when she's with her friends, but she's still just a little girl.

"Okay, fine," I sigh. "You watch *SpongeBob*. I'm going to exfoliate my feet." She gives me a strange look and then turns back to the television. I wander toward the bathroom, but on my way I spot a small white card just inside the suite door. I bend over and pick it up and squint at it. My face flushes with shame as I see it's the business card of a neighborhood dermatologist. My hands instinctively fly up to my face to touch my rash, and my first impulse is to be outraged. How dare they! The concierge must have slipped it under our door while Haven and I were reenacting *Chariots of Fire* on the treadmills in the workout room. I can't believe how rude . . . I stop and take a breath. I walk into the bathroom and look in the mirror.

Actually, I do need to see a dermatologist. I know this myself. Haven mentioned that I looked like a pizza when she saw me today, bless her little heart, and the rash is starting to itch. I feel like a circus freak. Why am I so proud that I can't take the help I so obviously need? I slide the card onto the counter. I'll give him a call tomorrow.

I dig through the gift basket for the sloughing cream, reminding myself to call Matt Sherwin first thing in the morning to thank him, when I hear sniffling from the other room. I walk into the bedroom to find Haven on the bed, still staring at the TV, tears streaming down her cheeks.

"Oh, Haven, what's the matter?" I ask, sitting down and pulling her into my arms. She buries her face in my robe and puts her arms around me.

"Is my sister . . . going . . . to be okay?" she gulps, trying to keep the sobs from overtaking her. She suddenly looks so small and frail. She's been such a good sport about all this I forgot she'd be worried.

"Oh, honey," I say, stroking her hair. The truth is, I have no idea if she's going to be okay. I don't know what's going on at the hospital, or what happened to get Olivia there in the first place. I know her ears are sensitive and an infection in them could be dangerous. I know Raquel is in her second trimester and the stress of this is bad for her and the new baby. And I know that even when everything is going right for you, your whole world can suddenly collapse around you. And yet, I think, looking around, the God who created us knows what we need and strips away from us the things that keep us from seeing straight.

"Everything is going to be fine," I say, kissing the top of her head. "Let's pray for her."

"**What** is that noise?" Haven moans, lifting her head up groggily.

"Ungh . . . ," I say, reaching for the phone on the nightstand next to my side of the king-sized bed. I open it and push the talk button just to get it to stop ringing. "Hulloo?" I whine into the mouthpiece.

"Jane? It's Raquel. Are you okay?" The sun is streaming in my window. Raquel's worried voice masks the vague noises in the background that suggest she's still at the hospital. "How's Haven?"

"She was sleeping like a baby until a minute ago," I say, sitting up. Haven puts a pillow over her head. "How is Olivia doing?" I ask, waking up a little.

"She's doing much better," Raquel says, tension draining from her voice. "They have the infection under control, her fever is down, and the doctors say she's going to be just fine."

"I'm so glad," I say, relieved. "When do you think you'll be able to take her home?"

"This afternoon," she says, sniffing. "But I thought I would come take Haven off your hands so you could get to work. Is it okay if I stop by your apartment in a little bit?"

Work? My apartment? Raquel either has stress-induced dementia, or, oh yeah. Wow. Has it really been that long since we talked? Or rather, has all this happened that quickly?

"Sure, you can come get her. But we're at the Four Seasons," I say, throwing a pillow at Haven to wake her up. She scowls and rolls over.

"Oh my goodness. Are you serious?" she says and laughs. "I'll never understand how you have such an amazing life, Jane."

"It was about three a.m. that it hit me," Raquel says, pushing a thick piece of French toast around the puddles of syrup on her plate. "They finally had Olivia stabilized and I was just pacing in her hospital room, praying about all the things I'm thankful for. And when I got to your name, I froze. It all came back to me." I smile sheepishly at her and shrug. She shoves a huge bite of her French toast into her mouth and then wipes it on the white linen napkins room service brought up with our breakfast. We have opened the curtains to enjoy the view of Manhattan and decided to have breakfast in bed, so all three of us are sprawled on the giant mattress, trying not to drip syrup on the eight-hundred-thread-count Egyptian cotton sheets. Haven finished her croissant in one minute flat and is now ignoring us for the television. "I'm so sorry. I'm not even sure what to say to make it right again." Her hands rest on her burgeoning belly.

"Say no more. I'm just glad everything is okay."

"Jane, you should be angry at me. In fact, I demand that you be angry with me. You called me when you needed a place to stay, and I practically hung up on you. That's really some kind of best friend you've got there."

I frown and then have a sip of fresh-squeezed grapefruit juice. "You didn't exactly hang up."

"You're right. I believe I ridiculed you first, denigrated your problems, and then I hung up."

I smile a little. "That might have been the order. But you were stressed."

"Does it matter? Is there ever an excuse to fail your friend?" Raquel throws her hands in the air in frustration with herself.

"You're right. I think we burn you at the stake later." I give her a little nudge, but she doesn't answer and won't look up from her breakfast. "You're being too hard on yourself."

"Jane, I wasn't there for you. And then I reversed the tables on you, and called you in my time of need and you didn't even hesitate to bail me out," she says, motioning at Haven at the foot of our bed.

"Please," I say. "I love hanging out with Haven."

At the sound of her name, Haven looks up from the cartoons.

"I said you're cool," I say to her.

Haven nods, unsurprised, and goes back to her television program. Apparently she gets that all the time. Then I look at Raquel, and she's still staring at her plate. I lean over and give her a hug and hear her sniffle a little in my arms.

Haven looks back again at the sound of the sniffling and cocks her head to the side. "Mommy, are you crying?" she asks.

I pull back from our hug and look at Raquel's tear-stained cheeks.

"No. She's not. She just has something in her eye," I say to Haven, who rolls her eyes at us and flips over onto her stomach. And then I turn to Raquel. "Raquel, I knew you were going through a tough time. And the hormones. You weren't yourself. You've got to stop beating yourself up."

She shakes her head. "I'm so sorry," she says. "I'll make this up to you somehow. I was selfish and stupid."

"I know you're sorry," I say, taking a sip of my juice. "And I'm chalking it all up to temporary insanity. We're all selfish and stupid sometimes." My mind instantly flashes to Ty, and I shake my head to make it stop.

"Thank you," she says, smiling at me. I smile back and thank God for her friendship.

"Are you okay now?" I ask.

She takes a deep breath and exhales. "Tell me something funny to snap me out of it. Otherwise I might continue to sit here and remember everything I did to you."

I look around. Something funny. Something funny. The Four Seasons is like heaven on earth, but it isn't particularly funny. I take another sip of my ruby-red grapefruit juice. "Um."

"Yes?" she says, eyes alight.

"Did you know that Tropicana is trying to brand grapefruit juice 'Sass in a glass'?"

Raquel and I exchange a funny look and laugh for a moment, and then she goes quiet and looks around the room with a funny expression on her face.

"A penny for your thoughts?" I ask.

"I was just wondering, who on earth is paying for you to shack up in the palace?"

I look at the balcony, the Jacuzzi, the marble flooring. "This isn't even where the story begins," I say and have a sip of coffee. I begin to fill her in on all of the sordid details of my cursed life, from the breakup to the sick dog to the roof caving in, even pulling the copy of *Star Power* out of my suitcase to show her. Raquel's mouth hangs open, and as I go on, she covers her ears and insists she can't hear another detail.

"This is so much worse than I thought. Tyson? Your job? I just thought you were having some kind of apartment trouble. Oh Jane," she says and covers her mouth. "And you thought he was going to propose," she says.

I look at my lap and swallow back the tears. How stupid I was. "I misread all the clues. There were clues all right. But they were spelling out 'He's leaving you, dummy.' "

She leans over and gives me a hug. "And the mugging? You got mugged at gunpoint? How are you even still standing?"

I shake my head. "I'm just trying to look at this as some kind of test from God. He has always been good to me. I have to trust him even now that my life is in shambles. I've decided he's working on something big up there, and I just don't know what it is yet." I nod and smile confidently.

Raquel nods and bites her lip. "I guess so. I'm really impressed with you. Some people might just give up and call the whole faith thing quits."

I look at my lap. "Whenever I start to pray, I feel like God is there."

Raquel grabs my hand and holds it, silently looking around the room. "Okay, I get the rest. But I still don't understand the hotel room." She looks around, shaking her head. "I sure didn't do it, and your parents are far too practical to do something like this. So who did? I mean, you're great and all, but really, all this?"

"Matt Sherwin."

"No," Raquel says, shaking her head. "Didn't you say he was a him-bo?"

I giggle, remembering the term my assistant taught me for male bimbos.

"This isn't the gesture of someone like that. Besides, how could he get away with it? Wouldn't that just make all the rumors look true?"

I bite my lip, shrugging. The only other person it could possibly be . . . No.

"Then I don't know."

Chapter 14

I wake up the next morning and sleepily look across the room. There is no sound. For a moment, I worry that I'm deaf. And then a wonderful realization settles over me. I'm not deaf. I'm just alone. I'm alone in the most peaceful place in the world. Well, maybe not *the* most peaceful place, as a monastery in the Alps where the monks have all taken a vow of silence and just make cheese all day might be a smidge quieter, but still it's very peaceful. I haven't been this relaxed in ages. I take a deep slow breath and lazily talk to God about all the goings-on in my life, curious to see if he has any thoughts he'd like to interject.

After an hour of lying around in bed, I saunter over to the Jacuzzi and begin to fill it up for a bath. As I stare out the bathroom window, though, I hear a knock. I open the door, and Lee bursts into the hotel room. I should never have given him the room number, but when I called to see about Charlie he demanded to know all the details.

"So it's true," he says, looking around. He walks to the window and takes in the view. "Wow."

"It's pretty cool, huh? Check out the minibar. Toblerone!" I laugh, pointing out the chocolate bar inside the mini-fridge. I pull it out and begin to unwrap the foil.

Lee spins around, taking in the sumptuous room. "You're telling me you really don't know who is paying for all of this, Jane?" he asks skeptically.

I take a bite of the chocolate and chew. I shrug.

"Dunno," I say.

He watches me. "When you find out who this sugar daddy is, can you make some requests for me? Meanwhile, I am going to do some research," he says, nodding. "And FYI, the contractor was pumping water out of your place all day yesterday. I peeked in, and you could probably come back now. It still smells a little funny, but it's technically livable again." I nod. Though the front desk told me I was welcome to stay as long as I needed, I do feel weird living off the generosity of an unknown donor. It's been nice, but I guess it's time to get back to reality.

"And I've decided to help you get to the bottom of this article about you in *Star Power*."

"Lee, aren't you supposed to be at work?"

"Sick day." He pretends to cough. "We have important business to attend to, Jane."

"What's that?"

"You wanted to clear your name, right?" He pulls a yellow legal pad out of his bag and sits down on the edge of the bed. I take a seat on the desk chair across from him and nod. "So we have to figure out who is responsible for the article," he says.

"You want breakfast?" I ask, tossing him the room service menu from the desk. "It's free."

He shakes his head. "Had a smoothie earlier," he says. "Your blender still works, by the way."

"Great."

"Who are the primary suspects?" Lee pulls out a pen and begins to chew on the end.

"I don't really have any suspects," I sigh. "That's the thing."

"Think, Jane. If we can figure out who planted that story and why, we can get them to print a retraction and clear your name." He picks up the menu absently and begins to read. "Then they have to give you your job back."

"That would be nice," I say. "But even if we do figure out who did it, I don't know if they will take me back."

"Of course they will," he says, undeterred. "You do want your job back, right?"

I look down at my hands for a second, thinking. "Of course I do."

"Good. Then I need you to think hard. What can you re-member about the times those photos were taken? What stands out to you? And can you call down for some croissants and mi-mosas after all?"

"Of course." I pick up the phone, ask Eric in room service to send up the breakfast, and turn back to Lee.

"The only clue I can think of is that there was this girl with red hair who was always around when I was with Matt Sher-win," I say, inspecting my split ends. "She had this curly auburn hair, and she was always watching him. But I don't know who she is or if there is any connection."

"Curly red hair. Got it. It's a start."

"Lee?"

"Remember anything else?

"Lee, I really appreciate this, but why are you so into clearing my name?"

"That's what friends do, Miss Jane," he says, putting his hands on his hips. "Besides, I have a vested interest in making sure you can pay your mortgage," he says and laughs. "If you leave, who knows what kind of psycho might move in? I might get stuck with some guy with a nutcracker collection living above me or something. Plus, I'd miss Charlie. So you see, I have to make sure you stick around." I laugh a little at his ridiculousness, but I sense there's something he's not saying.

"Lee," I say, pushing my hair back behind my ear, "how's your mom doing?"

He looks at me, then looks away quickly. He's quiet, and his silence speaks volumes. Oh, Mary Sue. All of a sudden, my problems seem ridiculously small.

"So where do you think we should start looking for the girl with the red hair?" he finally says, smiling. "I have a contact at Condé Nast, which owns *Star Power*, so I'll see if I can find anything out that way. Any other ideas?"

The smell of mildew still permeates the air, and the mold on the walls has spread, but the floor is dry, and the contractor has cleaned up most of the debris and nailed a thick sheet of plastic around the broken skylight. Elvis stands in the corner, silently mocking me. I sigh as I walk into the bedroom. It's not going to be pleasant, but I can stay here. I begin to strip the damp linens off my bed and replace them with dry sheets from the closet, but I stop. While I have been lolling about on Egyptian cotton, Mary Sue has been fighting for her life downstairs. I have to go see her.

I knock on Lee's door, but there is no answer. He must be at work, and I don't know if Auntie Di is still around or if she's gone back to New Jersey. I run upstairs, grab my key to Lee's, then slip it in the lock, and push the door open. The apartment is dark and cool, and Charlie is sleeping on the couch. I walk over to him and kiss and nuzzle him awake. The joy on his face brings tears to my eyes. And then I know that he can help me with my plan.

"C'mon, buddy," I say, and he follows me to Mary Sue's bedroom door, which is slightly ajar. I push it open to see Mary Sue, asleep on the bed. Her eyes flutter open, and she smiles weakly when she sees me.

"I'm just gettin' my beauty sleep," she says, pushing herself up as she smiles at me. She looks very pale and frighteningly thin in the dim light. "How are you, shug?"

I walk over and sit on the edge of the bed. I pick Charlie up, and just like a trained therapy dog, he kisses her face and nuzzles into her body for a little nap. She baby-talks to him for a moment.

"I'm fine," I say, smiling at her. "Just fine." She smiles at me, reaching for a glass of water on the nightstand. Her fingers tremble, and the glass slips out of her hand, landing with a crash on the floor.

"Oh fudge," she mumbles under her breath, but I motion

for her to stay where she is and walk to the kitchen to get a towel to wipe it up. On the counter is a whole row of little bottles filled with different pills.

After I have the spill wiped up and hand her another glass of water, I take a seat on the floral-print wingback chair in the bedroom that I know isn't Lee's. Mary Sue assures me that there isn't anything she needs and lies back against the pillows. And then I have an idea. I start out slowly at first because I'm really not much of a storyteller but after a while, I get the hang of it. I talk for a good while, regaling her with stories from my childhood, about the time I booby-trapped Jim's bedroom or when I fell down at my five-year-old dance recital and played it off as a modern dance move, hoping that I will take her mind off of things like she did for me that night. And after an hour, she has a small smile on her face. She pats my hand and looks at me seriously.

"Shug, there is something you can do for me if you really want to help," she says quietly. "I'd understand if you want to say no. But I'm havin' a hard time getting around these days, and while my sister was here, she helped me get a bath. But now that it's just Lee—well, you can see why he'd feel weird about that."

For a moment, I feel like I can't do it. God, I am not ready for this. I am not strong enough. What if she falls? What if something goes wrong? But I know I have to. I can do this for my friend. "Of course," I say and give her a smile.

And as I lower Mary Sue into the tub, I think about how

blessed I am, even now. Especially now. Sometimes, in our darkest hour, God gives us the most beautiful moments of grace.

After a seemingly eternal stay in the poshest waiting room I've ever seen, I am finally called into the examining room of the dermatologist the concierge recommended. At least I had time to call my insurance company to see how much of the repairs and furniture they would pay for. And I got in contact with the contractor working on my apartment, who told me they would be able to fix the skylight by the weekend. But my joy at the good news is crushed as soon as I see Dr. Singer's face. He looks at me and his eyes light up.

"I've never seen it this bad," he says by way of introduction, leaning in to get a close look at my skin. "That's amazing!" He turns on the small light over my head and leans in for a better look, a look of pure rapture on his face. "I'll be right back," he says, turning quickly and walking out the door. "Hey, Lenny, come get a look at this!" he yells, and I cringe. So it's true. I have some rare infectious flesh-eating disease, and I will be horribly disfigured for the rest of my life. Suddenly I feel for Cyrano de Bergerac. At least me and Elephant Man can hang out. Oh, wait. He's dead. I sigh. I'm all alone.

Lenny comes rushing in in a white lab coat. He breaks into a grin when he sees my rash. "What a mess!" he shrieks happily, looking closely. "This is one for the textbooks! China, get the camera!" he yells over his shoulder. A young nurse's aide comes into the room carrying a professional-grade camera, probably bought by the doctors in the hopeful anticipation of this very moment. I am a circus freak on display for the legions of dermatologists to come through medical school in the next few decades. Like Jessica Simpson, I am so bad that I am good.

"Is it treatable?" I ask.

Four pairs of eyes—who is this new doctor come to gawk?—turn on me at once. They look at me as if I'm a complete moron.

"Of course it is," Dr. Singer says, shaking his head. "It's just impetigo. Kids get it all the time." He shrugs. "All it takes is a round of antibiotics to kill it. It's so easily treatable that it never gets to be this bad," he says, leaning in again to admire the mutant nature of my skin. "Did you put anything on it?"

"I used some drying cream," I say. The room erupts in laughter.

"Drying cream?" the new arrival laughs. "That's the worst thing you could use. Drying cream!" He chuckles like it's the best joke he's heard in years.

Dr. Singer looks gleeful as he hands me a prescription. "Don't worry," he scolds, seeing my distress, "you'll be fine in a day or two." I swear I hear someone whisper, "What a shame."

"Really, immensely fascinating," Lenny murmurs from the corner. I slowly get up to leave, hoping these crazy people will leave me alone. China blocks the doorway with her gigantic camera. "Can we just get some more pictures before you go?"

———

I am still lying in bed at home when my cell phone rings. I reach over and grab it, then put it back down when I see it's my mom calling. Ugh. We haven't spoken since I left their house in a huff the day my roof caved in. I let it go to voicemail. I can't deal with her right now. I roll over and try to muster the energy to go to the library and e-mail my résumé for some job postings I saw online yesterday. I need to get a new computer, fast.

A few minutes later, it rings again. Mom. Great. She's stalking me now. I ignore it.

Three minutes later, it rings again. Why can't she just leave me a voicemail? What could be so important that she has to speak to me this minute? Did she have another revelation about how I can win Ty back?

The first ring of her fourth call is enough to drive me to distraction. I flip the phone open in desperation. "Mom?"

"Oh, hi Jane dear," my mom says. "Did I catch you at a bad time?" Her saccharine voice makes me want to scream.

"No," I sigh. She doesn't seem at all concerned that I have obviously been ignoring her calls.

"Honey, I know you're mad at me, but I really hope you can forgive me." I sigh. After how she treated me, I'm not sure I'm ready for this. But then, she is my mother. What else can I do?

"Okay, Mom," I say simply.

"Oh good," she sighs. "Because I have some big news. News I hope you'll be happy about. We're coming down to New York tonight."

"That's the big news?" I ask, rolling my eyes.

"No," she says. "We're coming down to tell you all about it. Please," she takes a deep breath, "try to be happy."

"Who is we?"

"Your father, Jim, and I," she says. "We have a reservation at Balthazar at seven. See you then?"

I pause. On the one hand, this is destined to be an uncomfortable evening of silent accusations and awkward apologies. On the other hand, they are my family, and they are promising me free dinner at a nice restaurant.

"See you then," I say.

Chapter 15

You're what!?" I yell. I am shocked. Horrified. Mostly shocked.

"Engaged!" Jim says and laughs. "Who would have thought? All those years I had a crush on Patrice and she wouldn't give me the time of day, and then, bang, we're getting married." His eyes light up as he talks about her.

My parents look like they have died and gone to heaven. I reach for my water.

"Wha—when did this happen?" I stammer. Jim, my brother. The man who wanted to join the circus and marry the fat lady. The one who dropped out of college because he couldn't be bothered to show up for class. He got stuck in a revolving door last year, for goodness' sake.

"Two days ago," he says.

"B—but the whole Patrice thing?" I ask. "When did you two . . ." He couldn't show up on time to work if his life depended on it. He doesn't even own a day planner.

"Oh, we started dating about two months ago." He smiles. "When I moved back home, we started hanging out again, and, well, we really hit it off." He grins again. I cringe. He's like the cat that got the canary. "It was like I had come down with a strange dread disease," he says and looks wistfully over my shoulder at nothing. "I couldn't eat. I couldn't sleep. I lost my mind. I kept the ticket stubs to our first movie. I have every e-mail she ever wrote me printed out and filed. I have fortune cookies from the Chinese restaurant where I first held her hand. I even saved the tissue she blew her nose on," he says and laughs.

"Gross," I say.

"Love," he says, a dopey grin on his face.

I stare at him. Jim's keeping weird mementos that make him seem like a stalker, and my mother seems delighted. Who are these people? Where is my nice, normal family? "So, um," I say slowly, trying to wrap my head around the fact that my screw-up brother convinced someone to marry him, "when did you decide you were going to marry her?"

"On our first date," he says, his eyes crinkling. "I took her out to dinner, and I watched the way she ate her salad, and I just knew."

"How could you possibly know by watching her eat a salad?"

"I just did," he sighs.

"Oh yeah?" I cross my arms across my chest. "And what about school? Are you still going?"

"Nah," he says, shaking his head. "I'm going to get a job. We're saving up for a house," Jim says. Dad smiles proudly.

"But how can you just not go to school?" I ask. "You already told them you were coming. It's totally irresponsible to give your word and—"

"Jane?" my mom says, her voice steady. "We're so happy for Jim. I know it isn't what you expected, but——"

"You can't always plan the way things are going to work out, kiddo," Jim says, taking a sip of the water. "I thought I finally knew what I wanted. And God had something else up his sleeve. The way he worked things out is so much better than what I had planned."

I force a smile at him, trying to be convincing. But everything suddenly feels completely backward. Jim has always bumbled through life, winging it from one misadventure to another. And now, he's the one who has it all together. As I look at him, beaming across the table, I wonder if maybe he's always had it a little more together than I ever gave him credit for.

"She wants you to be a bridesmaid," Jim says. "Will you?"

Will I? I guess I don't have much choice. He's my brother. And I want to be happy for him. I really do. But this is so . . . sudden. And what's all this God talk now? From the guy who once asked me in front of all my youth group friends where the verse about not having sex with donkeys was?

"So, um, this dinner wasn't about coaching me on how to get Tyson back?" I ask, quietly.

My mom looks at me as if I've just confessed to hating her pot roast. My dad looks confused. Jim looks crestfallen.

"Jane," my mom snaps. I look at her, and the expression on her face gives me the sudden urge to duck under the table and hide until it's safe. "Not everything is about you."

———————

"**Does** anyone else need anything before we start?" Raquel asks, gesturing toward the untouched table of snacks.

"You're sure you don't have any cucumber juice?" Caroline Truesdale asks, raising her perfectly groomed eyebrows in hope. Caroline is Abby's mom. As in Abby who will do anything for candy. All of a sudden things are starting to make sense.

Raquel shoots me a knowing look and calmly replies, "I'm afraid we're fresh out. But we have lots of cookies left if you want one." Caroline visibly shudders—all one hundred pounds of her—and picks up her ice water in resignation.

Apparently when Raquel invited all the Girl Scout mothers over for an emergency meeting, she forgot that these Upper East Side moms don't eat anything unless it's sugar free, fat free, carb free, hormone free, and pesticide free. I'm the only one who's touched her homemade Oreo balls or her chocolate chip macadamia nut cookies. At least Eleanor Pearson, Kaitlin's mom, bothered to ask if the cookies were made with carob, but upon hearing they were tainted with real fattening chocolate she contented herself with iced tea and Sweet'N Low. When Raquel noticed none of the snacks she spent all morning baking were being touched, she finally brought out some carrot sticks, which were a huge hit and disappeared within minutes.

"If everyone's set, then, why don't we go ahead and start," she says smiling sweetly. "I'm sure you know why I asked you here." Caroline and Eleanor look at each other and roll their eyes. Raquel clears her throat and says, "Jane Williams has been falsely accused and prematurely judged, and I wanted to give her a chance to defend herself."

Margaret Ann Markelson, mother of Bella and the woman who ruthlessly cut me off from my girls, sniffs and raises her hand. "I really don't see why we have to go through all this again, Raquel," she says. "We just don't want someone with loose morals teaching our children. Period." She smugly takes a sip of ice water. She's staring at me like I am the Whore of Babylon.

"I don't want anyone with loose morals teaching my children either," Raquel says. "So we agree on that. But I'm afraid there has been a misunderstanding here about Jane, who is the most moral and upright person I know." My heart swells to hear Raquel defend me. "But what I'm really concerned about is that when you were worried about the leadership of this troop, you took immediate action and did not even contact me about it. While I might not have been the leader of the troop at the time of the article's publication, I was, at the very least, Haven's mother, and I was not told," she says, glaring at Margaret Ann, who has elected herself the new troop leader. "I only found out after you ruthlessly fired Jane Williams as troop leader, a woman who has selflessly led this troop by my side for years now and was a very capable leader on her own. Now, as you all know, I stepped down because I'm having another child," she says, rubbing her belly. "And I felt completely confident leaving Jane in charge. She has been there for these girls through thick and thin. She has taught them and led them with patience and care, and has al-

ways made them and their safety the most important thing."
She looks around the room coolly. "Now, let's open the floor
for you all to ask Jane questions so that we can get to the bottom of all of this nonsense."

"Why were you running around with that celebrity when
he had a pregnant fiancée?" Margaret asks without missing a
beat. Ten pairs of eyes turn on me.

"Matt Sherwin and I were working together, not running
around together," I say. "I was doing PR for a charity campaign,
and he was the celebrity spokesman."

"So kissing celebrity spokesmen is part of your job too,
then?" she asks archly. Why is she so smug? She seems to be the
only one questioning me. The others watch in interest, but
none of them seem to have anything to add.

"*He* kissed *me*," I patiently explain. "On the cheek. Once.
Unfortunately, this one time was captured by a camera and
published in that gossip rag." Margaret Ann looks horrified that
I called it a rag, as if she honestly believed she was reading serious award-winning journalism.

"Then why were there pictures of you two in a hotel?" She
looks around at the other moms triumphantly, but they avoid
her eye.

"That was a business meeting. The location was his choice.
We talked, and I left," I say, fighting the urge to roll my eyes.

Caroline raises her hand tentatively. "Why should we trust
you? These are our daughters," she says quietly. Margaret Ann
beams. "There is nothing more important than who we leave in
charge of them."

I look around uncertainly. Why *should* they believe me? Caroline is right. There is nothing more important to these women than their daughters, and protecting them is their job. They're right to pay close attention to who they get to spend time with.

"I understand your concern, and I wish there was something I could do to prove to you how serious I am about this. But I can't." I take a deep breath. "All I can do is promise you I never had anything to do with Matt Sherwin aside from work. I never called him, never talked to him, never went out with him unless it was about the Strike Hunger Campaign. I loved my boyfriend. I respect what a relationship is. I would never do anything to break up a family." I look around uncertainly. They are eyeing me, but they are listening. "Your girls mean the world to me. They made me laugh, and I loved spending time with them. It wasn't until I found out I couldn't lead them anymore that I realized how much I really loved them. It would break my heart to never see them again. But even if I never see any of them for the rest of my life, please believe me when I say that I would never have done anything that would give them the wrong ideas."

"Please," Raquel says, "she's suffered enough. She already lost her job over this. And I have no qualms about leaving Haven in her care. Can we give her another chance?"

The women look around uncertainly. No one says anything. Caroline takes a sip of her ice water.

"We'll have to discuss it another time," Margaret Ann says, looking pointedly at me.

"Okay. Thank you for hearing me out," I say weakly.

Raquel smiles and gets up to start carrying her untouched sugary goodies into the kitchen. "I guess I'll go now." I start to stand up.

"One more thing, Jane," Eleanor says, and I sit back down. Oh no. What can she possibly ask that would make this better? Here it comes. I'm ready. Bring it on. Slowly, Eleanor breaks into a smile. "What's Matt Sherwin really like?"

"Yeah," Abby's mom says, leaning forward. "Is he as cute in real life as he is in the movies?" Everyone is smiling and nodding, anxious to hear what I have to say. I almost want to laugh. Aren't we fickle? Suddenly, I am a star.

"I've always had such a crush on him," Margaret Ann confides, giggling and shrugging her shoulders.

"I'm dying to know," Eleanor asks, winking at me. "Is he a good kisser?"

I put the key in my lock and open my front door. I inhale the smell of newly minted construction and see that the skylight is installed and the plaster around the hole is new. I resolve to begin my job search in earnest tomorrow. After all, I've been working in PR for a while now. I have a lot of contacts. It can't be that hard to find something new. I slip into my cute monkey pajamas that Mom gave me four Christmases ago and find my fuzzy slippers. There. That's more like it.

There's a knock at the door. It's probably Lee. I hope he has an update about Mary Sue. As I walk over to the door, I pull my hair up into a messy ponytail.

I swing it open and am staring at Tyson. "Huh . . . ," I gasp.

He stands there awkwardly. My mind flashes back to the last time I saw him. He wasn't there for me. He failed me. And I just let him slam the door in my face. After everything we've been through, I just let him slam the door in my face like I was some kind of stranger. All at once I decide that this time he's not getting off that easily. I walk forward and put a finger on his chest and press on it hard. "You. I have something to tell you, Mr. Denver." He takes a step back and rubs the spot on his chest, looking wounded. I go in for the kill. "You were every-thing to me, and you let me down when I really needed you." He stares at me blankly.

I take another step forward into the hall, and he drops a plastic bag and stumbles a little.

He looks down. "Jane—"

"Don't Jane me. Jane you." Okay, I'm not making a lot of sense right now. Stay focused, Jane. "I needed you that night. Do you have any idea what I had been going through that day?"

"I—" he stammers.

"Trust me, you don't. It was easily the worst day of my life. My roof caved in, Charlie almost died, I lost my job, I was mugged, I lost—" I realize that the worst part was losing him. I hesitate. After all, he dumped me. "And then to go to you in my time of need only to have you, who I loved, who I wanted to spend the rest of my life with, turn me away?" I stare at him, wild-eyed. "Well, Tyson, it was almost more than I could bear." I rock back on my heels, done for the moment.

"I'm sorry, Jane," he starts, tentatively. "That night, I was—I was stupid. I was upset."

I roll my eyes. "Trust me. You don't even know 'upset' until you walk around in these shoes for a while." I point down at my slipper-shod feet. "Well, not these shoes exactly, but other shoes. My other shoes. The black patent leather heels, maybe."

He frowns. "I'm so sorry. I hope you can forgive me," he looks at me like he's scared. "In time."

I take a deep breath and try to calm down. I can't believe any of this is happening. This is just not how it was all supposed to turn out. This is not how I had it planned. Even yelling at Tyson feels so wrong. For a full minute, we are both silent. The tension is palpable. I finally exhale and decide to be honest with him, to try to explain why I'm so angry, to calm down. "I loved you," I say, my voice shaking. I swallow and look at him. "You know that, right? That's why all of this hurts so much. I really loved you."

"Yeah," he says, nodding. "I know." He takes a deep breath. "And for what it's worth, I love you too."

I grimace a little and try to remember to breathe, glad we're at least talking now—wait, did he just use the present tense? I stare into his eyes searching for a sign that it was a mistake, trying to read what he's thinking. He meant to say "loved" too, right? I expect to see him staring at the floor or looking at me sadly, but instead he stares back, boldly. We fix eyes on each other.

"I love you," he whispers.

A jolt of electricity runs down my spine. I am locked in his gaze. He's so beautiful. And then he rushes to me, takes the back of my head roughly in his hands, and kisses me, deep and long, pressing me against the wall. My whole body wants to kiss him back, and I hold him against me. He stops, but keeps his face close to mine. I can feel him breathing on my cheek. I hear him swallow. He gently brushes his lips over my forehead, my nose, back down to my mouth, and then whispers, "I have to go. I fly out from Kennedy at nine tomorrow." I stay perfectly still and silent, afraid anything I do will make him leave. Stay, I pray. Stay. He finally pulls back from me. He looks at the ceiling. He takes a deep breath and then says, "Here," and hands me the plastic bag. I take it numbly. He turns and walks away. I lean against the wall and watch him go, unable to breathe, wanting to scream, Wait, wait, as he walks out of my life, but I can't get the air to do it.

I stay still for a while, trembling with shock. But eventually I peek down into the plastic bag he gave me. Inside I see a T-shirt that says "Plain Jane." I bought it at a thrift store in high school. It's charcoal gray and worn soft and thin. My signature T-shirt. The one I wore over one time to help him paint his apartment. It ended up living at Ty's place. Every time I hung out at his place after work, I would throw it on to relax and get out of my work clothes. I hold it up to my nose and it smells like his apartment, like him. I slide down the wall and sit outside my door. What on earth does this mean? Why would he return this? It's the worst thing he could have done. Does he really think I want this now, after everything?

"Jane?" I hear from the stairwell. "Are you home?" It's Lee. I open my door and throw the plastic bag with the T-shirt inside. I can't think about that now. It's too much.

"It's me," I call down to him. "Here I come in my pajamas," I say.

"What else is new?" he yells back.

I walk down the stairs, and Charlie follows behind me. When he sees Lee, his tail wags so fast and furious that I think it might fly off. Lee scoops him up, and he's wiggly with excitement. He kisses Lee all over his face, and I laugh.

"Listen, thanks for picking him up and keeping him for me. You got my note, right?" After I gave Mary Sue a bath, I left Lee a note that I was taking Charlie home. "I owe you," I say.

He shrugs. "You'd do it for me. And just wait until you see all the tricks I taught him. He can dance now. Just say, '*Baila!*' and he'll turn around in circles."

I look at Lee. "You taught him the command for 'dance' in Spanish?"

He shrugs. "*Baila* is a cute word. Don't you think?"

I laugh at him.

"And here," he says, ushering me into his apartment. "I've been doing some research." He pulls an envelope from his bag and takes a seat on the couch. I sit next to him as he pulls out some glossy blowups of a woman's face. They look as though they were taken on the fly.

"Where on earth did you get those?"

"Remember Brandon?" I nod, remembering his friend, a struggling actor who often starred in commercials and got bit parts on daytime dramas. "Turns out he and Matt Sherwin use the same talent agency. What luck, right?" He beams at me.

"Did he ever get past that whole fear of birds thing?" Brandon was set to star in a new daytime drama, but he withdrew when he learned that his girlfriend on the show had a pet parakeet who was integral to the plot.

"Not really." He smiles sheepishly. "But he's auditioning a lot, and something will come up. And he was a gold mine of information."

I sit down next to him and check out the snapshots. They are definitely of the red-haired girl we've been looking for.

"That's her! That's her, all right," I say, taking them from him. I remember how she looks like a wealthy socialite. "But wait. That still doesn't explain the photos. How'd you get them?"

"Easy. Matt Sherwin's agent is a friend of Brandon's. So I got Brandon to ask Matt's agent to figure out who the red-haired woman in Matt's life was."

"And he just had photos lying around?"

"No, silly. He just had a name and an address. I took these."

"Oh. Of course. How silly of me," I say and slap my head. "What kind of agent gives out that sort of information?"

"The kind who has a crush on Brandon." I look at him like

he's nuts. "What?" He really sees nothing odd about any of this. "So Matt's agent gave Brandon the red-haired girl's home address, and I waited until she came out and then snapped these. Apparently her name is Nina."

Nina. "That's his personal assistant. Matt Sherwin was always talking about her. That's it." I put it all together.

Lee smiles proudly, but the enormity of what he has done sinks in. He used his friend to get private information. He stalked someone. He clandestinely snapped photos of a stranger. "You have lost your mind," I say, but then a smile spreads across my face. My devious smile. "And I love you for it. Let's hope Nina has some answers for us." He laughs, handing me the thick envelope of papers.

"Hey, is your mom around?" I ask, craning my neck toward the bedroom.

"Oh," Lee says.

"What do you mean, 'Oh'?"

He takes a deep breath. "Mom's at the hospital. I guess I forgot to mention that." I nod, as if I actually believe he forgot. "She's had a setback."

"When?"

"This morning. They're worried it has spread. And then the drugs they had her on weren't mixing well, and she was really disoriented. It was scary. I took her to the emergency room," he says and his eyes start to water up.

"Where is she?"

"There are the apples of my eyes," Mary Sue says weakly when she sees us. She looks small and tired. She smiles as Lee and I walk in her room in the ICU and struggles to sit up. You're technically only allowed one visitor at a time, but we snuck in separately and are now hiding behind the curtain that separates Mary Sue's bed from the others. I come around and hug her. It's very quiet in here, except for the beeping of medical equipment.

"I just found out you were in the ICU," I say, "or I would have come sooner." She waves in the air like Lee does, dismissing this comment.

"Don't you worry your pretty head none. These New York doctors just have worked themselves into a real fuss over me. I'm fine. I promise. I feel just like the day I was born," she says, pausing a second to catch her breath.

"I wish I could have brought Charlie to cheer you up. I know he misses you," I say. "And thanks for helping Lee watch him."

"Lee, did you remember to turn off the oven before you left?" she asks.

"Mom, I haven't turned the oven on in a week."

"The iron?" she asks him and then turns to me. "I swear if I didn't watch that boy he'd burn the whole apartment down." I laugh.

"Yes, the iron is off," he says, almost patiently.

"Good. Now come give your mama a hug." He comes around and gives her a hug. When he pulls back from her she says in a loud stage whisper, "Did you remember to brush your teeth today?"

"Mom," he whines at her. I crack up at their little family drama but decide to help Lee out by changing the subject.

"Mary Sue, is there anything we can get you? A soda? Some ice?"

"Aren't you just the sweetest thing?" She smiles weakly at me. "Are you sure you don't want to marry Lee?"

I laugh while he groans at her.

"He could really use some help, you know. Why, I don't even know how he's managed all these years without me."

"By the skin of my teeth," he says, forcing a smile.

Mary Sue turns to me. "I'm fine, shug. Don't you worry about me. I got this real nice nurse, and she's got me all set up real comfortable here." She's probably charmed the entire hospital staff by now.

The curtain snaps open, and a nurse pokes her head in. "I'm sorry. Only one guest at a time. And visiting hours end in five minutes." She looks at us firmly.

Lee and I look at each other. "I'll just meet you in the lobby," I say to him.

"No, wait," Mary Sue says. "Lee, honey, can I have a moment with Jane? I want to have some girl talk with her." Her joke falls a little flat, but I try to smile anyway.

"Sure, Mama," he says. He kisses her good-bye and then follows the nurse out.

I go over to Mary Sue and hold her hand.

She takes a deep and labored breath. "Shug, I don't feel so well is the truth of it."

I squeeze her hand tight and fight back tears.

"I hope it's just a little setback, but if it ain't, can you tell me one thing?"

I nod. "Of course. Anything."

"Does Lee," she purses her lips and goes quiet for a moment. "Does Lee think I'm a burden? I don't want to be an inconvenience to him."

"Of course not, Mary Sue. He loves you to the end of this earth. He would do anything for you. He loves having you around."

"Are you sure?" she asks. "I know it's been hard on him to have me here all along. And I don't want to disrupt his life. I just wanted to see him. And I know I've been a bit, well, controlling, maybe. I just want to make sure he's okay. If I know what he's doing, I feel like maybe I can hold on to him a little longer."

I look down, not sure of what to say. "He's loved having you. More than anything."

"Now Jane, I'm no fool. But he, he—"

I look at her soft, wrinkled face.

"He doesn't really need me anymore. I guess all along even down in Charleston I was still living for him. When his daddy died, Lee was all I had left. I figured, okay, Mary Sue, your boy needs you. That's something to live for. But now I'm here and I see plain and simple, he doesn't need me. He's all grown up." A tear slides down her cheek. I place my cool hand on her forehead.

"Honey," I say in my best Southern accent, "you're plumb wrong about Lee."

She looks at me hopefully.

"I've never seen a boy who needs his mama more than Lee."

"Are you sure?" she asks.

"I'm positive. He's a mess when you're not around."

She smiles and I kiss her on her forehead and say goodbye. As I walk away, she seems so small and fragile.

Chapter 16

I ignore the stares as I walk through the terminal. I am carrying a giant pink stuffed elephant—so what? I hold my head up. This is New York. There are crazy people everywhere.

Last night when I came home from the hospital, I saw the T-shirt Ty returned and burst into tears. I pulled it on and crawled into bed, enjoying the smell of him. It was like having his arms around me again. I realized that he was really leaving. I thought about what it meant, about how I would probably never see him ever again, this man I thought I was going to marry. And then I thought about the kiss. We both felt it.

And I realized what I had to do. My mom was right. I couldn't let him get away. I had planned to spend my life with him, and I had to make it happen. I needed to make a grand gesture to stop him, show him I am serious about this. About us. No matter what it takes.

I got up at the crack of dawn and put on the jeans he loves so much and his favorite black top of mine. I took the train to Coney Island, praying that the vendors would still be there even though it's the end of the season, and then convinced a man on the pier to sell me a stuffed animal, just like the one Ty won for me on our first date, the one I got rid of after a week, because what kind of grown woman has a giant, pink stuffed elephant in her room? Then I called a car and rushed to Kennedy Airport.

I stop and scan the departure board. Good. His flight isn't boarding yet. I walk toward the security screening area.

"Ticket and ID, please," the guard barks at me.

"I just need to go inside for a little while," I say, smiling my best smile, trying to look as sweet as possible. I shift the elephant to my other arm. How did I forget about security?

"Can't get past without a ticket and ID," he says, waving me aside.

"Please, I promise I'll come right back," I say.

"Ma'am, this is a secure area," he says. "It is a violation of federal law to let you past without a ticket and ID. Are you asking me to break the law?"

I smile hopefully. He shakes his head no.

"Fine," I say, turning toward the ticket counter. I wait in the line, checking my watch every few minutes. I have to make it on time. After fifteen frustrating minutes, I make it to the front of the line. "How much is a ticket to Denver?" I ask at the counter. "On the flight that leaves in forty-five minutes."

"It looks like we have a seat available," she says, punching keys on her computer. "That will be eight hundred dollars." She looks up at me and smiles.

"Eight hundred dollars?" I mouth weakly. "But, I . . ."

"We have a later flight. Let me see if there is any room on that one," she says, looking back at her screen and smiling.

"No, that's all right," I say, turning to go but then stop. I take a deep breath. I hadn't intended to go to Denver, but if that's what it takes, that's what I'll have to do. I pull out my brand-new credit card. "I'll take it," I say and wince. I'll be paying that off for a year. But it's worth it. No price too high for true love.

Ticket in hand, I rush back toward security. The screener eyes me warily as I hand him my ticket and driver's license. He nods, and I rush past him, throwing the elephant on the conveyor belt. It doesn't fit through the opening.

"Ma'am, that won't fit in the overhead bin," the man behind the X-ray machine barks.

"That's ok. Hopefully I don't need it to," I say breathlessly, trying to stuff it into the mouth of the machine.

"It won't fit. Don't force it." I bite my lip. He looks at me, skeptically. "You can't bring that inside, ma'am."

"But I have to," I say, pushing on the pink fabric. I turn it over so its trunk is on the conveyor belt and give it another push. It slides under the lip of the machine, and I beam. "See! It fits!"

"You cannot bring that inside the boarding area," he says. I look at it on the little screen as it slides through the X-ray machine.

"Please," I say. "I need to bring Judy Garland in with me."

"Judy Garland?" he asks, raising his eyebrows.

"I think Judy Garland is a good name for her," I say. "Pinky was too obvious, and Poppy just didn't fit." He cracks a smile.

"How about Roger?" he asks, pointing to his nametag and smiling.

"She's a girl!"

"Fine," he says, shaking his head. "But ma'am, I'm afraid I can't let you bring Judy Garland inside the boarding area," he says, softening slightly. The man behind me in line clears his throat.

"Look," I say leaning toward him. "There's nothing wrong with the elephant. She checks out on X-ray, right?" He nods. "It's for my boyfriend," I say. "I mean, my ex-boyfriend." He listens. "And hopefully, my future boyfriend. I need to get Judy Garland to him before he gets on the plane." I look to see how he's reacting to my speech. He watches me. "Please," I say. "He's the best thing I've ever had." I look at Judy Garland, emerging from the other side of the machine. "I can't let him get away."

The guard looks at me. "This elephant is going to help you get your boyfriend back?" He laughs. I nod, tears pooling in my eyes. He has to let me in. This just has to work. The man behind me clears his throat louder this time.

"Fine," the guard says quietly, waving me through the electronic gate. "Take the elephant. But please be discreet," he says, as I pick up my hot pink stuffed elephant that blends in so naturally in this run-down terminal.

"Thank you," I say, blinking back tears as I look for gate A9.

"And good luck!" he yells as I start to walk away. I turn back and smile. He just shakes his head. I throw Judy Garland over my shoulder and rush toward the wing marked Gates A1–A15. He can't be on the plane yet. I still have time. I rush through the terminal, weaving around confused tourists and slow vacationers. I knock someone in the head with Judy

Garland's trunk and yell sorry without looking back. I'm almost there, and I slow down. I scan the boarding area.

There he is. I see the back of his blond head. He's looking out the windows and is slouched down in his chair, staring straight ahead, his headphones in his ears. I step out of sight behind a pillar and take a deep breath. I hadn't really planned what I was going to do at this point. Do I go sit down next to him? I wonder if I should sneak up behind him, set the elephant down next to him, and see what happens next. Surely he'll see it and realize he's making a mistake and stay. Or I'll get on the plane with him and surprise him in the air? Or is that a little too crazy? That's a long flight if he's horrified.

Judy Garland weighs more than I thought. My arms are getting tired. And then I study her and see how cheaply made she is. She's actually pretty hideous. Would anyone really want this thing? Why do I have this stupid animal, anyway? Maybe it's a kind of apology, an offer to start fresh. I guess I was hoping it would bring him back to our first date and help him remember what it felt like, that first rush of love. My mind drifts back to that magic afternoon—the sunshine, the salty air, the kiss— and I sigh.

I step forward to walk toward him when the woman at the gate announces that the flight is beginning to board. I see Ty look up and put his headphones away, then stand up and grab his carry-on bag. It's now or never. But as I try to walk forward again, I stop.

He loves me. He said it himself.

But is it enough?

Yes, I tell myself. I can't live without him. This was not how it was supposed to end. I have to stop him from leaving.

But I can't make myself go. This doesn't feel right. I sigh and look at Judy Garland. I notice she's not even the exact same kind of pink elephant that Ty won for me. Oh no. Why on earth do they give away more than one kind of pink elephant? I messed it up. But maybe he won't know. I should have just kept it the first time. Then I wouldn't be in this predicament. I look over at the line. Ty is at the back of it. I look at the stuffed animal again. But I didn't keep it. Does that mean something? Why didn't I keep it? What if the truth is, I knew even then?

Ty is three people away from the front of the line. I open my mouth to say something, but I can't make a sound come out. I look at my feet and tell them to move, but they are planted in place. I shift Judy Garland in my arms and look at her. All of my dreams of reconciliation seem childish. I'm standing in the airport with a giant stuffed elephant, and all of sudden I know it's not enough. This isn't going to work. Ty isn't ultimately the kind of man I want. The whole time, I guess I knew deep down that it wasn't going to work, but I was willing to live the lie.

I've been lying to myself.

I watch as Ty heads for the agent and pulls his ticket out of his pocket. I swallow back a lump in my throat as he hands it to the woman. I watch, helplessly, as he turns and looks around the terminal one last time. And a tear leaks out of my eye when he steps through the doorway and into his new life.

Slowly, I turn and walk away.

———

I check the address on the paper and hop out of the cab I caught outside the airport. Thank goodness computer centers are so common in airports now. I juggle Judy Garland in my arms as I pay the driver and slam the car door and march through the plate-glass doors of the SoHo loft building. I tuck the stuffed animal under my arm and hold my head up as I stride confidently past the doorman's slick mahogany desk and through the sleek modern lobby. I learned long ago that if you look like you know what you're doing, people tend to believe you. He doesn't stop me.

This is exactly the kind of place he'd live. The concrete floor and high ceilings speak to the building's former factory days, but the built-in flat-screen television playing images of ocean waves, the Eames chairs gathered around a tiled coffee table, and the modern art on the walls remind visitors that it costs a lot to live like you're poor in this city. The brushed-chrome elevator doors slide open soundlessly, and I step in. I push the button for the twelfth floor and look at my reflection in the mirrored walls. The jeans and black top aren't too wrinkled. I smooth down my hair and take a deep breath.

When the door opens, I step out into a long hallway with gray carpeting. I look for number 1214. I pass several doors with welcome mats and crayon drawings taped to the door, but 1214 is austere. The heavy metal door is tall and intimidating.

I raise my hand to knock, then bring it down again.

He's going to think I'm crazy. I can't just show up at his

door. I'm still holding this ridiculous elephant. I'd better just go.

I turn to go back toward the elevator when I hear noises inside. I lean in to listen. That's definitely Neil Diamond. I can't help but laugh. Okay. I can do this. Surely he'll be so embarrassed to be caught listening to "Sweet Caroline" that nothing I say will be a big deal.

Before I lose my nerve, I knock on the door. I hear footsteps, and I steady myself. The door opens, and he's standing there in dark blue jeans and a tight gray T-shirt. He looks . . . good. And he is smiling. Before he can ask me what I'm doing here, I blurt it out.

"I know it was you."

Chapter 17

You're a little later than I thought," Coates says, looking at his watch. "I had guessed two days ago." He shrugs. "But better late than never."

He expected me? Here we go again with him pretending he knows everything about me.

"All the same. I'm glad you're here." He smiles, his cold blue eyes almost kind. "Please, come in," he says, stepping back and gesturing me inside.

I step through the doorway and look around. Straight ahead is an entire wall of floor-to-ceiling windows. The view toward upper Manhattan is breathtaking. The living room is decorated with an annoyingly tasteful mix of modern and classic furniture. He has several large photographs hanging on the walls, and the kitchen is open and looks professional grade. He gestures toward the sleek brown leather couch, and I sit uncertainly, placing Judy Garland down next to me. I can't deny that he has a nice place. And, it's spotless. Surely he must have just cleaned it up . . . but he didn't know I was coming over. He's not telepathic. Oh well, I bet he has a maid.

"Can I get you something to drink? Coffee? Water?" he

asks, leaning against a granite counter and crossing his arms over his chest.

"I'm fine," I say, shaking my head. I balance on the front edge of the couch.

"Hungry?"

"Nope," I say, looking around. I tap my fingers on the couch leather. This is awkward. I usually think through what I'm going to say before I face an awkward situation, but I just came over so quickly, I hadn't really played out in my head how it would go.

He walks to the stereo and turns the music off without a hint of embarrassment, then takes a seat on the modern armchair chair across from me. He looks at me. "So . . . ," he says, raising his eyebrows.

"Why?" I ask. "Why did you do it?"

"Whatever do you mean?" He smiles at me.

I know he knows what I'm talking about, so why does he insist on teasing me? This man. Is he nice? Is he evil? How can those two qualities intermingle so closely?

"Look, Coates. The Four Seasons. All of that. Obviously you have money to spare, but we're not exactly the closest of friends, so I don't get it."

"Hmm," he says and gets up. He paces back and forth for a moment with a bemused look on his face. "I've known all along you'd someday come to me and ask this question." I stifle a groan. As if he knew that. "And even still, I'm not sure how to answer it. For the moment I would prefer to let you decide for yourself." He sits down next to me and breaks into a big, enticing grin. He's having the time of his life with this.

I have no idea how to respond to that. I change my tactic.

"Why did you make it such a big secret?" I ask.

"Aren't you supposed to keep your right hand from knowing what your left hand is doing?"

I shake my head. I could try to fight him, to insist that he tell me what he's up to, but I suspect that's exactly what he wants. I will not play along.

"So you're a Bible scholar now?"

"I know the Bible."

I look at his chiseled face next to me. "Indeed. You seem to know a lot of things. It's sort of what you do for a living, I realize now."

"Aha. I see you've been researching what an actuary does. I must say, it was quite a breakthrough when I finally found a career that perfectly tapped into my gift for—"

"Insulting others?"

He stands up and walks to the wall of windows, grinning. "From your mouth to God's ears, Jane."

"You hope to be insulting?"

He puts his hands in his pockets and looks out at the city. I watch him. "I think I might choose a different word than insulting, but yes, basically."

"You'd choose annoying? Dismissive?"

"I'm not sure. What's the term for waking people up to how things really are?" he asks.

I cross my arms over my chest. Fine. He did sort of have that effect on me. But did he have to be so unctuous during the process? "Fairy godmother of cruel reality?"

He turns and smiles at me. "It certainly has a nicer ring to it than 'actuary,' I suppose, though we're mostly men."

"Of course you are," I say and roll my eyes. "So how did you know that I like cookie dough and face masks?"

He laughs. "Every woman likes cookie dough and face masks. It's a stereotype, but the thing about a stereotype is that it's often statistically true."

"Glad I'm so predictable."

"Only on some things. Like I said, I would have thought you'd have come by at least two days ago, And I didn't expect you to have a pink elephant in your arms."

I watch him. He turns his head to look at me, then looks back at the window and takes a deep breath. "We didn't start off on the right foot, Jane."

"That's like saying Hitler wasn't such a decent chap," I say.

"You intrigue me."

"Why?" I shrug. I think back to our first encounter at Hamilton's party. "You had me all figured out by the end of our first conversation, didn't you?"

"Do you honestly believe five questions would be enough to tell me everything I want to know about you?" He walks to the kitchen and takes down two glasses, filling them with water from the refrigerator.

"You told me I was lying to myself." I accept the glass he

offers me and take a long, thirsty drink. I place the empty glass down on his dark wood coffee table. I bite my lip. I look at him. He's watching me intently. "And you were right."

He nods. "I'm glad you can admit that now."

I sigh. Why is it that just when I let my guard down with him and actually begin to like him, he says something insufferable?

"Now do you want to talk to me about the pink elephant in the room?"

I can't help but smile and start to think about how to explain about the elephant. But then I decide that it's really none of his business. "I don't know why I came here," I say quietly, looking down at my hands. "I should go."

"No, please stay," he says. For a moment, I almost think I can see a blush spreading across his face. "I mean, if you want to."

"I do want to," I say, standing, emboldened by my honesty. "But I have to go." He nods and rises, and I begin to walk toward the door. But I stop when my hand is on the knob. I turn back to him and look him in the eyes. "Oh. And thanks. I'm not sure if that's what I came here to say, but thanks. The hotel was what I needed."

"Don't forget your stuffed animal." He points to the couch where Judy Garland sits, incongruously bright in this masculine apartment. I pause, then pull the door open.

"Why don't you keep it?" I say, and walk out the door.

————

"**Now**, see, aren't you glad you came?" Lee asks, pulling me through the front door of Echo, the latest Manhattan hot spot. I would never come to a place like this but Lee insisted, begged, and finally demanded I come with him as payment for his keeping Charlie while I stayed at the hotel. Lee, understandably, has been having a tough time of it, and he wanted to go out and have fun for a night and forget about everything his mom is going through, so I didn't mention his statue was the reason I was homeless in the first place. And he always likes to be where the beautiful people are and would never be seen in anything less than the club of the moment. It didn't hurt that a friend of his who bartends there put us on the guest list. I'll admit it felt good to be pulled from the line snaking around the block and ushered behind the velvet rope, but as I look around at the hot, crowded room, I want to be anywhere but here. I remind myself that Lee needs this.

I follow him past the smooth-as-glass indoor pond, past the crowded bar area, and through the throng to a lounge area in the back where we manage to snag a table. I rest, leaning back on the low-slung padded bench, while Lee preens and looks around the room.

"Is that Lindsay Lohan?" I whisper, pointing at a waiflike figure shuffling across the room in big dark sunglasses.

"Shh, Jane," Lee says, pushing my arm down and rolling his eyes. "Please be discreet," he says. "No pointing."

"Fine," I say, signaling for the waiter. He comes over and smiles.

"I'll just have a glass of red wine, please," I say.

"Vodka tonic," Lee says, smiling at the waiter, who avoids his eye. He turns to go.

I shake my head and scan the room. The place is dark, loud, and hot, the dance floor is jam packed with writhing bodies, and the corners of the lounge area are shadowy and private. The VIP room is guarded by a bouncer and a velvet rope. I wonder what you have to do to get in there? I stare at the doorway, trying to catch a glimpse of whatever stars may be inside.

"It is so good to get away for a while. Auntie Di made these disgusting casseroles, and they're taking up my entire freezer, and not only that, I'm being forced to eat them for every meal. Tell me, Jane, do marshmallows belong in a casserole? I don't think so, and——"

"*Jen!*"

I look at Lee, who is staring in wide-eyed awe at the person who is apparently coming up behind me. I turn around. Matt Sherwin.

"Matt," I say as sincerely as I can and hop up. "Imagine meeting you here." I offer him my hand to avoid a kiss on the cheek and look around to see if there are cameras anywhere. That would be all I need.

"How are you doing?" he asks, taking a seat next to me on the bench. Lee is glaring at me, leaning in, practically begging for an introduction.

"Matt, this is my friend Lee," I say. Lee thrusts his arm out and beams with delight.

"Nice to meet you, man," he says, raising his hand for a

high-five. Lee meets his hand, but he appears too starstruck to open his mouth.

"So how's Chloe?" I ask, looking around to see if she's here.

"She's fine," he says. "She's at her mother's. She's like this amazing person, you know?"

I nod. I know.

"Well, good to see you, Jen," Matt says, rising. "Give me a ring sometime. And Lee," he says, extending his hand to Lee, "it was great talking to you." Lee, who has not uttered one word since he sat down, nods enthusiastically.

"You're, uh-huh. Yep," Lee finally manages to say as Matt begins to walk away.

"What did you just say?" I laugh as soon as Matt is out of earshot.

"Oh, can it, Jane," he says. "You're ruining this beautiful moment. I just high-fived Matt Sherwin."

"And you handled it so well."

"I did?" he asks hopefully, his eyes glazed over.

"Sure you did," I say. "You just sit here and bask. I'm going to find the ladies' room."

"Mm hm," he says.

I shake my head. I wind my way through the crowd to the back of the room, hoping I'm headed in the right direction. With the dim lighting it's hard to see anything. I get bumped and pushed and plow on ahead, gritting my teeth and thinking about how much Lee owes me for being here.

After a few dead ends, I find a hallway at the back of the room and duck down it. The bathroom must be down here. I follow it and stop short when I stumble upon a couple making out in a nook off the hallway. I know that head. It's Matt Sherwin's. I thought he said Chloe wasn't here? I decide to just put my head down and pass them when I catch a glimpse of shining red hair. The shining red hair. I stop and look, startled. Nina. Matt is kissing his personal assistant, Nina.

I freeze. Matt *is* cheating on Chloe. With Nina. As I put the pieces together, I turn around. I have to get out of here.

"Hey!" Matt says, as if delighted to stumble across an old friend he hasn't seen in years. "Jane. How are you?" So now he gets my name right?

"Shhh," I hear Nina whisper as I walk back past them. Nina glares at him, grabbing his arm and pulling him down the hall toward the bathroom. She doesn't look at me.

"See you later!" he yells as he's being pulled away. Nina whispers something angrily at him as they disappear around a corner.

I rush back to Lee, pushing my way through the crowd.

"We have to get out of here," I say.

"Jane, what's going on? We just got here," Lee says. "We haven't even danced yet."

"We have to leave right now," I say, pulling him to his feet. "I'll explain later."

"Fine," he says, sighing and looking at me like I'm crazy. "But this had better be important. This is a good song," he says, moving his shoulders.

"I promise I'll make it up to you," I say, a little calmer now that we're closer to the door. I take one last look to make sure Nina isn't around. The coast is clear.

"Hey, I think that really is Lindsay Lohan," I say, nodding at her as we pass.

"Jane, please," Lee says. "You're totally embarrassing me." He pulls my arm down and shakes his head. "You really need to learn how to act around celebrities."

Chapter 18

My head is inside my fireplace as I try to remember how to get the gas turned on. I've only used the fireplace once, at the fancy Christmas party I threw a couple of years ago, and even then it took Ty and me an hour to figure it out. This must be the first gas fireplace ever invented. No switch to flip, no easy instant-lighting mechanism. After another five minutes of hunting around in dusty soot, I spy a faucet in the back and give it a turn. The fireplace begins to fill with gas fumes, and I pull my head out. I grab a match and slowly but surely get a nice little fire going after a minor sneezing fit.

Pulling up a big pillow, I sit in front of the fire with Charlie, whose doggie instincts are telling him to stay far away from the heat. I look out the window and sigh. Thank goodness fall is coming on, otherwise it'd be too hot to do this tonight. And I have to do it tonight, or I'll lose my nerve.

Next to me, on the new couch I bought on credit last week, is my day planner. I wonder if it knows what is about to happen to it? Not that it has feelings or even a life force so, um, that was sort of a silly thought. I pick it up and flip through the pages, watching them fan in front of me. I guess it really did seem to me to have a life force. I read some sample entries.

I find a week where I apparently scheduled and resched-
uled a date with Tyson five different times. I shrug. That's the
nature of being a publicist. I'm not going to make myself feel
bad about it. You can't stop the world, and especially your
clients, from having crises. I keep thumbing through. I see that
I have church scheduled each Sunday morning. Why did I do
that? Did I think I would forget? I never oversleep. I run my fingers over my own precise handwriting and remember the answer. I just liked to fill in the gaps for the week, liked the
security of seeing it all written in front of me. No need to
worry about the future, Jane. You've got it all scheduled right
here. A small laugh escapes from deep within me. How foolish
I was.

For another hour I flip through my year, reliving all the
things I had scheduled with Raquel, Lee, Tyson, the Brownies,
work, my family, everything. And then, I move a little closer to
the fire. I take a deep breath. I have to do this. I have to learn
to let go. Normal people can use day planners in a healthy way,
but mine is a security blanket, a crutch. I slide a little closer and
tear out the first page. Charlie wakes up and tilts his head at the
noise.

"I know, Charlie. It's hard to believe." I take another deep
breath. "But here goes nothing." I throw the first piece of paper
in the fire. Watching it burn, I feel as though I might have a
panic attack, but I force myself to keep going. I continue to tear
out the pages in big chunks and throw them into the fire, causing it to blaze up and then calm back down each time. "*Thy word
is a lamp unto my feet and a light unto my path,*" I say again and

again, until the last curl of paper disappears and the last lick of flame has burned out.

All I can hear at the Chelsea Piers skating rink is high-pitched, little-girl glee. This is a trial event, a chance for the mothers of Troop 192 of Manhattan, New York, to see me with their children before they make a judgment. This is their chance to skewer me, an opportunity disguised as a friendly mother–daughter skating event. Predictably, the turnout is excellent. Everyone except Raquel, who's very pregnant and uncertain on her feet, is here, so Haven is my honorary daughter for the day. Of course Margaret Ann Markelson is in attendance with her darling little Bella, who has spent the last hour chasing a little blond boy around the rink threatening to kiss him. Our cute instructor, Sven, seems a little over-whelmed.

"Twwwweeeeee." Sven blows the whistle, and we all clutch each other and look at him, trying not to fall down. "Ladies, listen up," he says, hands on hips. I'm pretty sure he aced his Presidential Fitness Test every year. "Our goal is help you all learn the basics of ice-skating so that no one leaves here today a 'rail hanger.'" He doesn't have to define the term for me to know what it means, and judging by the nodding heads, everyone else knows too. "Now who can tell me the names of the two edges of the blade on your ice skates?" he asks.

I look around like he's mad. Who would know such a thing? But sure enough, I hear chubby little Abby, wearing her sock tassels even now, say confidently, "The inside edge and the outside edge." I see Kaitlin snicker, but the other girls look at Abby with envy and respect, even Haven, who is quietly singing Mariah Carey's "Always Be My Baby."

"That's right," Sven says. "And today we're going to learn how to make use of both edges so we can get you skating like the pros!" he says, bursting with athletic mania.

"I might accidentally fall down a lot today so that Mr. Peppy will come and pick me up," says Eleanor Pearson under her breath to Margaret Ann Markelson.

"Did you catch a load of those buns of his? Do you think it was the inside edge or the outside edge that did that?" Margaret laughs.

An hour later, we're skating around the rink drastically improved. Sven beams with pride at everyone. Everyone, that is, except Haven. As it turns out, Haven may be good at social politics, but she can't skate to save her life. Meanwhile, Abby, who I just discovered has been taking lessons since she was three, was allowed to go into the center of the rink because she was so bored with the basics, and Sven periodically drops by to help her perfect her salchow and lutz.

Haven wipes out again in front of me, and I think she might finally be reduced to tears on what must be her hundredth fall. Raquel's going to think Haven got a good paddling today with all the bruises she'll have on her bottom. I skate over slowly to help her up.

"Jane," she says, poking out her bottom lip. "I hate ice-skating. It's stupid."

I squat down next to her. "It's not stupid, Haven. It's just hard."

"How come it's not hard for Abby?" she pouts. Haven looks with awe at Abby, who is spinning like a top in the middle of the rink. Bella and Kaitlin are standing next to her, trying for all they're worth to spin too.

"Abby has worked hard for many years to be able to skate like that," I say. I put my arms under her armpits and hoist her back up. "If you practice, you can be really good at ice-skating too."

She crosses her arms across her chest and scowls at me. "I *am* good at ice-skating," she says. But then she looks around at the other mother–daughter pairs, and I know I don't need to tell her the truth. It's apparent. All over the rink, the women and the girls are skating hand in hand, trying out stopping correctly, slowly turning one wobbly circle. Our eyes travel back to little Abby, spinning as if nothing in the world made her happier.

I lean over and give Haven a hug. She doesn't tear her eyes away from the center of the rink.

"Jane," she says. "Isn't Abby beautiful right now?"

"Yeah," I say. "She really is."

I arrive at the tiny West Village restaurant Le Gigot about ten minutes late, or exactly as I planned. I open the little wooden door to the restaurant, which is pocket-sized and charming in its simplicity. Coates is sitting at the table in the back, and he stands as he sees me. I take a deep breath and try to walk over casually and elegantly. I'm dressed to kill.

When he called last weekend and asked me to join him for dinner, I wasn't quite sure what to say. He didn't use the word *date*, and I had no idea if that was what he meant. But I did something I've never done before. I just said yes. With Tyson, I practically forced the poor guy to ask me out so that by the time he finally did so, I already had it tentatively scheduled in my day planner. But dinner with Coates was foreign territory, and the moment I hung up the phone, I started freaking out. Dinner with Coates? What was I thinking? As I walk toward him now, my heart starts beating a little faster.

"Jane," he says. He's wearing a suit and tie, and I am struck by how handsome he is. "You clean up just fine."

He comes around behind my chair and pushes it in as I sit down, defeated.

"I clean up just fine?" I repeat. He goes around the table to sit down again.

He smiles at me and winks. "That is to say, your skin is all better now, isn't it?"

I touch my face. "Um, yeah. It was nothing." I cough. "But that's not really much of a way to start off the evening."

He inhales and nods to himself. "I'm afraid you may be right. I don't do this as often as you might have been led to believe."

I eye him. "I'm beginning to believe you on that."

"And I'm me," he says with a shrug, "which can't be helped." He leans in and pulls my hand across the table. "Tell me what was the right thing to say."

I pull my hand back immediately. Whoa. " 'You look amazing,' " I say. "That's what I thought you might say." He smiles at me, and I feel a little silly. "I mean, that's what people have said, um, people say, I've heard sometimes that they say that." I laugh a little. No. Don't let him win. Be tough, Jane.

He looks me dead in the eyes and says slowly, "You look amazing." A chill runs down my spine. But I can't help thinking about the *Times* article and the lawsuit against him, and I hate myself for being here at all.

"This place is charming, just like the review said." He smiles as he looks around. I try to picture him researching restaurants online. "Have you ever been here before?"

"Once," I say, nodding. "Ty and I came here for our anniversary."

"It's supposed to have an excellent wine list," he says smoothly, as if he hasn't heard me. "Would you like to look?" He hands me the drink menu.

The waiter comes and gets our drink order, and Coates gives me a look that seems to say that he is very amused by all of this. I remind myself that he is arrogant and condescending, that I'm not over Ty, that this is not the sort of person Jane Williams dates.

The waiter returns with our drinks and the bread, and we place our food orders, then fall silent. I realize I haven't had French food in a long time because Ty always thought it was too rich. That night we came here together was a concession to me. Coates looks at me silently, seemingly unbothered by the lack of conversation. I clear my throat, trying to think of something to say.

"I have a job interview next week," I say.

"That's wonderful. What's it for?"

"Do you mean who's it with? I'm going to stick with PR."

Coates studies me for a moment. "Okay. That's fine. It's funny, though. I just can't see you in PR."

I laugh. "My West Village mortgage sure can see me in PR."

Coates shrugs. "Just don't choose your job by the zeros at the end of it. As an actuary, I can tell you that everyone who does regrets it at the end."

I laugh at him. "A Glassman is lecturing me about how it's not about the money? That's rich," I say and take a sip of water. I decide to change the topic. I don't really want his unsolicited advice on my career. "And I got rid of my day planner."

"Do you mean you put it away in a box and next week in a moment of weakness you'll get it back out again?"

"No. I went cold turkey. I burned it in the fireplace."

Coates gives a deep-bellied laugh. "Jane, you amaze me. And how long has it been since your last entry?"

"Two weeks, three days, and four hours. I really think the worst of it is over now." I take a piece of bread and put it on my plate.

"Really? I can't believe you know that."

"No. Not really," I say. "Wait a minute. I got you!" I point at him. "I got you! You thought that was true but it wasn't."

"I can be wrong," he says. He takes a piece of bread and

then a tiny piece of butter. "I can't actually see into your life. I just take guesses."

"And predict when I'm going to die."

"That's not exactly how I would phrase it." He smiles mischievously.

"You work for an insurance company, calculating projected life spans, right?" He nods. "You ask all these questions to figure out someone's life, or, actually, death."

"Basically, yes."

I take a sip of my wine and study him across the table. "I want to try," I say, as I watch him buttering his bread with precision. How can anyone take so long to butter one piece of bread?

"Oh, I'm not going to die for a long time, Jane."

I ignore him. "I'm going to study you for a moment, and then I'll tell you stuff about you I 'know,' " I say.

"All right," he says and stops the buttering process. "Study away."

"Go right back to what you're doing there, mister. I'm not studying you doing nothing. That's not how you learn."

He raises his eyebrows at me. "My, my. They grow up so quickly." We lock eyes, then he goes back to the buttering. He spreads it evenly all over the slice of bread, right up to the crust. Then he takes a small bite and chews it for a full minute. "Are you getting all of this?" he asks.

I cross my arms over my chest. "Okay, I'm ready. The doctor is in."

"Please proceed," he says and gestures forward.

"First of all, you are a little bit OCD."

He nods. "Very impressive. Correct. And how did you decide that?"

"You have the second-cleanest apartment I've ever seen, after some woman named Jane Williams. And have you ever thought about your buttering technique there? It's a little neurotic."

"You see, you're more intuitive than I gave you credit for," he says. "Anything else?"

I look askance at him. "You dress like Prince William, but actually you find clothes a bore and simply buy what the saleswoman suggests for you."

"Good. I like to brag that I can get my shopping for the year done without ever showing up. Just send some things over from Saks, and I'm fine."

"You're a little obsessive about staying in shape," I say.

"Aha!" he says, after finishing his bite of bread. "Now, there you are wrong. I have to force myself to work out, and I only do that because my doctor is upset about my cholesterol." He sits back and beams at me. "I've never been on this end of things. It's exhilarating. Keep going."

"Okay," I say, reaching for one last sip of water. "You come from a wealthy, prominent New York family."

"That's cheating. You already knew that."

"You don't need to work, but you do just for the challenge."

"Wrong."

"In college, you were the kind of guy who took a lot of

philosophy classes and thought that you were above the silly pep rallies and frat parties."

"They're pointless, don't you think?"

"You don't like modern art."

"Even I could draw that."

"But you do have a soft spot for opera."

"Hate it."

I take a bite of bread and chew thoughtfully. I look at his shiny dark hair, his clear, tan skin. He is good-looking. I guess I can admit that now.

I think back to the article I read about him months ago.

"Why are you here?" I say slowly.

"That's not how the game works, Jane," he says, smiling at me. His eyes sparkle in the candlelight.

"Fine." I brush my hair behind my ear. Now that I'm here, he doesn't seem like Satan incarnate. But he's still an arrogant rich boy. And even if I were to begin to think otherwise, that doesn't change what I know. "How about this. You're being sued for mistreating women."

His smile fades, and the sparkle drains from his eyes. He stares at me, lifting his chin. "You observed that just now?" he asks, setting his jaw.

My breath catches. I look away, but I still feel his gaze on me. I play with my napkin. He didn't deny it.

Coates takes a deep breath as the waiter sets our plates down in front of us. He looks down at his food, and he doesn't look up.

Later that night, I sit on my rooftop deck, staring up at the stars with Charlie in my arms. I have a blanket wrapped around me because the fall seems to really be coming on fast this year. We probably won't have too many more nights out on the deck, and I need to clear my head. I'm even more confused than ever after seeing Coates. Luckily, it's unlikely I'll ever have to face him again, but the whole evening was kind of . . . unsettling.

I think about what he said about not seeing me in PR. What would I do if I didn't do PR? It's the only thing I've ever done with my life. It makes the best use of my God-given talents—the gift of gab, strong organizational skills, and decent public speaking. Granted, I don't exactly get to help people very often. Is there some way to do something like PR but also help people? I think about how I feel when I'm with the Brownies. Those are some of my happiest times. A day-care worker? No. I admire day-care staffers, but I don't think I could do it. Those places seem like hothouses of germs and crying kids. A missionary? No. Too extreme in the other direction. I get nervous at the farmer's market, and when I actually leave Manhattan it feels like my throat might be closing up.

I hear my porch door open and see Lee coming out. "Hey, Steel Magnolia," I say. "Long time no see."

He comes over and sits at the edge of the chaise longue

I'm reclining on. In the moonlight I can see the tears running down his face. I sit up, throw my blanket around the three of us, and hug him for a while. I listen to him sniffling and say, "There, there. It's okay," like my mom would always say, but in my heart, I know that something must really be wrong.

After a while, he stops heaving and looks me in the face and frowns.

"Talk to me," I say.

"I didn't know. She kept it all from me. I didn't know." He begins to cry quietly again, and I hold him and wait.

After a minute or so, he tries again. "Today, my mother got an e-mail from my Auntie Di. I've been checking her e-mail for her while she was at the hospital. So I open it up to read and find out—" His voice fails him. He swallows hard. "I find out that she's gone, Jane."

"Who's gone? What?"

"*She* is gone. She's already gone."

"Mary Sue is gone?" I ask. How could this be?

He shakes his head violently. "Not yet. They gave her three months to live in Charleston. That's why she came up here. She only had three months this whole time, and she didn't tell me. And now the cancer has metastasized and is in her lungs, her stomach, everywhere."

I hold him again and listen to him sobbing on my shoulder.

"Why would she have kept it from me?" he asks.

I pull back from our hug and look at him. I think about the last time I saw Mary Sue and what she said about Lee. "Honey, she still sees you as her little boy. Just like I don't tell Haven bad things. You keep things from your children because you want to protect them from the hurt and pain of life."

He looks into his lap. "I would have done it all different if I had known that we only had three months together."

I rub his back. "That's exactly what she didn't want. She wanted her last months to be as normal as possible with you. She didn't want to focus on the negative. It's her way."

Lee looks at me. "I can't lose her. I still need her."

I smile at him. "First thing tomorrow morning, we'll go and tell her that."

Chapter 19

My future sister-in-law and her mother are clutching each other as if neither is able to stand without the support of the other's willowy frame, dabbing their eyes ever so gently with matching monogrammed linen handkerchiefs. They are crying in elation at the first dress brought out by the svelte woman at Barney's, who is our personal wedding dress shopper.

Patrice called last week to "beg" me to come to help her pick out a dress for the wedding. She positively refused to do it without me, her new "sis." I have been avoiding my family like the plague, so I had half a mind to refuse, but Patrice is so sweet and kind that denying her requests is physically impossible for anyone born with a heart. I remember the time she baked me a cake when I broke my arm in second grade, hoping it would make me feel better. As I recall, Jim devoured most of it before I even got home from the doctor's office. Patrice reminds me of a little hopeful bunny, so I relented, even though she'd told me that our moms would be there, and my mother is about the last person I want to see right now.

"Isn't this exciting?" my mother asks and squeezes Patrice's arm. This is the fifteenth time my mother has said this. I'm keeping count in order to stay focused. Poor Mom. I think she's out of things to say at this point. She glances at me for help, but I look away.

"Mom," Patrice says to *my* mom, catching me off guard, "this is the happiest day of my life." Patrice hugs my mother again, and my mother returns it. This is the eighth hug of the morning. If she starts jumping up and down, holding my mother's arms, it will be the second time. Definitely the highlight so far.

"It sure is, honey," my mother says. And then "Morg," Patrice's mother, starts whimpering all over again and I nearly lose it and laugh.

Luckily for me, according to the Lovell ladies, the only proper place to buy a wedding dress is Manhattan, so it didn't take too much for me to roll out of bed this morning and meet the other women for a coffee at Starbucks to "talk strategy." And when I say coffee, I mean nonfat, no-whip, sugarless, grande, vanilla latte, extra hot. There, Patrice's mother, Morgan (please-call-me-Morg) Lovell, brought out a thick binder and listed all of the places we had appointments at that day. Barney's was our third stop. We'd already been to Bergdorf-Goodman and "Vera." At Vera, Morg had pulled me into a corner and demanded to know from me, a true New Yorker, if Vera was "over" or not. Didn't everyone go to Vera? Hadn't she become a bit, well, common? I waffled until she pressed me harder and harder, and I realized I was going to have to come down on this (non)issue one way or another. I took a deep breath and pronounced Vera "not over" and then cited the example of a recent starlet using Vera Wang for her wedding. Morg was quite relieved.

The saleswoman holds the dress aloft and clears her throat. Here comes my favorite part: the long, gibberish description. "A strapless, modified mermaid gown, with reverse pleating, taffeta sash, English net overlay, and ruching detail. Emanuel Ungaro." Well, then. That certainly cleared things up. And before me is a dress that I and anyone who has not drunk the laced Kool-Aid wedding punch would describe as a "long, white, poofy gown. Overpriced Designer."

"Ungaro," Morg says dreamily.

"Different," says Patrice, nodding.

"Like him."

"Love him," Patrice says.

Our personal shopper smiles. "Then let's begin by trying this piece. I have more to show you, of course."

Morg and Patrice walk over to a dressing room that's bigger than my living room and go in together. I was a little surprised the first time this happened, as my mother and I have an unspoken contract to never be naked in front of each other, but now it's come to be just another fun aspect of Patrice and Morg. Does my brother know who he's marrying? Does Morg know that Jim doesn't work at Deloitte & Touche?

My mother and I sit down awkwardly on a giant, round pleated silk ottoman and rest. I won't look at her, so I look around. It's funny. Just a few months ago I had thought it would be me in here trying on dresses for my marriage to Ty. I shake my head, a little sad. Those dreams seem to be from another lifetime.

Mom and I both look up when we hear Morg and Patrice whimpering again, and even though I'm not really talking to Mom, I can't help but glance at her to exchange a look.

"They're kind of something, aren't they?" she says. She laughs and then pulls her purse up on the ottoman when a Barney's employee frowns at us as she passes by.

"Putting it mildly, I'd say." Am I really ready to be friendly with Mom again? I look at the corner and tap my foot impatiently. And then I look around the room. Something catches my eye. In Mom's purse, in plain sight, I see a hardcover book called *She's Thirty and Single: How to Talk to Your Modern Daughter*. My face flushes in embarrassment.

"Mom, I'm not thirty yet," I say, pointing at the book.

She snatches her purse into her lap and hugs it to her, covering the book. "It's on the bestseller list. I heard it was good."

I sigh. "I can't believe that's how you see it."

"You *are* modern, Jane." I roll my eyes. Modern is code for spinster.

Patrice comes out of the dressing room, looking like a big vanilla meringue pie, but the look works for her. She really is stunning.

"Patrice, that one is just gorgeous," my mother says, rising. "You're going to be the prettiest bride to ever walk down the runway."

I look at Patrice's baffled face.

"I think she meant to say 'aisle,' " I say.

"Oh yes, sorry—aisle! Of course. How silly of me," Mom says. I smile at her, and she shrugs at her mistake.

Patrice slowly turns on the platform in front of the three-paneled mirror. "I do like the way the skirt moves."

Morg stands by her with her arms crossed. "I just don't think this bodice is flattering, though." She shakes her head slowly, brow furrowed. "Patrice has very narrow shoulders, just like me, and she has to be careful about the bodice." Morg walks away from the dressing room. "Where is that woman? I need to talk her about our bodice concerns."

My mother volunteers to go on a mission to locate our personal shopper with Morg. I walk over to Patrice to get a closer look. This one really is more beautiful than some of the others we've seen.

"I think I really like this one," I say.

Patrice frowns at herself in the mirror and looks even cuter than before. For some reason I can't stop myself from imagining little bunny ears on her head. Hey, they'd match.

"Do you think Mom likes it?" she asks.

I turn around, wondering where the moms went off to. "She seemed concerned about the, uh, bodice thing, but I've never thought you had particularly narrow shoulders." Nor have I thought anyone had narrow shoulders.

"Oh no," she says, laughing. "I mean your mom, Mom. Did she like it? I want her to like it too. I want all of us to love the same thing."

I smile at her kindness. This woman is amazing. How on earth did Jim talk her into marrying him? "Mom loved it," I say. "And so do I."

Patrice flings her arms around me and gives me a hug. I

hug her back in what seems like the longest hug ever given until finally the moms return. I never thought I'd be so happy to see Mom and Morg.

"Patrice, let's get you out of that ill-fitted frock. The consultant and I had a little chat and agreed it was all wrong. She's adjusting our next selection with our bodice concerns in mind."

I look at my mom. I see that she's miserable too and smile.

I sit with my hands in my lap, trying not to fidget. Why am I so nervous? It's just an interview. I never get nervous.

On the other side of her desk, Annie Myers, the YMCA director of after-school programs for the entire Northeast, reads my résumé. She is all business. Even her phone message to schedule this interview was curt and precise.

"I see you don't have any experience working for a non-profit," she says and then looks at me over her reading glasses.

I place both hands flat on my thighs to calm myself and try to think of my comeback to that. I prepared for this. Okay, what did I plan on saying? Oh right. "That's correct. But as you can see, I've helped lead Brownie Troop 192 for three years now." I don't mention that I may no longer be a member of the troop.

Annie looks at me with cold brown eyes. She's got curly brown hair that's a little wild, and she's wearing billowy black pants and a loose top made of some kind of rough fabric. "Yes, I see that," she says. "But I don't think you realize how different this is."

"I realize it's not the same thing as being the after-school coordinator for a branch of the YMCA, but if you've ever gone camping with twelve eight-year-olds, you'll know what I mean when I say I now feel I can do anything." I smile, hoping she'll laugh at my little joke. She doesn't.

"These children come from all walks of life," she says simply. Okay, so my troop is a little privileged. "This program is what keeps many of these kids off the streets. There is no parent at home in many of our families until nine or ten at night. It's up to us to be their surrogate parents. I'm just not sure you have the . . . background to relate to them."

"I assure you, I am prepared to give my heart and soul to these kids," I say quickly. "I can relate to all kinds of people."

"Is that a Marc Jacobs suit?" she asks. I nod, simmering. So I have nice clothes. So what? Does that make me unqualified to work with these kids? As she looks over my résumé dismissively, I begin to wonder if she's right. Maybe I'm not cut out for this. I don't know anything about keeping kids off the street.

"The person who is awarded this position will be responsible for coming up with a full after-school curriculum, everything from staffing the tutoring center, to organizing outings, to regularly scheduled intramural sporting events. We're looking for someone who is organized, quick on her feet, tough, and excellent with children." Annie raises her eyebrow at me. Maybe I should just stick to PR. I've already got one company putting together an offer for me in writing. I'm not even sure why I came on this interview. I'm wasting this busy woman's time. She sees that I'm not remotely qualified. What was I thinking? That's the last time I listen to Coates's advice.

Annie slides a piece of paper to me. "Perhaps you can look

over our current curriculum. I need to step out for a moment and check in on our older kids. We're short-handed today. When I come back, we can have a discussion about changes you'd make to this schedule."

The door closes behind her, and I begin to panic. What's she pulling? Putting me on the spot? I roll my lips in and start reading the list for the after-school programs. It's a pretty standard lineup of crafts, basketball, tutoring in the computer lab, and swimming lessons in the pool. I have nothing to add. It's going to be terrible when Annie comes back to find out I have no original ideas at all. Okay, focus, Jane. Think about the girls. What would Haven like to see on this list that isn't here? You know a lot about kids. Don't let her suggest that you don't. I tap the page with the pen for a moment. Oh! What about Friday night movie night? We could rent kid-friendly movies and pop popcorn and sit around on beanbags. That'd be fun. Haven would definitely approve. What else? What about Bella and Kaitlin? What would they like? Dress-up. There is nothing they like better than to imagine themselves as sophisticated adults. I'll bet we could get the neighboring community to donate a bunch of fancy old clothes and have a big dress-up tea party once a month. I write down on the paper "movie night" and "tea party." Oh no, the boys. What do boys want? Think, think. Oh. Water volleyball tournaments. We can divide them into teams and have a bracket system. It would only cost us for the net and the ball since they have a pool. Maybe some variations with inner tubes. That's something, maybe.

What an amazing job this would be. No more staring at a computer screen all day, answering e-mails. No more placating demanding, rich clients. I could give back to my city. I could play with kids every day, see them find hobbies and passions they love, develop skills they're going to need.

Annie knocks on the door and sits back down behind the desk. "Good thing I checked on them. Anarchy was developing. I'm afraid our time together must be short. Can you tell me what you've come up with?"

I tell her my ideas. "We'd never get permission to keep the children overnight," she says. "Anything other than swimming lessons in the pool is a legal liability our insurance doesn't cover, and . . . I'm afraid 'dress-up' isn't quite as fun when many of these children can't even afford decent clothes of their own. Do you have anything more . . . economically appropriate?"

I am dumbstruck. How can she just shoot all my ideas down? And what is she implying—that I'm some spoiled rich kid who doesn't get it?

"Tell me, Jane," she says. "What brought you here today?"

How dare she? Why am I here? I'll tell her why I'm here. "I've learned a lot lately," I say. "You're right. I was privileged. I had everything going for me, and then it was all taken from me." I stop to swallow. "I had to look hard at life and figure out what really made me happy at the end of the day. And what I came up with is helping people. Because you know what? It's not a very happy world out there," I say, my voice rising. I think about me and Ty, about all that Raquel's been through, about Mary Sue. "It's hard and painful, and people you love might hurt you or disappoint you, and your possessions aren't going to make you feel better about any of that. And when I think about all the kids in New York who are alone, and afraid, and unloved, and just overlooked by society, I want to help them."

There is a long silence. I look up defiantly. Annie is studying me, frowning. Finally, she leans forward, puts down her pen and takes off her reading glasses.

"I used to be a day trader," she says and breaks into a big smile.

On Thursday night I'm sitting on my couch drafting a formal letter of complaint to the building management company about the roof expense. The insurance company is going to come through to replace the furniture, though I'm still waiting on that check, but the roof is another story. I know I should be grateful to have my roof back at all, but I am not letting them stick me with that bill. I look up when I see something slip under my door out of the corner of my eye.

It's a little envelope. Charlie barks at the envelope for a second. He sniffs it. I walk over and pick it up. The outside says "Read me." I obey.

Inside is a little printed card that says:

spon-ta-ne-ous
Pronunciation: spän-ˈtā-nē-as
Function: adjective
Etymology: Late Latin spontaneus, *from Latin*
      sponte, *of one's free will, voluntarily*
1: arising from a momentary impulse

I read it again, trying to make sense of it, when I hear a knock on my door. I peek out the peephole and see Coates standing there. What on earth? After our horrible date, I figured we both understood that it was over. I must have been half insane to agree to the date in the first place. Besides, I'm in my pajamas. I crack the door and lean out, but Charlie escapes. After sniffing Coates a moment, he tries to jump into his arms.

"Um, hi?" I say, annoyed. Coates leans over and scoops up Charlie. I need to teach that dog to be a little more suspicious of strangers.

"Jane," he says, smiling devilishly. "I believe this is yours." He hands Charlie back to me. I stay planted in the door and take Charlie back.

"Are you concerned about my vocabulary today?"

"A little, particularly where it pertains to that word." His eyes take in my pajamas. "Could you get your coat? I'd like to get on with our date."

I shake my head. "I wasn't asked on this date. Nor did I accept."

"Isn't that thrilling?" He rakes his fingers through his dark hair. "I don't like to follow the rules."

"Me either," I say. "So, good-bye." I shut the door in his face. I can't believe he'd just show up here like that. We don't click. Why does he want to try again? I shouldn't have answered the door.

I sit back down on my couch and turn back to my letter. Another envelope slides under the door. I roll my eyes and go back to typing, but soon yet another one slides under the door.

Charlie is looking at them and at me and at them again. He gives a small bark at them. I give in and go over to retrieve them again.

I open the first one. He has written:

Please?

I open the next one:

You won't regret it.

"You're not funny," I say through the door.

"I've got fifty envelopes out here," he says back.

I swing my door wide open. "How did you get my address?" I ask.

"It's really lovely out tonight. The air is so crisp and clean."

"Why are you doing this? Remember our last date?"

"So this is a date, then?"

"Argh!"

He smiles at me and waits.

I shake my head at him in defeat and say, "Come in. I'll go throw some jeans on." Coates comes in and plops on my couch. Charlie jumps in his arms and begs with his little brown eyes to be petted. As I walk to my room I call out, "Don't suppose I get to know where we're going?"

"Didn't you read the first card?" he calls back to me.

I pull on my favorite jeans and a top and grumble, not quite to myself, "I hate this kind of thing."

Chapter 20

Coates is wandering the aisles with a look of glee. I'm following behind him, feeling snookered. Some wonderful spontaneous date this turned out to be. We're cooking together. Hurrah. If only he had called me and checked with me first on this one I would have had the chance to tell him that I don't know how to cook at all, that I once burned scrambled eggs, that my idea of making dessert is pouring a bowl of Count Chocula, that I've only been grocery shopping in New York twice. That I don't date men who are being sued. But instead here we are stumbling around in Whole Foods, which is, from what I can tell, the Henri Bendel of grocery stores, with me wishing that we could just go pick up something to go. I already pointed out the section with precooked meals, but Coates laughed like this was some kind of good joke. At least someone is having fun.

"While I go and inspect the olive oil selection, why don't you work on getting the arugula," he says.

"Sure," I say and smile.

"We'll need two cups of it, chopped."

I nod confidently, wait until he walks off, and then begin to wander around. What is arugula? I think it's a vegetable of some kind, but I really can't be sure. I think it was on some-thing I had at a restaurant once, but there was a lot of stuff on top of that tuna steak. There was some leafy stuff, a drizzle of something red, there were some crunchy nutlike things, I think one of the things on top was maybe in the mushroom family. That's it! Arugula was that weird mushroom thingy. I wander over to the mushroom section and look for a sign that says "arugula." I need two cups chopped, I repeat to myself. This isn't that hard. Okay, let's see. There's Portobello, baby Porto-bello, shiitake, morel, button . . . no arugula kind. I frown. Then I see someone who works at Whole Foods and tap on his shoulder.

"Can you please show me where the arugulas are?" I ask. I motion behind me at the mushrooms.

The worker cocks his head a little. "I'm sorry?"

"I'm looking for the arugula mushrooms please?"

He puts his hands on his hips. "You want arugula or mush-rooms? Both?"

Maybe it's not a mushroom. I blush. "Look, I just need two cups of arugula."

It dawns on the employee what's going on, and he smirks. "The arugula is over here with the *greens*," he says,

Green what? Everything over here is green. I follow be-hind him obediently until he deposits me in front of a big sign that says "Arugula." How did I miss that? "Do you need arugula or baby arugula?"

Baby arugula? I don't want baby food. "I just need regular arugula."

He points at a big stack of green leaves and walks away. I hold one up and inspect it. It's covered in dirt! I gasp and throw it back down, rubbing my hands together to try to get the dirt and water off.

"How's it going?" I hear behind me and jump. This whole nightmare experience has really gotten me ramped up.

I turn around and try to smile at Coates. "I, um, found . . . the stuff." I gesture at the arugula sign.

"Indeed. Could you get two cups' worth for me? Just put it in the baggies there," he says, motioning at a big spool. I suddenly have a hazy memory of my mother doing this once when I was little. This is really her fault. She never cooked either.

I stride over, wrestle with the baggie spool for a while, pull off two bags by accident, and then come back to get two cups of arugula, chopped. But it's not chopped yet. It's, well, it's just kind of big, long, and green and looks kind of like where Cabbage Patch Kids come from.

Coates is watching me, smiling from ear to ear. I won't let him make a fool of me. I bravely pick up a bunch of arugula and put it in the bag and then try to hand it to him.

"I'm afraid that's not even close to two cups chopped," he says.

I lean in to him and whisper, "Are you sure we should be buying it here?"

He looks around and then leans in to me. "Why?" he whispers back.

I pick up another bunch and bring it over to him. "It's dirty. Do you see that?"

He lets out a big belly laugh. "Jane."

"What?"

"Where do you think arugula comes from?"

"An arugula tree? An arugula chicken?"

"It grows in the ground. That's why it's dirty, as you say."

I stuff one more bunch into the bag while he guffaws in the greens aisle. What fun being spontaneous is turning out to be.

"**We're** making pizza?" I ask, raising my eyebrow at the recipe in front of me. "You do know this is New York, right?"

"Is that right?" he asks, and then looks out his window in mock surprise.

"Hello, McFly. Pizza grew up here. There are probably twelve pizzerias on this block alone. Three of them claim to be the Original Ray's," I say, walking past the granite counter into the living room. I see a splash of pink plush and freeze. Judy Garland, my elephant, is in there. In the corner. Just behind his entertainment center. I take a deep breath and turn back to face him. "There is a whole world of good pizza out there," I say, recovering. "Why bother to make it? It doesn't make any sense."

"Why indeed," he says. "Would you please hand me the yeast?" I rummage around in the shopping bag and find the little yellow packets. I toss one to him. He adds it to a bowl of flour and begins to knead the dough with his hands. I watch. Making our own pizza. Who ever heard of something so ridiculous?

"Your turn," he says, extracting the ball of dough from the bowl and handing it to me. I take it tentatively.

"What am I supposed to do with this?" I look down at the dough and up at him.

"Knead it," he laughs, sprinkling some flour on a wooden cutting board in front of me. I place the ball of dough gingerly on the board and poke at it with my index finger.

"No, silly," he says, coming up behind me. I flinch. He wraps his arms around mine and places his hand on top of mine, then guides my hands toward the dough. My heart skips a beat. He smells good. He moves my hands gently, showing me how to push on the dough and work it around. I lean back slightly and feel him subtly lean in to me. Maybe making pizza isn't so bad after all. We work the dough together. I can feel his warm breath on my neck. Focus, Jane. You hate this man.

"By Jove, I think she's got it," Coates says softly, pulling away. He walks to the sink and turns on the faucet, rubbing his hands together under the water. I don't look up. "You keep doing that for a few minutes, and I'll get started chopping the arugula," he says as if everything is normal. I start to breathe again, nodding.

The kitchen is quiet. I can't meet his eye. I glance at the recipe again so I look busy. "Three-Cheese Pizza with Onion, Sage, and Arugula." Hm. I run my eye down the ingredient list. "Oh no, Coates!" I say, panicked. He looks at me, smiling calmly. "We forgot the Gorgonzola."

"No we didn't," he says, unfazed, turning off the faucet. He reaches into a cabinet and pulls out a bottle of red wine.

"But it calls for Fontina, Parmesan, and Gorgonzola, and we forgot to buy the Gorgonzola, so how can we—"

"I don't like blue cheese," he says, shrugging as he opens the corkscrew. He places the tip against the cork and begins to twist. "All the mold and the veins. I figured we'd just leave it off." My face must register the shock I feel, because he continues, his face softening. "I hope that's okay. If you really want it we can get—"

"How can you just leave out an ingredient?" I ask. I may not cook much, but I know you are supposed to follow the recipe. "You can't do that."

"Why not?" he shrugs, pulling the cork out with a satisfying pop. He reaches into another cabinet and pulls down two red wine glasses.

"Because," I stammer.

"This is our pizza. We can make it however we want," he laughs, pouring ruby-red wine into the glasses.

"But . . ." I stop. Why not? I look at Coates.

"Come on, Jane," he smiles. "Spontaneous. You can do it."

I look at the recipe and back up at him. I look at my hands in the dough.

"Fine," I say. "It's totally fine." I try to sound sure. "It doesn't matter to me."

"I knew you could do it," Coates says, handing me a glass. I reach for it and take a sip, then put my glass down and turn away. He takes a sip and raises his eyebrow slightly. "You know, Matt Sherwin is really not your type."

My face flushes, thinking about that stupid article. "Thank

you," I say, throwing my hands up in the air. "*That's* what I keep telling people. Sure every woman in the world thinks she'd just jump at the chance to date Matt Sherwin, but trust me, spending quality time with that man is like brain drain."

"Plus," Coates says, turning on the oven, "I have a policy of never believing silly lies about people."

"Me too," I say with a nod. Why couldn't my boss be this sensible?

"Whether they are published in some silly tabloid like *Star Power*," he says, "or even the lofty *New York Times*."

He looks at me, and his gaze pierces right through me. Oh. I see what he's getting at. I knead the dough. But the *Times* is not *Star Power*. What they say is well-researched fact. Coates stands close to me.

I bite my lip. Do I want to hear this?

"That article was not entirely false," he says, but I don't look at him. "Yes, I am being sued by two previous assistants. Yes, my conversion to Christianity did anger my family." He takes a deep breath. "Yes, many people over the years have found me—let's see, what were the words they used?—'impossible, arrogant, and stubborn.' "

I look up, but I can't meet his eye. I look at his mouth and focus on what he is saying. The article was true.

"But I have never mistreated someone and not gone back to apologize. I know how I come across at times, and I am working on it. And the two young women who are suing me simply saw an easy mark."

I roll my eyes.

"Jane, listen to me." He touches my shoulder. "Just today I got word from my lawyer that the judge threw the case out. They have nothing against me. Their claims are preposterous."

Oh. I frown at myself.

"Coates, I——"

He raises an eyebrow at me.

I swallow a lump back in my throat. "I owe you an apology," I say, my mind racing. It is beginning to dawn on me that even while I was convicting Coates for crimes he did not commit, he was arranging for me to get a roof over my head. In my darkest hour, he was the one who knew what I needed most and provided it discreetly with not so much as a thank-you from me.

He shrugs. "Let's drop it. But I could tell it was bothering you. I handled it wrong when you brought it up before, but forgive me. I had no idea that anyone even believed that article."

"It was in the *Times*," I say, shrugging. "I don't believe it anymore."

"Good, then we'll put both of our allegedly sordid pasts behind us and move forward from this moment on."

"Agreed," I say and put out my hand for him to shake. He takes one look at my flour-covered hand and shakes his head. "Of course, the arrogant part is still true." I plunge my hands back into the flour, pouting.

I see the flour hit his face before I register that I threw it. He looks at me, stunned. He looks so comical, standing there in his well-appointed apartment with his perfect gleaming teeth and a big burst of white powder on his tanned face. There's only one thing to do now. I laugh and grab another handful from the open bag and launch it at him again. He ducks, breaking into a smile, and the flour falls softly all over his spotless kitchen. He reaches toward the bag, but I block him with my body, and grab another handful myself. Within minutes we're both covered with fine white powder and laughing hysterically. He's holding on to my waist as we slump against the counter. I am gulping for air.

We sit next to each other on the floor, and all of a sudden our laughter seems to die. I can hear him breathing next to me and smell the good, clean smell of his detergent on his clothes. I turn my head slightly and look at him. He reaches a hand out and uses his thumb to smudge a little powder off my cheek.

"Got yourself into a little mess, I'd say," he whispers, resting his hand on my thigh when he's done.

I smile at him. "The way I see it, it's not really my fault," I say at normal volume.

He cocks his head at me. "Really? Shall I refresh you on how all of this started?"

I laugh. "But I was just caught up in the moment," I say and put my hand on top of his. We lock eyes and fall silent again. A long moment passes.

I look down at my clothes, covered in flour, and I lean forward to him. I don't think I mean to kiss him, but for some reason, I just want to be closer, to be touching him. He leans in too, and we both pause, our faces an inch apart. I can smell his cologne faintly, and his breath is warm and slow on my cheek. And then I shut my eyes and lean in to kiss him. We kiss slowly, delicately, a still, sweet, longing kiss. I pull back and look at him again.

"Being spontaneous isn't so bad after all, is it?" he asks as I lean in to kiss him again.

Chapter 21

Raquel, are you okay? How are you doing? How much longer do you think it's going to last?"

Raquel raises herself onto her arms, takes a deep breath, and winces at me. As soon as she called, I flew out the door and, after a quick trip to the drugstore, caught a cab uptown and raced to her side.

"About seven weeks," she whines. "Bed rest. Can you believe it?"

"What did the doctor say? Is the baby . . . ?"

"He's going to be fine." She smiles. "I just went into labor a little early, but as long as I stay put, they say we're both going to be fine."

"I'm so glad."

"But seven weeks, Jane! I'm going to lose my mind."

"I'm sorry," I say, pulling a chair up next to her bed. "Um . . . here. I brought stuff that might help pass the time." I reach into the shopping bag I brought. "Clue. I always thought Colonel Mustard was kind of sexy, didn't you? And Connect Four." I place the boxes on her bed. "*People* magazine." I reach down into my shopping bag. "Let's see. What else? Berry Smackers lip gloss." Raquel bursts out laughing. "And this romance novel, *Love Is Torture*. Well, actually, now that I think about it, that doesn't sound like a very fun book, but they had a whole rack of romances, and I didn't know the difference, so I just picked one. And, um, oh here's the medicine for Olivia. Let's see . . ."

"You didn't have to do all this, Jane," she laughs, unscrewing the top of the lip gloss and giving it a sniff.

"Trust me, after a few days, you're going to thank me."

She nods. "I don't know what I'm going to do, Jane. I can't take care of a toddler like this."

"You know, when I came in, Haven almost looked like she had it under control," I shrug. "I mean, obviously, she's not going to be able to do everything you do, but she and Olivia were both munching on peanut butter and jelly sandwiches, and though your kitchen might never be the same, they looked unharmed."

"Were they watching TV?"

"*Dora the Explorer*. Olivia was speaking Spanish like a native."

"That's good. That will keep them busy for a while. But I don't know what I'm going to do when they get bored with that."

"Do you have to stay in bed every minute?"

"As much as I can. And Jack can't really take any time off, what with his job uncertain anyway," she sighs.

"Let Haven try," I say. "She's old enough to be able to at least help. I bet if you show her you trust her, she'll really come through for you."

"But she's just a baby," Raquel says.

"Raquel, she's not a baby anymore," I laugh. "Give her a chance to show you how mature she can be."

Raquel nods uncertainly.

"And I'm still unemployed," I volunteer. "I'll be here as much as you need me."

"Thanks, Jane," she says quietly, looking down. "That means a lot. Especially . . ."

"Stop it," I laugh. "But I have to warn you, I'm a master at Connect Four. You're never going to win."

"Duly noted." She smiles at me sadly. "I have some more news, Jane."

"What's that?"

"The Brownie moms had a meeting this morning. I was there. That meeting was probably what sent me into labor. We took a vote. It was 8–4, in favor of having Margaret take over the troop."

I feel like I've just been punched.

"I'm so sorry, Jane. If it helps, Abby's mom spoke very passionately about the change she's seen in her daughter and how much Abby talks about you, but it wasn't enough." She sighs. "I did my best."

"I know you did, Raquel." I take a deep breath. "Thank you."

"At the end of the year, I'm pulling Haven out of the troop," she says. "Margaret went on about her new vision for the troop, and well, let's just say she mentioned manicure parties and a field trip to Toys 'R' Us."

"She didn't."

"Oh yes," she laughs. "And no more camping. Her SUV came back mud splattered and she doesn't really see the point."

"Did anyone mention that SUVs are made to go off road?"

"I didn't dare," Raquel laughs. "Oh, and get this. They will only be selling low-fat Girl Scout Cookies from now on."

Hearing this breaks my heart, but I still can't help it. I laugh until tears are streaming down my face, and Raquel laughs too, smiling wider than I've seen her smile in months.

I sit in the café where I used to meet Tyson. I am fuming as Nina walks in the door. It's not like I wasn't expecting her, but as she sits down across from me, I'm still livid. How could she? Never mind ruining my life by planting that story about me in *Star Power*. She is having an affair with Matt Sherwin when his fiancée is pregnant with his baby. This is such a violation of the contract of female friendship that I want to throttle her with my bare hands for poor pregnant Chloe.

I look at her and try to remember who I really am. All I need is for her to agree to issue a retraction and I'll never have to see her again. "Thanks for coming," I say slowly, careful to let no errant words of hate escape.

She shoots me an ugly look. "Not like I really had a choice, Jane. You practically forced me, and you've got major blackmail material over me right now so I just need to know your price. That's why I'm here."

I used the information Lee had to call Nina at home and

tell her to meet me here today. I've been fretting about this moment all week.

"It's not about a price, Nina. I want you to admit that you planted that story to distract people from Matt's real affair with you. All I need is a retraction from the magazine so I can get my job—". I falter. "My life back," I say, finally.

The waitress comes over and I get a cappuccino, but Nina just shakes her head.

"Sure. I admit it. I started hearing rumors that he was cheating on Chloe, but obviously I wasn't about to be blamed for it," she says, rolling her eyes. "And I didn't really think it would get you fired. So, I guess, sorry about that. Who knew your boss was such a prig?" she says and yawns. That was probably the least authentic apology I've ever received. "But I'm afraid I can't get the retraction. Not only is it not in my power, *Star Power* never issues retractions. Ever. I'm not risking my neck to fight for something that won't happen."

I take a deep breath and think about what Jesus would say to her. He would say, 'I forgive you.' But the thought of uttering that makes me sick to my stomach.

What about the affair? This is my chance to stop it, right? And what about her ruining my life? I look at her and smile. If she doesn't agree to the retraction, revenge is mine. I'll call up *Star Power* and get them the real story. Chloe will find out and justice will be served. She'll pay for what she's done.

The waitress brings over my drink, and I take a sip of my cappuccino.

Nina looks at her watch. "Can you speed up this whole angry introspection thing you're doing? I have a job to do."

I look down. I can't get revenge. That's what I'd like to do, sure, but definitely not the right thing to do. I have the urge to reach across the table and slap her hard and scream, *Do you know what you did to me?* I take another sip of my drink.

Nina sighs dramatically. "Seriously. What is your price? This isn't that hard." She digs in her handbag and gets out her checkbook. "I'll make the check out to 'cash' so you can't use it against me." I stare at her. "I'm not an amateur like you."

"Nina, I'm a person who has a strong faith in God."

"Great," she says, rolling her eyes. "This is all I need today," she mutters under her breath.

"I'm not judging you. All I'm asking for is the truth."

"Really?" she says. "Shocking. I found the first nonjudgmental Christian in the world." She starts to write "CASH" in very big letters on a check.

"I don't want your money."

"What do you want, then? I already told you, there's nothing I can do."

I watch her. She is breathing heavily. She looks desperate. She looks . . . scared. And it hits me. If I go to the press with what I know, her life will be destroyed like mine was. And as much as I would like to let her know how it feels, let her squirm a little just so she gets a taste of what she did to me, I know I can't do that to her. In my worst moments, my faith sustained me. What will sustain her?

I know what I have to do.

What was done for me.

"Nina, I forgive you."

"Great." She rolls her eyes. "Can I go now?"

I look at her sadly and nod.

I am taking the flourless chocolate cake out of the oven when my phone rings. I grimace when I see it's Patrice. She's so sweet. So sweet it hurts. I just can't deal with another conversation about whether she should have strawberry or raspberry filling in the wedding cake. Really, I just don't care. No one cares. No one likes wedding cake. No matter what the filling flavor is, the cake is always terrible. I steel myself. She's going to be my sister. I have to talk to her.

"Hi Patrice," I say with as much enthusiasm as I can muster. "How's it going?"

"Jane!" she cries, as if delighted to find herself talking to me. "How are you? How's New York? How's your dog? What are you doing? Did I tell you, Mom and I—I mean my mom Mom, not your mom Mom—we went shopping again on Saturday and I think we finally found the perfect dress. It's from Carolina Herrera, and it has the most gorgeous tulle underskirt you ever saw, and . . ."

I place the phone down on the counter. She'll be going for a while. I check on my cake. It seems to be fine. And the pasta is all ready to go and the salad will be finished as soon as I toss in some pine nuts. I lean toward the phone and hear Patrice say,

"It's diamond white, but eggshell really looks better with my skin tone, so I don't know if I . . ." I let her go on. I check on Charlie, who is asleep on my bed, and close the door so he's not tempted by the smell of food. I walk into the living room to light the fire. I turn the gas on and step back and watch the flames lick at the ceramic logs. I look around my living room and smile. I just need to change, and I'll be all set. I walk back into the kitchen and grab the phone. "Jane? Are you there? Jane?" Patrice is asking.

"I'm here," I say. "Sorry, I—I had just taken a sip of water, and, um . . . So, what's up, Patrice?"

"Well," she giggles. "The reason I'm calling is that I thought and thought and I just couldn't decide on wedding colors. They're just all too pretty. So I decided to go with a 'Rainbow of Roses' theme for the wedding. We're going to have flowers of every color, and we'll decorate colorfully, and it will just be so beautiful," she says, sighing.

"Who are you talking to, Lovepat?" someone says on her end in a voice that sounds suspiciously like my brother's.

"What did he just say?" I ask.

"It's your sister," she says away from the phone. I hear him grunt. "Sorry, Jane. I'm back. Jimmy calls me Lovepat," she says to me. "You know, like my names, but backward." I make vomiting noises in my head. "So anyway, I picked out a dress for all the bridesmaids to wear, and it comes in all these colors, and I thought I would let the girls all pick out whatever color they want," she says, giggling. "So what color do you like to wear?"

"Black," I say absently, lighting a candle on the mantel.

"Oh, you," she laughs. I pause. It really is what I wear most. It's New York. Everyone wears black. "Black at a wedding," she says and laughs. I sigh. I decide to play it off as a joke.

"Yeah. Just kidding. Ha ha ha. Bet they don't make it in black. How about blue?" I say. Blue sounds safe.

"Great. There's turquoise, aqua, sky, periwinkle, royal, pool, sapphire, ocean, and navy. Do you have a preference?"

"Wow. So many choices. Okay. What colors did the other girls choose?" I have it on good authority that I am one of ten bridesmaids so we should be quite the bouquet up there.

"I'd really like to see some of the girls in pink, lavender, and seafoam," she says.

None of those are blue. So much for my preference. "I guess I could—"

"And yellow. Someone's got to wear yellow."

Bye-bye blue. "Yellow sounds fine," I say.

"Oh Jane," Patrice laughs. "You always were such a kidder. You know yellow won't look good with your skin tone."

My mouth falls open in shock. Did I know that? I drop the phone by my side for a moment and take a deep breath. I hold it back to my ear. "Oh, well, how about—"

I hear a knock at my door.

"You know, Patrice, there's somebody at my door, so I have to go now," I say quickly. "We'll figure this out later, okay?" I try to sound cheerful.

"Of course," she says, genuinely disappointed. "I'm so sorry. I didn't even ask if you had a minute to talk."

"No problem," I say.

"I'll just put you down for the seafoam for now."

I frown from ear to ear. "Talk to you soon, Patrice," I say and close the phone. I toss it on the counter and yank the door open. "Thank God," I say to Coates, who is standing in my doorway holding a bouquet of tulips. Oh no. I never had the chance to change out of my grungy clothes. Oh well. Didn't I read somewhere that men like women who feel comfortable being casual?

"Most women aren't as direct as that, but I do suppose some of them thank their maker when they see me."

"I just had an entire conversation about which shade of pastel goes with my skin tone," I say, grabbing the flowers from his hands. He smiles at me, and I freeze. I had forgotten how his eyes crinkle when he smiles.

"Definitely not yellow," he says, striding confidently into my living room. "It smells great in here."

I walk the flowers to the kitchen, where I take down a vase and begin to cut the stems. "You are going to be so proud of me," I smile. "We have fresh linguine, and I prepared a salad, and I even made dessert."

"I am impressed," he says, laughing. "All this from the girl who didn't know the difference between cream of tartar and tartar sauce a week ago?"

"Who uses cream of tartar these days?" I shrug. "Thanks for the flowers."

"You're very welcome," he says, reaching to take the cut stems from the counter and walks to the trash can. He steps on the metal foot and pauses as the lid lifts.

"Jane?" He grins at me.

Uh-oh. I try to look innocent.

"Next time you pretend to cook, be sure to hide the take-out containers better."

"Takeout containers?! How did those get there?!" I say, my face reddening. I look at Coates. He's not buying it. "I did make the salad," I say. "And the dessert. Smell the oven if you don't believe me."

Coates leans over and kisses my forehead. "I can't wait to try the dessert," he says, winking. And though I know I should hate him, I can't help but smile.

"**That** was disgusting," I say, gagging.

"Truly terrible," he agrees, nodding.

"I swear I didn't know there was a difference between baker's chocolate and semi-sweet."

"I believe you." He grimaces.

The lights are low, and the fire is smoldering in the fire-place, and I feel content. I take a sip of wine and smile, enjoying the sense of peace. Coates smiles at me and leans in, his face only inches from mine.

"So what's with the T-shirt, Plain Jane?" Coates asks, smiling at me. I look down. Oh no. I had forgotten I was wearing this old thing. "You're not plain," he says, stroking my hair.

"It's ironic," I say. I cross my legs and face him, leaning forward just a little.

"Or false advertising," he says softly, touching the sleeve. He trails his fingers down my arm. I don't pull it away.

"This is my around-the-house uniform." I say, looking up at him. "I've worn it for years. Isn't it hilarious?" I beam at him. "Plus, I only just got it back. Tyson had been holding it hostage—" Coates flinches. "Anyway, I have it back now and I wear it when I'm just hanging around, or when I'm cleaning, or, like, when I am pretending to cook dinner." He leans back and looks at me, like he's studying me. I shift away uncomfortably. It almost looks like he's frowning.

"Tyson." He nods. "I confess, I hadn't factored him in. I'm good at reading you, but I guess I'm not perfect."

"It's just something I used to wear at his apartment," I say, shrugging. The mood of the room had changed perceptibly. Time to change the subject. "He's gone now. He lives in Denver." I get up. "Would you like some coffee?" I ask, going around the counter. "I have regular and decaf, although I will admit I'll think less of you if go for decaf," I laugh. He doesn't smile.

"You're not over Ty."

"What? Yes I am," I insist, sitting back down, my voice getting higher with each syllable. "I'm completely over him."

"What color are his eyes?"

"Blue," I answer, and immediately regret it. Coates is narrowing his eyes, looking at me. "We dated for over two years. I have to know that," I say. He doesn't move.

"When was the last time you heard from him?"

I sigh. Do we really have to go into all of this? "Last week. I was on a group e-mail with about a hundred other people."

"Saying?"

"He's coming back to town. He's giving a reading from his novel in the East Village next week." I shrug.

"Are you going to go?"

"I hadn't decided."

"Hm." He looks down at his hands.

"He drinks decaf."

The joke falls flat.

We're both silent. I stare at the fire, watching the flames dance and spin. Is there a grain of truth in what he's saying? I get up quickly. "How about that coffee?"

"Yes, please," he says without looking up. "Decaf."

I slide behind a table in the back of the bar just as Ty begins to read. His blond hair falls over his eyes, and he pushes it aside absently with his hand. His voice is quiet. Faltering. He's nervous.

I look around slowly. The interior of the bar is dark and crammed with tables stuffed in every square foot of the room. A stage is set up with a microphone up front. Off to the side is a table loaded with autographed books for sale. A young man in a tie, who I recognize as Ty's editor, is flipping through a stack of papers. Some of the tables are occupied by young-looking hipsters with greasy hair and tight, dirty jeans. I recognize a few of Ty's friends from college and look away quickly. Maybe they won't see me.

The turnout is pretty good. A few empty tables, but the bar is definitely doing good business by having Ty read here tonight. I signal the waiter and order a red wine.

I am not sure why I am here. Of course I am proud of Ty. And I am excited for him. And, well, with all the time I spent listening to him talk about the book, rejoicing with him when he found an agent, and struggling through the revisions with him, I guess it just feels like this book is partly mine too.

Maybe I shouldn't have come.

Ty coughs, and the microphone amplifies the sound. I hope he's not getting sick. He always gets sick this time of year.

The waiter places my wine and a little napkin in front of me. I take a sip gratefully. This feels weird. But it is good to see him again. I watch him intently. He begins to relax a bit, visibly straightening up, and his voice gets louder and more natural as he gets used to being onstage. He looks up and glances around the front of the room. He continues to read. I remember when he was writing this part about the baby. He looks up again and sees me in the back of the room. He catches my eye. He smiles, then looks back down quickly. One of his college friends turns around to look and, seeing me, gives me a small wave. I wave back and then slide lower in my chair.

When he finishes, the bar erupts in applause. Ty beams, his handsome face lit up with pleasure. I grab my coat and purse and make a break for the door.

"Excuse me," I say to a man at the table squashed next to mine, motioning that I would like to get out. He is too busy clapping to notice. "Excuse me," I repeat, louder this time. He turns and gives me a look of annoyance. Slowly, very deliberately showing how difficult I'm making his life, he grasps the edge of his table and slides it over a few inches. I try to edge through the space between the tables, but it's far too small. He looks at me. "I'm sorry," I say. He sighs loudly and stands up, pulling the table back just enough for me to slide through. I don't bother to thank him as I hurry toward the door.

"Jane." I stop. It's him. Behind me. "I'm so glad you made it," Ty says, putting his hand on my shoulder. I turn around to face him. He looks happy.

"Congratulations, Ty." I don't know what else to do, so I lean in and give him a hug. He wraps his arms around my waist and pulls me close. "You did an amazing job," I say, pulling back.

"Thanks," he says, his deep voice so familiar. "Are you leaving already?"

"Uh," I say. "I have this thing I have to get to, and—"

"Stay," he says, cocking his head and smiling the same charming smile that made me fall in love with him. "Please?"

I am tempted. This is his big night, the night we dreamed of for two years. And he's being so sweet. He's my friend, after all, a part of my life for so long. And the way he's looking at me . . . I look around at the crowd of people waiting to give him their congratulations.

I nod. "I'll be here," I say, pointing at a new table. I'm not going near that grouchy guy again. Ty beams, then turns back toward the crowd. I sit down, pull a book from my purse, and start to read.

I don't look up again until the crowd has thinned. Ty is

smiling for pictures with his friends. He catches my eye and gestures that he'll be right over. Five minutes later he pulls out the chair across the table and sits down. He smiles at me.

"So," I say, placing a bookmark between the pages. "How's Denver?" I put my book back in my bag.

"It's nice," he says, looking down at the table. "The mountains are beautiful. I've got a giant apartment, right downtown," he says, looking back up at me. "It's less than half of what I was paying here." He smiles. "And I got a dog."

"A dog?"

"A mutt I found at the pound," he laughs. "I named him Brian." Ty reaches for the napkin lying on the table and starts doodling on it nervously with his book-signing pen.

"Have you been writing?"

He looks at me through the bangs still hanging over his eyes and shakes his head. "I haven't been able to write much." He takes a deep breath. "Jane, I miss you."

I look down at my hands, resting on the table. I don't want him to see the terror in my face or the tears welling up in my eyes. "Jane, I—" he swallows. "I think I made a huge mistake."

I swallow the lump in my throat and panic for a moment. I must think of something else. Anything else. I look at my hands again. My fingernails. Good. Perfect. Look at those cuticles. I need to do something about that.

"Jane?" I can hear the quiver in his voice.

It's definitely time for a manicure. That's what I'm going to think about. Manicure. Not man. Manicure.

"That night, at your apartment . . . You felt it too. I know you did."

Maybe I'll go for something dramatic to announce how carefree I am. Fire Engine Red.

"What are you thinking?" he asks.

What am I thinking? I try to block out this question but it gets through. I am thinking that this is the man I thought I would marry. That this is the man who broke my heart. That I know better now.

"I went to the airport, Ty." I look up from my hands and into his beautiful blue eyes. I take a deep breath. Ty leans in closer. "I went there to try to win you back." He places his hands on top of mine, and I am too bewildered and distraught to know what to do about it. "I brought an elephant." The confusion is apparent on his face, but he doesn't interrupt. "I wanted to stop you from getting on the plane. So I went. I bought a ticket for your flight and everything." He begins to rub my hands with his thumb, and he leans in closer. I sit silently for a minute.

"But I couldn't do it," I say finally. "I couldn't make you stay. It wasn't going to work, and I knew it." I shake my head. "I mean, what would you have done if I had come up to you in the airport, holding a giant pink stuffed elephant I got at Coney Island, and asked you to try to make it work one more time?"

He looks at me intently. "I would have said yes." He rubs my hands and smiles at me, and I can't make myself look away. "I knew even then that I was making a mistake. That I could never be happy without you," he says, interlacing our fingers. "Why didn't you stop me?"

I bite my lip and pull my eyes away from his. I look around the room slowly. A girl with a guitar is setting up on the stage. The bar is getting more crowded, and . . . I freeze. By the door, in a long black coat. Coates. Watching me and Ty. He looks me hard in the face. He turns quickly, holding his head up as he walks out the door.

"Because somewhere deep down, I knew all along that no matter how much I loved you, it wasn't going to work," I say, watching Coates disappear. "And I was finally honest with my-self."

Chapter 22

I hear a knock at my door and open it to Lee, his face swollen. I don't say anything, but take him in. He holds a long, crumpled piece of paper and a pen. He is barefoot and wearing gray sweat pants and a T-shirt. His eyes are bloodshot, and his always-immaculate hair is greasy and flat on one side.

"Hi," I say. I dread what he will say. Something in my gut tells me that I already know what this look on his face means. It speaks of one thing. Death.

He nods at me. That is our sign. It's finished. Mary Sue has succumbed to the disease. I shut the door behind me and hold him. I hear him drop the paper and pen to cling to me tighter. I feel incapable of tears. I'm stunned and feel hollow inside. But he sobs angrily into my shoulder. I hold him tightly and think of her. I remember how Mary Sue smelled. I remember her talking about her cotillion, and I remember her teasing Lee, playing with Charlie, making me feel like it was all going to be okay.

How small my problems really are. How brave she was.

"I'm so sorry," I mumble, knowing it can never help. "She was an amazing woman, Lee."

"Don't," he says simply.

I nod and continue to hold him, letting the tears fall freely. We stand like that for a long time, holding each other, when Lee finally leans back and wipes his nose on his T-shirt. He sniffs and brushes his hair back from his face.

"Why is this happening to me, Jane? It's too much."

"Lee—" I say and put a hand on his shoulder.

"You know, when my father died, I took that well. Sure I was the only kid without a father in middle school, but I was brave. I still had my mother, and she was so amazing she was practically a father *and* a mother to me."

God, what can I do to help him? Guide my words.

"But now, now, the universe takes her from me. The only parent I have left." He begins to pace a little in the hallway. "We're only in our twenties, Jane. A grandparent might die, sure, that happens, but not our parents. Not yet. And not mine," he yells as he finishes. He punches the wall with his hand and then cups it into his stomach in pain.

I go to him and look at his red hand. His face is tear-streaked and blotchy. He takes big gulps of air, trying to recover from the crying and yelling.

"I'm so sorry," I whisper, tears running down my face.

"It's not fair." I look down and think of how soft Mary Sue's hands were. I think about her wonderful, ladylike laugh, the way her stories always had a moral hidden inside. He covers his face with his hands and breathes in and out a few times. Then he stumbles back and, coming in contact with the wall, slides down. He coils into a little ball on the floor. I squat down next to him and put a hand on his forearm.

"Lee?" He doesn't look up. I rub his arm a little. "She was in a lot of pain." I cringe at the image of her attached to machines. "She's free from that now. She's in a better place."

Something about that seems to get through to him. He looks up from his knees and sighs. "She did believe that, you know," he says. "She told me she was ready to go because she knew that the other life was a good one." He seems a little relieved to think of it. I nod and help him up. We hug in the hallway for a while, crying on each other's shoulders.

"Jane," he says through sobs. "I need a favor."

"Anything," I say.

He stoops down and picks up the pen and paper he had when he first came up. We open the door to go inside. I stub my toe on the couch because I can barely see through the film of tears in my eyes.

Lee sits on my couch and takes a deep, shaky breath. He holds my hand and rolls his lips in to steady himself. "She looked good, Jane. At the end. She looked good."

I sob quietly, unable to look up at him.

"I had never seen death, but at least," his voice trails off for a moment, "for my mom it looked sweet and peaceful. I never got to see my dad like that."

I nod and go to get my box of tissues. We both help ourselves to big handfuls of them. I need to be stronger for Lee. He needs me now. Mary Sue told me to take care of him. I finally make eye contact with him.

"What can I do?" I ask.

He points to the beaten-up piece of paper in my hand. I look at it. It is tearstained and covered in beautiful, delicate cursive penmanship. "She left me that."

Lee Bordereaux Colbert,

If you are reading this then I've finally slipped on the great banana peel of life and landed smack dab in the grave. That's a joke, shug. Try to laugh. Please don't sit around too long making a big ol' fuss over me. Remember a small fuss is respectable. Anything more than that and you're just a-wasting your precious time and probably making a fool of yourself to boot.

I know I'll be happy on the other side, drinking lemonade with your dear, sweet daddy again, watching you get up to all kinds of trouble and being proud of you. Shug, we both love you with all our hearts and will always be with you. You know how when you pass someone or a restaurant or a store and something about it, boom, shoots through you and makes you think of home, or biscuits, or the bicycle you had growing up? Well, that's just us passing you by, tapping you on the shoulder, telling you we're always thinking about you, son.

You were the best boy a mama could have hoped for and I'm real proud of you. So stand tall and make us proud of you from Heaven. I know you will.

Love,

Mama

*P.S. On the back of this you will find a list of people you
are to call and invite to the funeral. I figured I'd better
write it out for you. You'd forget your own head if it
weren't attached to your body.*

By the time I finish the letter my face is streaked with hot
tears. When Lee sees me it sets him off too. We grab more tissues, pull ourselves together, and then sit quietly for a moment, while I feel her presence there in the room with us.

"She was really one of a kind, Lee," I say.

"I know," he says. "The postscript just about sums it up."

I nod and try not to well up with tears again.

"I just hoped that maybe you could sit with me here while
I made the first call," he says.

I flip over the paper and see what must be close to one
hundred people he needs to contact.

"I'm scared," he says. I reach out and hold his hand. "I'm
scared to call people, I'm scared of life without her."

I give his hands a squeeze. I swallow back a big lump in my
throat and muster all of her I can in my voice. "She raised you
right, Lee. It's going to be fine. And I'll be beside you."

He looks at me with a half smile.

"I promise," I say. "Now go get that phone. We have to
throw her a funeral that Charleston will never forget."

Chapter 23

I knock on Coates's door. I hear the peephole cover slide away and smile at him. A long moment passes and then I hear it slide back in place.

"I know you're in there. C'mon. Please open up. We need to talk." Another moment passes. I'm prepared for this. I suspected I wasn't going to be able to just waltz back into his apartment after he had been refusing my calls for the past few days.

"Coates, you were right," I say.

I hear the dead bolt unlock, and then footsteps as he walks away. Okay, I guess I can just let myself in. I open the door and look around. I see that Judy Garland is still in her spot, looking as garish as ever. Coates is sitting on his couch looking tired. I walk over there slowly, dreading this conversation. I never know how to begin these things. I sit down next to him, and he slides over to get away from me but cloaks it as a polite gesture to make room for me.

I sigh. How do I start? "Look, that night, I—"

"I shouldn't have gone. I felt so bad for even being there. But my heart was telling me that you would be there. I shouldn't have. I know it was a violation of trust, but I needed to go. I had seen the flyer in the bookstore a week earlier. I was obsessing over it that night so I thought, I'll go. It won't matter because Jane won't be there. And even if she is . . ." His voice fails, and I see a flash of what Coates must have seen as he came into the bar: Ty and me holding hands.

"Coates, I was trying to tell him it wasn't going to work. I told him to stop trying, that we had been lying to ourselves. We were over."

"How can I even trust you, Jane? How am I supposed to know what to think anymore? I come to your ex-boyfriend's reading and there you are in a dark corner holding his hand."

"Look, it's not what you were thinking. He had just grabbed it. It just looked bad. I decided to stay afterward to get some closure, make sure he knew that I had moved on, and then you appeared, I saw you, and I just knew all the more that you were what I wanted. You were who I need to be—"

"Why did you even go?"

I shrug. He rolls his eyes.

"Did he ask you to be there?"

I shake my head.

"Did he contact you at all beyond a mass group e-mail?"

I watch him. He turns away.

"Did you go because, deep down, you had some doubts about letting him get away?"

"No," I say quietly. "That's not why I went."

My phone rings in my purse, and I reach my hand in and silence it without looking at it.

"Then why did you go?"

Coates is looking at the floor. Should I slide over closer to him and put my arm around him? Should I just give him space? We sit in silence for a minute or two.

"I don't know."

My phone rings again, and I silence it again, then toss it back in my purse. It's probably my mom. Why doesn't she just leave a message? I need to tell her to stop doing this.

Coates takes a deep breath. "Jane, I think I need some time to consider it. I want to believe you, and I think I do, but you need to see how it looked to me." I look at him and nod.

My phone bleats out again. "I'm so sorry," I say. "My mom." I open the purse and pull it out. The screen flashes *Tyson* and I freeze. I can hear my heart thump-thump-thumping. Not now. This can't be happening. Why is he calling?

Coates stares at my phone as though I'm cuddling a snake. "I honestly can't believe you, Jane," he says. Coates tears across his room for a coat, marches to his door, and slams it on his way out. The phone continues to ring in my hand as I stare at it in horror. I silence it again.

I sit on Coates's couch for a while, praying that he will come back. Thirty minutes later, I realize that I'm kidding myself. I pick up my things to go and dial up my voicemail.

"Jane. Hey. It's Ty. I don't know why I'm calling you really, but I just got back to Denver, and it looks like my apartment was ransacked while I was gone. My stuff is everywhere, and my computer is gone, and, well, you always know what to do." He pauses. "I didn't know who else to call."

———

"Jane Williams?"

"Who is this?" The caller ID lists the number as Unknown.

"Nina. Nina Federici." I don't know if it's the loud music on her end or my tear-soaked brain, but it takes me a minute to place the name. "Matt Sherwin's assistant."

Why would Nina of the illicit affair be calling me?

"Did you have something to do with this?" she asks without preamble.

"With what?" I ask, confused. I am lying on a lounge chair on my roof deck in an ankle-length down coat, wrapped in a fleece blanket. I wanted some air.

"It was supposed to be Greece!" She shouts into the phone. "Ancient Greece! Graceful white columns. Hot waiters in togas. The full pantheon of gods. Zeus was supposed to give the toast!"

"What?"

"It was supposed to be elegant and classic. We're asking these people for money, for crying out loud," she hisses.

"Nina, I'm afraid I don't know what you're talking about," I say, pushing myself up into a sitting position.

"The kickoff party for the Strike Hunger Campaign," she says, her voice heavy with contempt for my ignorance.

"Nina, as you know, I no longer work for Glassman and Company," I say, sighing.

"That imbecile Natalie who took over for you is nowhere to be found," she screams into the phone, as if it's somehow my fault.

"What's wrong with the party, Nina?" Despite my disgust

for Nina, I still care about World Aid and what they're trying to accomplish. Maybe this is my chance to redeem myself to them.

"Jukeboxes!" she screams. "Leather jackets and poodle skirts. There's a John Travolta look-alike dancing lasciviously and a group of girls walking around in pink satin jackets handing out cigarettes!"

"They organized a *Grease* party?" I can't stifle my laughter.

"We have all the Hollywood A-listers drinking milk shakes and listening to *Summer Lovin'*," she says, practically spitting. "Reese Witherspoon is wearing saddle shoes. This is awful."

"How's Matt holding up?"

"Right now he's wearing a jacket that says Rydell High and is jumping all over the car with flames painted on the side."

"Sounds like he's having a blast," I laugh. "So why are you calling me?"

"Because I need you to fix it," she says, professionalism trumping her obvious dislike for me. "You still have all the right contacts. You can get it straightened out." She pauses. "You will be compensated, of course."

"Nina, I can't."

"Ohmygosh. You're so petty. This is about him, isn't it? You're not going to do this because of that tawdry little affair? Please."

"Nina, that's not why I can't help. It's just that I—"

"I'm through with him, if you must know. I ditched him. He's so over, anyways. I'm dating a Baldwin now. They're coming back, in case you haven't heard."

I smile, both relieved that she and Matt are over and amused at the thought that the Baldwin brothers, any of them, are coming back.

"So help me, Jane. Do something!"

"Nina, just go with it."

"What?"

"Go with it. I could call some people and have Greek gods at your party in half an hour," I say, taking a deep breath. "But if they're having fun, why?"

"Eeekk!" she screams. "Gwyneth Paltrow is doing the hand motions to 'Greased Lightning,'" she whispers into the phone.

"Is she smiling?" I try to picture the amazing scene Nina is witnessing right now. Some people have all the luck.

"Yes," she says.

"Enjoy the party, Nina," I say, pushing the Call End button with satisfaction.

I arrive at Lenox Hill Hospital in a suit and heels. So much for seven weeks of bed rest. I got Raquel's call that she was going into labor again just as I was leaving my second interview for the job at the Y. The director of the Y had been out of town, so they had delayed doing the second round of interviews. I am one of three final candidates, which was a huge shock to me. Luckily, my cabbie is good, and I arrive at the hospital in fifteen minutes flat.

"Hi. I'm Jane Williams," I say to one of the women behind the long desk. "I'm here for Raquel Hardaway. She's in labor."

The nurse looks up and smiles. "Right this way. We'll need to get you scrubbed in immediately. She's not taking her time with this." The nurse eyes my outfit.

"I was called out of a meeting," I say, shrugging. "But why do I need to scrub in? I was just going to say hi and give her a good-luck hug."

"You said Jane Williams, right?" she asks, looking down at a clipboard. I nod. "I have your name right here as one of the 'coaches' during delivery."

I laugh. "I'm sure that's a mistake. She's very private. This is her third child, and for the other two, I just waited out here."

The nurse looks down again at her clipboard. "No. Your name is clearly stated right here with the doula's name."

I laugh again. "Aha! That proves it. She doesn't have a doula. I'm her best friend, and I'd know." The nurse cocks her head at me. "Wait. What's a doula?"

"A doula is a quiet, nonjudgmental presence in the delivery room."

"A what?"

"A kind of friend and coach," she says. "Can I see your ID? Perhaps you're right that there's been a mistake."

Great. Now the nurse thinks I don't even know Raquel. And what is this business about a doula and wanting me in the delivery room? Raquel is adamantly against that sort of stuff. I hand the nurse my ID. "Please let me go see Raquel right now." What if they've got her drugged and are making her agree to weird stuff? I have to be there for her.

"Then that brings us back to the beginning of our conversation. Let's go get you scrubbed in."

I sigh. "Okay, lead the way."

I walk into the delivery room and see Raquel, along with Jack and a strange, stout, stern-looking woman whom I assume must be a doula. So much for nonjudgmental. I run over to Raquel in my new seafoam-green scrubs and footies. "Raquel! I'm so excited!" I say.

"Shhhh," the stern woman says. "Please stay calm."

I look at Raquel to make the crazy person signal, but she just laughs. "Jane, this is Dolores, our doula."

I turn to her and extend my hand. "Dolores the doula. Nice to meet you-la," I say, laughing.

Dolores doesn't break a smile and stares at my hand. "I'm sterilized so I can't shake your hand." I nod at her, stifling a laugh.

Jack and I exchange greetings, and I notice that for the first time ever, he looks a little terrified, maybe even a little smaller.

"I'm going to get you some more cool water," Dolores says and marches out of the room. I see this as my chance.

"Raquel? What on earth is going on?"

She looks at me, and then recognition registers across her face. "Oh. I forgot to tell you. It all happened so fast. And of course we thought we'd have a few more weeks to prepare you." She turns to her side and smiles at Jack. "But this one isn't waiting for anything. We decided late last week that we'd like to try to have this one *au naturel*."

I look at Jack, but he's staring with adoration at Raquel. "Raquel, um, are you sure you've thought this through?"

She looks at me funny. "Of course I'm sure."

"One word for you," I say, putting my hand on my hip. "Highlights."

"What?" she says.

"Okay, more words for you." I take a deep breath. "Highlights, manicures, Brazilian bikini waxes, laser hair removal, eyelash extensions, teeth whitening—"

Raquel starts laughing so I stop. "I know I'm not exactly the crunchy, organic, have-your-baby-in-a-bathtub kind of person. Maybe it was sheer boredom that drove me to it. But I don't know. I just want to try it. This is probably going to be my last one, Jane." She winces as a contraction racks her body. Jack grabs her hand, and she squeezes, a look of determination on her face.

"Okay, just one last question for you," I say as the pains pass and she relaxes back against the pillows. "I'm here because?"

"If I do this," she gives me a thumbs up, "you have to tackle Dolores and go find a doctor to give me enough drugs to keep me under for the first year of the baby's life."

I slip in and steal a peek at Robinson Hardaway, the new addition to the Hardaway clan. Raquel is now in a private room and her perfect little baby boy gets to sleep in his own little bassinet next to her. Raquel has been asleep for hours, worn out from her successful natural childbirth, and Jack left an hour ago to get Haven and Olivia from their neighbor's place and take them home. I promised to stay a while with Raquel and the baby. I go over to the little hand sanitizer station and clean my hands and then walk back to Robinson, sleeping so peacefully. I put my pinky finger near his hand, and he grabs it without waking. My heart soars.

I watch the perfect new baby, and in the quiet of the still hospital, my own life floods back to me. With everything that has been going on, I haven't had a chance yet to really stop and process Mary Sue's death, or the hours that Lee spent on the phone calling his family and Mary Sue's friends. And I remember the time I spent with her, her time in the hospital, her final letter. Somehow it feels so fitting to be thinking of her with little Robinson sleeping soundly before me. I am reminded that God has a wonderful plan for our lives, and even when it doesn't make sense and it feels cruel, he's still there. He's weaving it all together in an elaborate and indiscernible pattern. A birth. A death. And so it goes in his time.

Chapter 24

I am sitting in Carter Associates of Manhattan hoping that Mr. Glassman will be able to work me in today. I made the poor, nervous front-desk woman with the tight bun even more anxious by asking her to tell Mr. Glassman that I will not be leaving today until he meets with me. She hung up the phone and said to me, "He said, 'Perchance.' I'm—I'm not really sure what that means." I told her I'd just keep waiting.

But one hour and four *Cosmo* magazines later, I'm wondering if I should really wait much longer. If Coates would just let me talk to him one more time, I could make it all okay. I know I could. I've even got my cell phone turned off now.

Fifteen minutes later her phone rings, and she waves her arms at me. I walk over to her desk. "Mr. Glassman will see you now," she says. "Just walk through the glass doors and his assistant will escort you the rest of the way."

I thank her and then walk through glass doors to another waiting drone with a tight bun and low navy pumps.

"Right this way, please," she says and walks me down a long hall of cubicles filled with even more women, exactly like the others. I'm wondering if they are self-replicating robots when we reach Coates's office. I go in without being asked and shut the door behind me, and he stands up in some sort of automatic, polite gesture.

I lean against the door, and he is frozen behind his desk. I go to talk, but nothing comes out of my mouth. I'm stunned by the sight of him. He's so gorgeous in his suit, a little self-conscious and embarrassed by my visit.

Without thinking about it, I rush over to him and lean forward and kiss him hard on the mouth. The moment my lips touch his, he puts one arm around my waist and pulls my body to his and holds my upper back in his other arm. We kiss a long time as if he is just back from war and I am the first woman he has seen in two years. At last, he pulls back, panting, and says, "Wait." He sits down and motions to the chair across the room. "Go, sit."

I hit my leg on the corner of his desk while I make my way to the chair. I am still panting a little from the kiss when he pulls it together enough to say something.

"Now, talk," he says.

I look at him and can see that he feels it too. We may not exactly make sense, but we have that. We have it. We click. I just need to explain to him somehow that there's more than that between us.

"You're the person I want to call in the middle of night when I have that dream where I forgot to put my clothes on and everyone is laughing at me at work," I say.

He looks at me, his brows knitting together. I decide to just keep going. "You, you make me angry," I say and he sighs and rolls his eyes so I hurry to continue, "but it's often because you're right. I think it's good that you challenge me." He looks at me warily. "You make me better. That's what I mean to say."

Coates clears his throat and almost smiles at me. I need to keep going. "You turned my whole world upside down, and that's the kind of thing I hate, only, I don't. I mean, I should, but this time, it's different somehow." I sit on the edge of my chair and reach for his hands. He gives them to me.

"But what about—"

"No, shh," I say. "This is my turn to talk. What about Tyson? It's over. It's been over for ages. In fact, you made me see that we never really even began. He was this ideal, this perfect guy I had always thought I'd end up with—except, well, I wasn't thinking. I was measuring him for the tux before I stopped to consider whether he was the kind of man I wanted to spend the rest of my life with. But then you came in and made me see that it's not about having a warm body, a Prince Charming, who happens to be the right size for the tux. It's about someone who smashes everything up and makes you look at it with new eyes. More like Humpty Dumpty than Prince Charming."

Coates raises an eyebrow at me and I try to smile confidently at him. He seems to be looking for something in my face, studying what I'm saying.

"And I think you are my Humpty Dumpty. I don't know what this relationship will look like, and I don't know where we'll end up, but I don't even care as long as we're together."

He remains impassive.

"I'm sorry about the mistakes I've made, but I'm not

sorry for one moment I've spent with you," I say. And then I look down and add, "I'm not sorry for that kiss when I came in either."

"May I talk now?"

I nod, a little embarrassed at all of what I have said, feeling it filling the room now.

"Not good enough."

My phone rings and I put the cashmere sweater back on the table. I pull the phone out from my purse. I can't afford the sweater anyway, and it's not like I'll need lots of cashmere at the YMCA, or wherever I end up working. I should have known better than to come to Saks. I look down at the phone and see that Lee's name flashes across the screen. Ever since the Tyson incident, I've gotten a lot more careful about looking before I leap, or flip the phone open, as the case may be.

"Lee? How are you? Is everything okay?" I ask breathlessly. I expected him to call me after Mary Sue's funeral, but I haven't heard a peep since he left for Charleston. I turn and walk toward the door.

"I'm fine. We're all fine." Wait, this can't be Lee.

"What's going on?"

"Child, you just aren't going to believe how wonderful it is down here," he says, only it's not Lee. I would swear it's Mary Sue, but this voice is definitely a man's.

"Lee? Did your accent go up a few notches since you left? Or is that just my imagination?"

"Oh Jane," he says, still drawling like a big, ripe South Carolina debutante. "You always were such a card." I'd heard that sometimes people pick up accents when they go home, but this is ridiculous.

I shake it off. "How is everything going down there? How was the funeral? Did the lacy coffin look exactly like she wanted? Did you make sure to get the deviled eggs from Lurlene's? Did your Uncle Bob come through with his famous boiled peanuts for the reception?"

Lee laughs. "You have a photographic memory."

I push the sleek glass door open and step out onto bustling Fifth Avenue. "Not really. The instructions for Mary Sue's funeral read better than fiction, so I can't help but remember them."

"Everything came off just beautifully, if I do say so myself. And I got to see all of my cousins I hadn't seen in years."

"That's great," I say, stepping away from the door and resting in front of one of Saks's famous picture windows. This one shows a family gathered around a fireplace with stacks of presents all around.

"But I have something big to tell you."

"Oh?" I say. I'm so glad to hear him feeling better. When I packed Lee off to Charleston he still looked like a broken man. Going home does everyone good.

"I might be moving."

"Where to? Brooklyn? The porch envy finally get to you? I said you could use it whenever you wanted."

"No, Jane. Really move. Mama left me the house."

I nearly drop my phone. Lee can't move to Charleston. We live here. We're a family. A family doesn't split up. I put the phone to my ear again. I will be calm. He's not in his right mind. His mother just passed away. "Um, honey," I start. There, I'll speak his language. Win him over. "Have you really thought about this? A free house is nice, but your life is here in New York."

I hear Lee talk to someone in the background. "Sorry, Jane. Got some family over right now even as we speak. What were you saying?"

"You can't move," I say, putting my finger against my free ear to block out the noise from the street. Lee will listen to me. He always does.

"I'm not sure yet. I'm just thinking about it. But the thing is, I just can't sell the family place."

I try to picture him in a big wooden house in sunny South Carolina. I see him in a rocking chair on the front porch, sipping lemonade. "Don't sell it, then. Keep it in the family. No one says you have to sell it. But your life is here. What would you do down there?"

"I play winner," he says in the background. "Sorry, Jane. We've got this heated game of backgammon going among all the older cousins. Mama was the best so I'm killing all of them." And he drops the phone again, and I hear him say, "I was taught by the best, Randy. You're a goner."

"Lee, listen to me," I say, leaning against a high-rise. "I know you're upset, but you can't move down South. I need you," I say.

"Aren't you a sweetheart," he says. "But I need to go. It's my turn. Kiss Charlie for me."

"I will," I say, shaking my head in confusion.

My mother and I walk into the Geller–Zumdahl wedding at St. Patrick's Cathedral dressed in our Sunday best. We had a rough start this morning, since we're not exactly BFFs right now, and when she wasn't at the Starbucks fifteen minutes after the appointed meeting time, I almost turned around and went home. But she seemed genuinely apologetic when she arrived, and I couldn't really fault her for being delayed by helping at the scene of an accident on the way down here, so I decided to grin and bear it.

We take two programs at the door and step inside the foyer. Our eyes go up to the ceiling at once. It soars high above, glowing with an ethereal light. This church is breathtaking. The floors are stone, the intricate glasswork is brilliantly colorful, and the outside looks like an ornate Gothic wedding cake.

"What's the waiting list like to get married here?" I whisper to Mom. There. An olive branch.

"It's best to put your child's name in right after her baptism." She smiles shyly, breaking the ice. "She has until she's twenty-five to find the guy and then after that she's out in the cold."

"So this means I'm getting married at McDonald's?"

"Worse. Burger King. But I hear they give out free crowns to the both the bride and groom, so that has its merits." We both chuckle and walk over to the ushers. As we approach, a short, balding man offers my mother his arm and asks, "Bride or groom?"

She looks at me, and I shrug.

"Bride," I say.

"Groom," she says at the same time.

He looks at us warily. I clear my throat, place my hand on his biceps, give a little squeeze, and flutter my eyes at him. "Ha ha. That is, we just love him so much now that we think of him as our friend too."

"Who?" the usher asks.

I look at my mom to cue her to bail me out. I see her glance subtly at her wedding program. "Why, Brendan, silly!" She laughs awkwardly and then I laugh with her. We guffaw loudly together and the usher laughs too.

"But we're really friends of the bride," I say.

He smiles at us, buying it, and then leads her down the aisle of the most beautiful cathedral in New York. I trail just behind them, taking in the red carpet we walk on, the dark wooden pews, the ornate tile flooring. This place is overwhelmingly beautiful. I can only imagine the devotion of the people who built it.

Mom and I settle in a pew, and she hands me a pen.

"Don't forget to take notes, Jane. We're not here to pick up chicks," she whispers.

I burst out laughing, and she shoots me a look. "Sorry," I mumble.

She shushes me, then looks around. I look around too but find myself focusing on the hats of ladies around us. I honestly didn't know people still wore hats with birds on them, but it looks like an entire flock has touched down around me.

"How does Patrice know these people again?" I ask. My sister-in-law-to-be doesn't understand drawn-out family drama and has talked Mom and me into this. We're here on a secret spy mission.

"She doesn't," Mom says and then writes down on her wedding program. "Four candelabras. Looks garish."

"What?" I hiss at mom. "Are we crashing this wedding?" I am going to kill her.

Mom looks back at me innocently. "Jane," she says with indignation. "Really. I wouldn't crash a wedding."

I give her my "Get serious" look.

"What? I wouldn't. Patrice's wedding planner, Anton, did this wedding too. He asked her to attend, but since she's undercover at the potential honeymoon resort, she couldn't come."

I look around, groaning. "So where do the friends of Anton sit?"

"What do you think of the red carpet?" Mom asks, trying to sound chipper.

I lean over to get a better look at it again. "I like it."

"Not too I-think-I'm-Princess-Diana?"

"Huh?"

"Patrice said to keep in mind that she doesn't want to come off as showy at her wedding."

"No red carpet then."

"Got it. Too Diana. What do you think of the poem by the bride and groom on the back of the program?"

"Gag," I say, laughing a little. I'd forgotten how fun Mom can be when she wants to. She draws an arrow to the poem and writes "Gag us."

"Mom, you can't write that."

"What? That's what you said."

I grab her pen from her hand and scribble it out. Next to the poem I write, "Too much?" I whisper: "Let's try to be diplomatic."

She looks around and then sniffs, "I don't know these people. What do I care?"

I turn around and peek down the aisle. I see four little flower girls in pastel dresses with miniature parasols giggling. "Write down, 'Absolutely no parasols.' "

My mother obeys and stares at the flower girls herself. "That looks a bit like a kindergarten production of *Gone with the Wind*."

I laugh. Maybe we will make it through this day after all.

"It's hard to believe we all thought you would be the one getting married, isn't it?"

I take it back. I am going to kill her.

"What?" I finally manage to squeak.

"Oh no," she says, her cheeks reddening. "Jane, I didn't mean it like that."

"Mom, why would you say that?" I sniff as my eyes start to tear up. "If you had any idea how hard losing Ty was, you'd never say something like that." I look away. "Or do you just not care?"

"Jane," she says, putting her hands on my shoulders and

turning me to face her. "I'm sorry. What I meant was, it's funny how life works. How things change," she says. "For the better."

"What?" I wipe the tears away from my eyes.

A woman in the pew in front of us turns and hands me a tissue. "Don't you just love weddings?" she sings, turning back to examine her program again.

"Jane, what I was trying to say is, I was wrong. I wanted you to make the choices I would have made, not the choices that were right for you. I'm sorry." She puts a hand on my shoulder. "And I'm proud of who you are."

"You have a strange way of showing it," I say, shaking my head.

"Jane?" She looks at me nervously. "Sometimes I wonder what my life would have been like if I had been born a generation later. Would I have married your father? Would I have had a career of my own?" She shrugs. "I just didn't have the choices available to you, and it's exciting to see what you'll do with what you've been given. I'm not always the best at expressing that. And sometimes I can get hung up on how I did things, wanting you to do it the same way."

I nod and stare at my lap. She always jokes that her choices were nurse, secretary, or teacher. I wonder, what would Mom have done if she'd had any career path in the world available to her?

"I have made mistakes," she says, "and I am sorry. But I want you to know that I love you, and I just want you to be happy."

I look at her and study her face. I swallow my pride. "Thanks, Mom. That means a lot."

We sit in silence, thinking, until the prelude music begins. Finally, I turn to my mother.

"So if Jim and Patrice are getting married in June," I say, trying to make a joke to lighten the mood, "then that means Mrs. Lovell has had this reserved for her since baptism?"

"June? You mean next June, right?"

"What? No. I thought they were getting married this June. As in June-June."

My mother smiles at me, suppressing a laugh. "Oh no. You are mistaken. They aren't getting married until next June."

"But it's only November. That's a year and a half away."

"I know," Mom says. She scribbles, "Don't invite guests prone to hat wearing."

"But what about the dress shopping?"

"Mmm-hmm."

"And the undercover research?"

"Eighteen months."

"She has the invitations ordered already."

"Next June."

"And the wedding planner who acts so frantic all the time?"

"Jane, it's next June."

I can't help it. I dissolve into quiet giggles. This is too much. "This family is insane."

Mom looks at me and, for a moment, a weird look crosses her face. Oh no. I shouldn't have said that. We were finally starting to get along better. But she winks at me and says, "Mixing our blood with the Lovells certainly isn't going to help matters. Those people are mad as hatters."

I sit at the café table, nervously tapping my fingernails on the wood. He's late. He's probably doing it to torture me. I bet he's not even coming. I bite my lip, trying to calm myself down. He'll be here. He's the one who asked me to come. And it's not like I have anywhere to be.

I distract myself by thinking about my conversation with the building management company today. After endless letters and phone calls, it turns out all I had to do was mention that my dad is a real estate lawyer to get them to approve my request for full reimbursement for my expenses from the flood. When the check comes, I'll pay down my credit card, and maybe replace my television and—

"Jane?"

I look up. Coates stands in front of me stiffly, wearing his coat and tie from work.

"Hi," I say and smile. I can't read his face. He's so stiff and nervous. Has he come to yell at me? Make up with me? "Want to sit down?" I ask, pointing to the chair across from me. He sits, and looks at me seriously. I frown. Whatever he is here to say, it doesn't look good.

"I thought we should talk," he says. "Thank you for coming."

I nod, waiting for him to go on, bracing myself for the barrage. He reaches down and opens his briefcase.

"I wanted you to see these," he says, pushing a stack of printouts across the table to me.

I look at the stack and then at his face. Is he suing me? Is this a long, angry letter? I should have known better than to trust someone who doesn't like blue cheese. That's always a bad sign. His face is blank and he looks exhausted. I reach for them and look uncertainly, flipping through the stack.

"Apartment listings?"

He nods and breaks into a big smile. I could be wrong but it almost looks like he's ready for me to swoon and fall at his feet for such a romantic gesture.

"Um?" I say, laughing. "Thanks. But why? I'm not moving." This is not exactly the direction I thought this conversation would go. At least he doesn't still seem mad at me.

He looks confused.

"I thought you were pretty sure you were going to get the job at the YMCA." He softens a little.

"Yeah," I say quietly. I cough. We haven't talked since the scene in his office, so I haven't told him the news. "I got it. They called Tuesday."

"I knew you would," he says, all business.

I wait. And . . .

"Oh. And congratulations."

"Thank you," I say, still baffled.

"And I thought you mentioned it was a significant pay cut," he says. I nod. "I don't want to assume, but as you know, math is one of my strong suits, and I must say, I don't think you can afford your place anymore."

I sit up straighter. "Yes, I can." I cross my arms across my chest. "You don't know what my finances are like. It's going to be fine. A little tight, but fine."

He raises his eyebrows to me. "Sorry. Maybe I shouldn't have assumed. I'm sure you have it under control." He looks down, and we are both quiet for a minute. My head is reeling.

"A little cutting back, of course," I say. I pick at the wooden table with my fingernail. Is he right? I hadn't stopped to think about that. Technically I can still pay my mortgage. But what if something happens? I won't have any buffer. And there's my credit card debt.

"Of course," he says, nodding. "Sure."

I look up at him. "I love that apartment."

He looks at me, and I think I detect a hint of tenderness in his eyes.

"I know," he says, exhaling. "But it's just an apartment. It's not what makes you happy."

I roll my eyes. "Easy for you to say."

"Money is not what makes me happy, Jane."

"Sure." My spirits deflate. My apartment. My home.

"All the money in the world couldn't make me fall asleep last night," he says, taking my hand in his.

"No, but it can buy you a lifetime supply of Ambien." I start to pull my hand away, but he tightens his grip.

"Jane?" He looks at me. "I'm being serious. I can't sleep. I miss you, and I wanted to see you, no matter how many times I tried to convince myself otherwise." I watch him. "And I realize that perhaps I overreacted. I was upset, Jane." I nod. "I'm sorry. And today, I thought I'd make it up to you."

This is how he wants to get back in my good graces? Talk about practical gestures. "With apartment listings?" My head is spinning.

"I pictured it differently somehow," he says, frowning. He looks like he's beating himself up. "It made you feel worse though, huh?"

I shake my head. What is it with this man?

"Okay," he says, standing. "We're going to try this again. I messed it all up. Meet me here tomorrow morning. Nine a.m. sharp." He scribbles an unfamiliar address in Brooklyn down and hands it to me.

Chapter 25

As the propeller whirs above our heads, I grab Coates's right hand, clutching it with all my strength. Through my headphones I hear him say, "Ouch, ouch. Stop it, Jane. I need that hand to fly this thing." I laugh and transfer my hand to my knee, gripping it so tightly that it seems plausible my whole leg might snap off. But in my defense, I've never been in a helicopter before, and as much as I like Coates, I'm not confident that he knows how to fly one.

We lift off above Brooklyn from the helipad, and my heart and stomach do a little wobbly dance. I swallow down the queasy feeling in the back of my throat and slowly, as we sway back and forth a bit in the air, I open one eye to peek out the window. Below me is all of New York, and I can't help but gasp aloud, open both of my eyes, and press my face to the window. Coates hears me gasp through his headset and smiles at me.

"It's really gorgeous, isn't it?"

We both sound like we're using walkie-talkies in this thing and it's tough to hear him over the sound of the propeller, so I just nod back at him and look out the window again, ignoring the fact that he's doing the flying. I've never even seen him drive a car before, so watching him fly a helicopter is a little more than my logical left brain can take.

He swoops the helicopter across the East River and heads toward downtown Manhattan. I see my Lady Liberty in the distance, and I give her a small wave. I miss having her as my client. I hope my replacement, Natalie, is taking care of her.

As we near downtown Manhattan, I can't help but grin. No view is more beautiful to me than downtown Manhattan. Keep your leafy forest or painted desert, you can have your sugarlike sand beaches or rugged coastline; for me the delicate, glistening skyscrapers of New York, patched together like an elaborate puzzle, teeming with busy, happy life, are the ultimate scenic view.

Coates continues flying north, straight up the center of the island. He points at a silver Art Deco building, gleaming in the sun. "The Chrysler Building." I look down at it and am surprised how close we are.

"How safe is this?" I ask.

He looks at me, smiles, and shrugs. I roll my eyes.

"Does this thing have a parachute?"

"Relax, Jane," he says. He leans over, pats my knee. I push him back.

"Focus, will you," I say, hoping that I sound like I'm joking, even though I'm not.

Soon we are hovering above Central Park. I see Sheep Meadow, where I love to lie on the grass and nap on a quiet spring day. We spy two cops on horseback meandering on the Bridle Path. And we can see all the people twirling and holding hands at Wollman Rink. I love Central Park this time of year. No tourists, no leaves, just naked trees and hushed silence on the walkways. And, when God smiles upon us, beautiful, peaceful snow.

By the time we fly past Central Park, I have relaxed and become accustomed to the feeling of hanging in the air. We soar over bridges and miles and miles of residential neighborhoods, choked with tall gray buildings, and I marvel at the sheer number of people who call this glorious city home.

As the city gives way to parklike Westchester County, with its cute wooden houses and tree-lined streets, I wonder what I have been doing with my life. How can this be my first helicopter ride? Hey, wait—I've never taken a hot-air balloon ride either. I try to come up with risky things I have done. I'm selling myself short, right? I'm sure I've done plenty of risky things over the years like, let's see: I went to Columbia after high school, but not because I was scared to leave New York— no, because it's a great school, and because I wanted to stay near my family. I interned at Glassman & Co. the summer of my junior year and they offered me a job when I graduated, but I would have been crazy to pass up that kind of opportunity. I bought an apartment. There; that was risky. The real estate market is never stable. I'm changing careers—that was risky too. But a little voice in my head reminds me, I was forced to change careers and the apartment pretty much fell in my lap one day when my parents' friend put it on the market. I cross my arms across my chest and then turn my focus back outside again.

"Where are we?" I ask.

"We're almost to Fritz Farms," he says, looking out his window.

"What?"

"Outside of Fritz Farms really. It's in Saratoga County. I need your help with something."

"What is Fritz Farms?"

He looks at me and smiles. His dark hair gleams in the winter sunshine. "A Christmas tree farm."

We touch down in a big, grassy field that Coates swears to me is the local helipad and airport and then hop into the back of a hay-lined trailer hitched to a big red truck that drives us to Fritz Farms. Each day during this time of year, they stop by the airport and the bus station to pick up visitors. The trailer already has a few other New Yorkers like us huddling together for warmth and taking deep gulps of the country air. I can't stop smiling.

Once we arrive at the farm, we walk through long rows of Christmas trees to pick out our very own. Coates insists that we cut it ourselves. At first I am very nonchalant about the errand. It isn't my tree, really. But, after a while, I get over the initial shock of seeing so many trees in one space and scour the aisles for the perfect one. It turns out I'm a Fraser fir kind of gal, and, well, I like 'em tall, just like my men. After an hour of wandering around the farm and getting down on my hands and knees to peek up each potential tree's skirt to look for thickness, and pinching all of their needles, I find the perfect tree for him. It has big, thick, soft needles and climbs eight feet in the air. Thank goodness Coates's apartment has twelve-foot ceilings.

He bends down to begin to saw the trunk in two, but I stop him. I want to give it a try. I saw and saw for ten minutes straight, but don't make much progress. Plus my hands are now sticky with sap, so I relent and let him take over. After we cut it down, we drag it up to the staff so that they can ship it overnight to his place in New York. Then they invite us to go and take part in the festivities.

I take a sip of my spiced apple cider and slide in a little closer to Coates at the picnic table. It's cold out today, but the sun is shining and we are both bundled up, watching women select the perfect handmade candles and holiday wreaths at the outdoor stand. Children are running around in unfettered delight and a group of carolers in period costumes serenade the customers waiting in line for a real old-fashioned sleigh ride. It's a perfect winter day.

"Want any more of this donut? I'm going to finish it all if you don't hurry."

I slide the paper plate with the still-hot apple-cider donut closer to me and cut another piece off. This is not the kind of day when you worry about your diet. I have had apple-cider donuts at the Union Square farmer's market on occasion, but this one beats them all. It is fresh, hot, and positively coated in cinnamon sugar.

I slide the plate back to him and bury my face in his big winter coat.

He looks down at me, and I smile. "I'm so happy," I say. "I just can't get over how good life is."

Coates takes a sip of his steaming cider. "And here I thought you might not be talking to me by the time we got here."

"Why?" I say.

"I wasn't sure how you were going to take the helicopter surprise," he says. "But the new Jane is surprising even herself."

I smile at him, proud of myself. "It was fun," I say. "If a bit nerve-racking at first. How on earth did you figure out how to rent a helicopter?"

"Rent?" he says, looking at me sideways.

I put down my cup of cider in shock. Wait. What?

"Jane, that's the Glassman family helicopter. I've been flying it since I can remember."

I stare at him in shock, feeling my face redden in embarrassment. We're from such different worlds. My parents will be paying the mortgage on their house until they die, and his family owns a helicopter. "Oh," I say. "Sure, of course."

He slides over a little on the picnic bench to be able to look me in the eye. "I'm sorry. I thought you knew that. It's no big deal," he says.

I nod, trying to recover from my shock and act normal. What happens when he meets my family and sees the carpet in the hallway that should have been replaced years ago, or Dad's collection of tacky coffee mugs from around the country, or Mom's handmade scrapbooks? And what will I do when I meet his parents? Will it be on their yacht? Will I accidentally use his father's bread plate? I put these thoughts out of my mind. He loves me. I love him. It doesn't matter about the money. It's just going to take some adjusting after having dated a starving artist for so long.

"It's not a big deal, right?" he asks. He nudges me a few times in the leg with his leg.

"Are you kidding me?" I laugh. "No way. I just wish I had known earlier about the helicopter. Imagine the shopping possibilities," I say.

"Good," he says and slides back to my side to get warm again. "I'm glad." He kisses my forehead and takes one of my mittened hands in his.

"Are we okay, Jane?"

I look at him, his delicious profile lit by the setting winter sun. He looks hopeful. I take another sip of my cider, and it fills me with warmth.

"We're okay." I nod. He smiles and leans in toward me. The kiss we share is more than okay.

Chapter 26

I sit at my desk, an old hunk of metal from the late sixties, squished into a tiny closet of an office, and look at my giant plastic wall calendar to see what's on the schedule for today. Aside from the daily homework help, arts and crafts, and organized sports, today we have optional foreign-language classes, a water balloon volleyball game, a treadmill distance race, and a performance by the drama group that meets Tuesdays and Thursdays. Under my carefully handwritten list of activities, one of the kids has scrawled "Pizza Party" in blue marker, apparently in the hope that I might mistake the handwriting for my own and call in an order for a dozen pizzas. Hope springs eternal around this place.

I make a note to start working on reserving fields in Central Park for our softball teams this summer and decide to check my e-mail. While I used to sit hungrily in front of my computer reading every e-mail the second it came in, now I'm away from my desk so much that I instituted a policy of only checking in at my e-mail account twice a day and dealing with all the messages then.

I open up Outlook and I see a message from the Wickham

Charitable Trust, to which we've applied for a grant for the money to replace the broken floor of the basketball court, and one from Coates, confirming our dinner tonight. I click on that one first and start to write him back when a tiny head pops into my office.

"Yes, Michael?" I smile. Michael was one of the first kids I met at my new job, and he latched on to me right away. His hardworking mother holds down two jobs to feed and clothe Michael and his two brothers, so he spends mornings here and then goes to a babysitter's later in the day. While he always has a blast with the other kids, I suspect he's looking for a little adult attention, and so even though he's not technically part of my after-school program, I always make an effort to say hello to Michael. This little guy is a handful, but he has a smile that could end world wars.

"Ms. Williams, can I have a basketball?" He grins at me.

"Didn't I just give you a basketball a few minutes ago?" I ask, narrowing my eyes at the child who I suspect is the culprit behind the broken soda machine in the lobby.

"Um," he says, rolling his eyes up as if searching for the answer above him. "I guess so. But I lost it." He looks as if he's trying to look sheepish.

"How did you lose it between here and the gym floor?" I eye him suspiciously.

"I don't know," he says, shaking his head, his eyes wide. He looks so earnest that I can't help but laugh.

"Why don't I come help you look for it," I say, trying to

look serious. His face lights up and he nods, reaching out to grab my hand as I stand up. I smooth my jeans and then take his little hand in mine.

"Thanks, Ms. Williams!" he laughs, pulling me out the door and grinning like he's just won the lottery. Somehow, I feel like maybe I just did too.

I look at them all standing there, wearing their little brown uniforms, solemnly holding three fingers up and reciting the words to the Girl Scout pledge. They look so serious. Even Bella is wearing her full uniform, including sock tassels, for this momentous occasion. The crowd is made up entirely of proud parents and a few beaming grandparents, and they clap politely as the girls all swear to live by the Girl Scout Law. I may not be the leader of Troop 192, but I was invited, I am told, at the request of the girls, who insisted I be there for their big day. And since Raquel is the only one who has led a bridging cere-mony—or in civilian terms, Brownie graduation—before, she was asked to officiate, so I don't feel completely out of place. This whole ceremony is totally dorky, but the girls seem to be loving it.

"I'd like to welcome you all," Raquel says, turning to the parents, "to the final meeting of Brownie Troop One-ninety-two." They clap politely. Little Robinson sleeps soundly in Jack's lap. "As many of you know, the bridging ceremony is a long and hallowed tradition in the history of Girl Scouting," she announces, flicking her eyes down to her note card. "It is a celebration of all that we've learned in the past year, and a way to look forward to where we will go next." Eleanor Pearson, sitting in the front row, wipes away a tear.

"And this is a very important day for our accomplished girls. This has been an exciting year, and we'd like to share with you a few of the things we've learned." She nods at Kaitlin, who steps forward confidently and explains to the audience how we studied the forest and lakes on our campout, and then points to her Outdoor Adventurer badge on her uniform vest. Bella steps forward next. She explains our recent experiments with static electricity and shows us her Science Wonders patch. I smile as the girls talk about their achievements. Abby only stumbles over her words a few times as she explains how they learned about math by keeping track of the hundreds of boxes of cookies they sold this year. It feels good to see them happy in what they have done.

Haven steps forward, and I take a deep breath. Raquel told me that while they were practicing, Haven had always stridently refused to recite the paragraph assigned to her about their Sounds of Music badges. Whenever it was her turn to practice, she launched into a heartfelt rendition of *Oops I Did It Again*, which the other girls found continually uproarious. But today she steps forward solemnly and recites, word for word, how we listened to and learned about music from all over the world. The parents clap appreciatively, and the girls beam.

Then they turn and walk slowly, just as they practiced, to the base of a little wooden bridge. It is just a simple wooden structure with a small platform and railing, but the girls are looking at it with as much awe and excitement as if it were the pathway to Tommy Drake's heart. Raquel stands on the other end of the bridge and waits until they are all lined up.

Raquel nods at Kaitlin, who is the oldest and consequently always the first in line. She steps onto the platform uncertainly and walks across the bridge. When she steps down on the other side, the crowd erupts in applause and Raquel pokes the little golden wings into her vest that signify she has "flown up" to Juniors, the next level in the Girl Scout hierarchy. One by one, while the parents record every second on their digital cameras, the girls march across the bridge. Abby holds her head up proudly as Raquel pins the wings onto her little vest.

"Now will you please join me," Raquel says, turning to the parents, "in congratulating the girls on their achievements and welcoming the newest members of Junior Troop One-ninety-two?"

The parents stand up and cheer for the girls, and even though I catch Margaret Ann elbowing Abby's dad out of the way for a good camera shot, my heart soars. The parents have hurt me, but these girls have worked hard.

And then I hear Haven singing. I cringe. Couldn't she hold off on Britney's Greatest Hits just a few more minutes? Just until the ceremony formally ends? I stifle a groan as Bella joins in, but then I pause. I know that song. They can't really be singing it voluntarily. They told me it was dorky. I turn and stare. Haven puts her arms around Kaitlin's shoulders, and the other girls catch on and do the same. This can't be happening.

But sure enough, I watch in shock as Bella slides her arm

around Abby's shoulder. "Make new friends," they sing out, swaying back and forth, "but keep the old." I am stunned. They don't even know any cool dance moves to this song. But there they are, singing their little hearts out, as if one thing, if nothing else, has actually sunk in this year. "One is silver and the other's gold." They start the song over, Bella and Kaitlin singing their own ear-splitting version of harmony this time, as we all stand, watching in confused but pleased silence.

I am so shocked and proud of them I don't even notice Raquel until she is standing right in front of me.

"Thanks, friend," she says quietly, as the girls sway to their own music in front of us. I know from experience that it's only a matter of time before they sway so much they all end up in a pile on the floor, but for now, I decide to just enjoy the moment.

"**Lee**, are you sure these lights are okay to use outdoors?" I ask, straining to read the fine print on the box in the dark night without letting the wool blanket fall from my shoulders.

"They'll be fine, Jane," Lee laughs, draping a strand of white Christmas lights over the top of my lounge chair. "Now help me with these. I want them to look like icicles." He is wearing a hat and gloves and a big down coat, but he still has my cashmere throw wrapped around his shoulders for extra warmth.

"If we stay out here much longer, *we're* going to look like icicles," I say, grabbing the strand he's holding out to me.

"Now, Jane, where's your Christmas spirit?" He pulls the lights up the railing at the edge of the patio and beings to drape them from the top.

"Right now?" I ask, looking at him. "It's probably halfway to Charleston by now."

Lee looks up at me. He drops the lights and comes over to me, wrapping me in a big hug. "Oh, honey," he says. "I'm sorry." He pulls back and looks at me. I look away quickly before I start to cry. "But you're moving too, right?"

I nod. "But I'm just moving to the Upper East Side. Not to a whole different state." I pout.

"Jane, thank you for caring." He sits down on the edge of the lounger. "It means a lot to me. But you know this is something I have to do."

"I know." I nod. "I just wish you could wait until after Christmas to move all your stuff out," I sigh. "It feels so sudden. So final."

"I know," Lee says, shaking his head. "It's all kind of fast for me too." He grins at me. "I just don't know how I'll ever get all my shoes packed up in time." I roll my eyes. "But the broker says I can list my apartment now and sell it from down there, so I don't see any reason to wait. And I can't stay here for Christmas," he says sadly. "I need to be with my family for the holidays this year."

I nod. I know this is the right thing for Lee, but that doesn't make it any easier to see him go. My New York family is breaking up. I listed my apartment with a broker just this afternoon, and since everything was just redone after the flood, he thinks I'm going to be able to get much more for it than I paid. Still, as I signed the forms, I knew I was ending a chapter of my life I could never revisit. I had some good times in this apartment. It isn't easy to say good-bye.

"I'm sure going to miss this place," Lee says, looking around at my little patio, blessedly peaceful on this quiet winter night.

"You'll have a huge porch." I sit down on the other lounger, pulling the blanket tight around me in a futile attempt to keep out the cold night air.

"But it won't have my favorite neighbor to keep me company."

"That's what you think," I laugh. "You'd better believe I'm coming down to visit you and sit on your veranda and drink sweet tea."

"Jane, you don't know the first thing about the South," he laughs, shaking his head. "All tea is sweet. I have so much to teach you." He stands up and grabs the strand of lights. He finds the end, plugging it into the outlet on the wall. The lights flick on, bathing the patio in a soft glow.

"You've already taught me so much," I say softly as I lean back in my chair and look up at the clear night sky.

Chapter 27

"How long do they keep this thing up?" Raquel asks, nodding at the famous Christmas tree in Rockefeller Center. I take a sip of my delectable Dean & DeLuca hot chocolate and shrug.

"I guess until after New Year's probably," I say. With only a few days left until Christmas, it looks magical, lit from top to bottom with white lights and colorful glass ornaments. Below it, ice-skaters race around the rink, enjoying the crisp night air.

"I suppose after you chop down a two-hundred-year-old tree, you'd better enjoy it for as long as you can," she laughs. I nod, remembering ice-skating with the Brownies. I am sure going to miss those girls. "So how did the meet-the-parents weekend go?"

"Oh, you know," I say, taking another sip of my drink. "At first they were a little standoffish, because, you know, he's not Ty, so that's a major strike against him." Coates left for Italy yesterday, where the Glassman clan always spends Christmas in their villa, so we celebrated early and took a trip to my house so my parents could meet him. "But Coates brought my mom flowers and a bottle of single-malt Scotch for my dad, so they melted."

"They liked him, then?"

"Loved him. Thankfully Jim was away with the Lovells at their house in Aspen, so he wasn't there to bring out the embarrassing baby pictures. But Coates and my dad talked about mutual funds for hours. And my mom kept bringing him cookies and refilling his glass and making sure he was comfortable. And he asked for seconds on the roast for dinner, and when he asked for her recipe, I thought she was honestly going to swoon."

"Sounds like it went well."

"A little too well, I think. Mom kept mentioning how Jim is finally settling down and hinting that she would like me to do the same. She mentioned how much she loves weddings probably a dozen times. Coates was totally great and played along with her insanity, but it was pretty mortifying. When she casually mentioned how much I used to love the little house we used to rent on the Cape and that she'd always hoped I would get married there, I cut her off."

Raquel laughs. "Did he like the cuff links?" She rests her arms on the handrail.

"He gave a good show if he didn't. I'll bet it's the only pair of cuff links with a pizza on them he's ever seen."

"And what did he get you? Something fabulous, I bet."

I bite my lip and lean over the railing. "He got me a Palm Pilot."

"No." Her eyebrows rise, and her mouth falls open. "He knows better than that. What was he thinking?"

I shrug.

"That thing is OCD in a box. You're a goner. You can

program in every number you're ever going to need. The calendar functions are amazing. You can plan out the next ten years of your life on there. And I thought we'd just weaned you off of schedules."

"He said I'm finally ready for it," I laugh.

"You don't give crack to a recovering addict." She shakes her head.

"It's hardly the same as crack, Raquel. I think you're being a little dramatic."

"Am I?" She stands up and looks at me. "I don't know." She takes a deep breath. "You've changed a lot in the past few months, Jane."

"I know. I had a streak of bad luck and flipped out, but I've been better for a while," I smile.

"No, that's not what I mean." She pauses. "You've, I don't know, mellowed out." She takes a sip and stares out at the ice.

"So I'm a little calmer. Big deal."

"I used to think you had it all. And I still do, but in a different way."

"Then you're delusional."

"I don't know," she sighs. "I guess what I'm trying to say is that you were really down and out. But even when you were falling apart, there were some things you never let go of."

"My grasp on reality, for one."

"No." She shakes her head. "You totally lost that. I mean, things that really mattered. The people you cared about. Your . . . attitude, I guess. It's just funny to see how God works." I watch her.

"I guess when everything I thought I wanted was gone, I saw what it was I really needed."

"You learned to let go." She looks away.

"I guess, in a way, I did." I nod. "There are things I'm never going to be able to control, but God can."

Raquel looks thoughtful. "And you honestly believe you're not going to rely on your calendar to control your life anymore?"

"I suppose that remains to be seen," I laugh. "Anyway, are you ready to head back? I've got my shopping done."

"No way, Jane," Raquel says seriously. "The babysitter's free until six. We're not heading back one second earlier." I can't help but laugh. Moms really do need a break now and then. I don't know how they do it. "Let's go get our nails done or something."

"Fine," I say, standing up straight. "I don't have anything else on my calendar all day."

Coates is going to be here in ten minutes, and I have no idea what I am supposed to wear. I panic, surveying the piles of clothes littering my bedroom floor. I got so desperate I even tried on my graduation gown, as if that might be appropriate.

New Year's Eve and I are not friends. Everyone always makes a big deal about it, and I've never had a good one. Last year Ty and I got into a fight about time zones. The highlight might have been the year a sparkler set my hair on fire. Needless to say, I was planning to just hide from it all this year. But

Coates just got back in from Italy and said he had tickets to a fund-raiser and wouldn't take no for an answer. I have prepared myself for a frustrating evening, and so far my closet is obliging.

I hear a knock on my door, throw on the black Valentino, pray it's appropriate, and walk out.

"**So** what's your weird fascination with the Four Seasons?" I ask as the bellhop opens the door for us. So far this night may change my relationship with New Year's. When Coates picked me up in a limousine, I was only vaguely surprised, and extremely pleased that he looks as good in a tuxedo as I remembered. And when we went on a tour of the city by limo, I felt as if I had died and gone to heaven. There is an electricity about New York, a sensation of excitement in the air tonight. Though we steered clear of Times Square, where the infamous ball will drop in just a few hours while the world watches, we saw people out everywhere, enjoying the evening, trying to savor every last moment of the dying year. A mighty good year despite it all, I realize as we walk through the opulent hotel lobby. I nod at Cal the concierge as we walk through the cavernous room and marvel at how different this is from when I first tried to check in here.

"My father owns a lot of stock in the hotel group that owns it." He shrugs. "Being a major shareholder comes with a lot of benefits."

"Oh," I say, realization sinking in. "Like free hotel rooms?"

We step into the empty elevator, and Coates pushes the button for the penthouse.

"You didn't really think I paid for that room, did you?" His eyes widen at the thought.

"Um, no," I laugh. "I mean, I don't know."

Coates shakes his head. "Oh Jane," he laughs. "You're amazing, but I would never pay fifteen hundred dollars a night for a hotel room for you."

"Hey!" I don't know whether I should be offended or relieved, but as I look at his face, I realize he's joking, so I just smile. The elevator doors slide open, and the sight in front of me takes my breath away. The wall straight ahead is one vast window, providing a breathtaking view of the twinkling lights of Manhattan. The ballroom is filled with round tables drenched in elegant flowers and white tea lights. Each place is set with more silverware than I'll ever own. A grand piano in the corner fills the room with soft music, and the beautiful people milling around are dressed to the nines. I silently thank God for the Valentino. I've been to nice parties before, but this is breathtaking.

Coates takes my arm and leads me through the room, smiling at a few people as we go.

"Coates, this place is amazing."

"See that white-hair over there?" he whispers, nodding at a small woman wrapped in a fur stole. "Watch out for her. She bathes in Chanel Number Five. You'll smell like it for a week if you get near her."

"Noted." I file away the image of the small woman for reference. "What's this benefit for, anyway?"

"The Glassman Foundation."

"The what?"

"Would you like something to drink?" Coates gestures to the bar set up along the back wall, and I nod, too stunned to do anything else.

Coates manages to drag me to the dance floor after an exquisite six-course dinner. While I was talking to the editor of *The New York Times* business section, who was seated on my right, Coates was busy entertaining the young head of a major hedge fund, seated to his left. Now, swaying to Sinatra, I rest my head on his shoulder and drink in the night. I watch the lights spinning around us and the people chatting comfortably.

What am I doing here? Can I ever really fit into this world?

"I'm impressed, Jane," Coates finally says, waking me from my trance.

"I told you I was a decent dancer," I say, pulling back and looking him in the eye.

"Not about your dancing," he laughs. "Though you are nimble." He raises his arm, and I twirl underneath it.

"About what, then?" I laugh. "I haven't even shown you my gymnastics routine yet."

"I'm impressed because you haven't been obsessively using the calendar I gave you."

"How do you know?" I ask, putting my hands back on his shoulders.

"I'm reading the clues. That's my job, you know."

"I know, I know." I roll my eyes. "What clues, Encyclopedia Brown?"

"For one thing, you haven't noticed what I programmed in."

I look at him for a second, confused. "I noticed the verse you programmed in. Jeremiah 29:11. Very clever. But I'm guessing from your reaction that that's not what you meant."

"See, you're getting good at this too." He smiles.

"What is it that I should have noticed?"

"On the contrary, I was hoping you wouldn't notice it," Coates laughs. "Your utter confusion tells me that you really have changed, and that you're ready."

"Ready for what?" This game is getting tiresome, and I was hoping to grab some more champagne before the clock strikes midnight, so we only have a few minutes left.

"June tenth."

I sigh. He's not about to just spit it out.

"What happens on June tenth?"

"That's the day we get married," he says, smiling at me.

I freeze.

"The day we what?"

"We could always go the St. Patrick's route, but really, I don't know that we want a big elaborate wedding. We can do something smaller, more low key if you—"

My mind is reeling. What is he saying? I stare at him, and I can't figure out what to say. I realize people are starting to stare, so I blurt out the first thing that comes into my head. "We'd never be able to get St. Patrick's."

Coates laughs. "I was thinking something more intimate might be better. What do you think?"

What do I think? "June of this year?"

He nods. "Why wait?"

All around us, people are starting to scurry and hush each other, and I flush until I realize it's not us they're getting excited about. With only one minute till midnight, people are looking toward the stage where Herb Glassman is ready to begin the countdown to the new year.

"What are you talking about?" My head spins.

"I'm talking about you and me," Coates says calmly, oblivious to the excitement around us. "I'm talking about how you make me laugh. How you challenge me to grow. How you force me to push the boundaries of what I consider normal." He looks deep into my eyes as the excitement builds around us. It must be very close to midnight. "I'm talking about how I knew, from the very first time I saw you, that we were meant to be together."

"Then why were you such a jerk?" I ask, closing my eyes to block out to commotion around us. I need to think. He touches my cheek, softly, and I open my eyes to look into his.

"Because I was completely flustered," he admits, blushing. "You were there and I knew I had to talk to you and I had no idea what to say." I bite my lip. "And then you had that boyfriend, and I knew he was wrong for you because I knew, Jane," he takes a deep breath. "I knew that *I* was right for you." I stare at him as he talks to me, acting as if there is no one else in the room.

I don't know what to say, so I just lean in to him, but he

pulls away. "I love you, Jane." And suddenly, he drops down to one knee.

"What are you doing?"

"What I wanted to ask you tonight, Jane," he says, smiling up at me, "was, will you marry me?"

"*Ten . . .*" The countdown begins from the stage as he takes a small black box out of his coat.

"What?"

"*Nine . . .*" He opens it and pulls out a gorgeous princess-cut solitaire ring. A few people around us notice and turn to stare.

"*Eight . . .*"

"I want to spend the rest of my life with you, Jane."

"*Seven . . .*"

The couple next to us whistles and points.

"*Six . . .*"

I notice a lot of heads turning to look at us.

"*Five . . .*"

"Jane?"

"*Four . . .*"

I look at the crowd, now turning and looking at us. I know I should feel embarrassed, but I don't. I feel . . .

"*Three . . .*"

Happy. I feel like this is right. And I know, with a certainty that I have never felt before, that God is good.

"*Two . . .*"

God is good, and wants what's best for us, even if he has to strip away our own desires to get us to see it.

"*One . . .*"

I love this man, and suddenly I want the world to know it. As the year ends, I bend over and kiss him, and the crowd erupts in cheers.

As the first notes of "Auld Lang Syne" float across the ballroom, Coates stands up and wraps his arms around me. I sink into his warmth as I think about how mournful this song is. I know that *auld lang syne* means "time long past," and I think about what it means to say good-bye to another year. I think about all the dreams that died this year, and the pain, and about the friends who have gone away, some forever. And I also think about the good that I've seen—the new life that's come into the world, and the deep ties of friendship, and the hope for better things to come.

I hear the people around us, still cheering as we sway to the music, but all I can see is Coates. I've never seen his smile so big. I laugh, and thank God for a new year. A whole new start for us all.

Acknowledgments

As always there were a lot of brilliant minds that helped us with this book. Thanks to our amazing agent, Claudia Cross, for giving us great comments and never minding when we e-mail you every day. Thanks to Trace Murphy, the kindest, straightest, malest chick lit editor in the business. Thanks to Darya Porat for being a huge help and funny to boot. Thanks to Carly Fraser and Preeti Parasharami for pitching our book all over town. Thanks to Beth Meister for keeping us honest and being the best friend two knuckleheads could have. Also to Haymaker, for being the other Beth. And thanks to Shannon Hill at Waterbrook for being our friend and editor-at-large.

Anne: Mom, you're the choice of a new generation. Dad, you're just what the doctor ordered. Nick, don't ever forget you can't beat the feeling, and Peter, you can't beat the real thing. Jeff, I like the Sprite in you (and thanks for reading). Wayne, with you, life tastes good.

May: Thanks to Dad for swearing people are crazy when they don't hire me. Thanks to Mom for being the original bookworm in the family. Thanks to Matt and Diem for not taking the name Walker. Thanks to Isaac and Aaron for being the life of the party. Thanks to Sandy, my partner in crime. Thanks to the Bransfords for making Buster your "granddog." And thanks to Nathan. I know I'm a handful, but you make it seem like you're having fun.

About the Authors

© Wayne Adams

Anne Dayton graduated from Princeton University and is earning her master's degree in English at New York University. She works for a New York publishing company and lives in Brooklyn. Another publishing veteran, *May Vanderbilt* graduated from Baylor University and went on to earn a master's degree in fiction from Johns Hopkins University. She lives in San Francisco, where she is a freelance writer.

Also by Anne Dayton and May Vanderbilt

Emily Ever After

Can a small-town girl find love and happiness amid the temptations of the Big Apple? Find out in this "classic story wrapped in the sweetness and comedy of Chick lit" (*Relevant*).

Consider Lily

A delightful couture adventure about a down-to-earth young woman on the verge of being swept away by San Francisco's hip, high-fashion scene.

The Book of Jane

Jane's got it all—the perfect apartment, dreamy boyfriend, and fast-track job. But when a chain reaction brings it all tumbling down, will her faith remain standing?

To find out more, visit www.goodgirllit.com